THE GUARDIAN

BILL EIDSON

FORGE®

A TOM DOHERTY ASSOCIATES BOOK
NEW YORK

This is a work of fiction. All the characters and events portrayed in this
book are either products of the author's imagination or are used
fictitiously.

THE GUARDIAN

Copyright © 1996 by Bill Eidson

A Tor Book
Published by Tom Doherty Associates, Inc.
175 Fifth Avenue
New York, NY 10010

Tor Books on the World Wide Web:
http://www.tor.com

Tor® is a registered trademark of Tom Doherty Associates, Inc.

ISBN: 0-812-54444-7
Library of Congress Catalog Card Number: 96-24233

First edition: November 1996
First mass market edition: June 1998

Printed in the United States of America

0 9 8 7 6 5 4 3 2 1

For my mother, Mary C. Eidson

ACKNOWLEDGMENTS

I would like to thank the following people for their help and encouragement: Donna Eidson, Bill Eidson, Sr., Catherine Sinkys, Frank Robinson, Richard Parks, David Hartwell, Tad Dembinski, Paul DiPaolo, Rick Berry, and Steve Bentley.

CHAPTER 1

You're sure you want to wear that beret?" Greg said to his daughter as they walked into the convenience store.

A bell jingled over the door, and Greg nodded to the owner, a round-faced man wearing a white apron who smiled back.

"Yup," Janine said, hopping up to look at her reflection in a sunglasses display mirror. "Looks good."

Behind them, Beth laughed quietly. "Give it up, Greg. You know your brother gave it to her."

Greg went along with it. "Oh, well, if Ross gave it to you, I wouldn't expect you to part with it at least until . . . high school. How about then?"

Janine giggled, shaking her head. She was nine. "College. Maybe."

He reached under the beret and mussed her hair, and she leaned back into him and elbowed him lightly in the belly. "Stop."

The two of them headed toward the ice-cream freezer in the back while Beth went for milk and bread. Janine immediately pulled open the freezer door and started pointing to different flavors: "Chocolate Supreme . . . no, Heath Bar Crunch . . ."

"Keep the door closed until you decide." Greg thought to himself that so much of raising his daughter involved saying the same kinds of things at similar times: "Are you hungry?" "Are you too hot?" "Too cold?" "Put your sweater on."

"Close the door," he repeated.

Greg felt the slightest twinge of jealousy over how she'd taken to his younger brother, now that he was back. Ross was definitely the exciting new man in her life, while Greg was just Dad.

Comfortable.

That's how he envisioned she saw him. He didn't feel that way himself, God knows, with his worries about his business and money.

Greg watched his daughter's lips move slightly as she read the different flavors, her eyes flickering from label to label. He felt the warmth that was already there intensify and trickle through him like balm. Knowing that she was about to turn . . . which she did, right then.

"Rocky Road." She nodded, decision made. Janine had her mother's dark hair and blue eyes.

Greg was faintly aware of the bell jingling again behind him. "You're sure?"

Janine's eyes widened, and she looked past him.

Greg turned around, and felt like he'd just been punched in the stomach.

Two men with guns had just walked in the store.

"Oh my God, oh my God," the man at the counter was saying. "Don't do this. You don't need to do this—"

"Shut up!" the bigger of the two yelled. They were both wearing ski masks, green flak jackets. The smaller one was wearing tight black jeans, and Greg realized abstractly that it was a woman. Greg stood in front of his daughter. His thinking became very clear. He told himself that all they wanted was money and what he had to do was keep his family out of it.

Out of it.

Beth. He looked up the end of the aisle to his left and saw her standing there, frozen, too. She was pale, and nodded to him slightly. She raised her finger to her lips, for Janine.

Greg felt an incremental amount better. They were in sync. Shut up and let this pass.

"The register. Now, you fat fuck." The man's voice was hoarse.

Greg saw the man's arm out of his sleeve was white. He was wearing cotton gloves. High leather boots, steel toes. No insignia on the flak jacket.

"We've got snoops, here," the woman said, and Greg realized with dismay she was looking right at him. Their ski masks were the same: screaming red faces on black.

"No," Greg said. "Just go. We didn't see anything."

"Shit!" The gunman marched down the aisle, his sawed-off shotgun at hip level. "You nosy bastard, I'll chop you into hamburger."

"Let them alone, please!" the store owner called. "Just take the money and go!"

The gunman was big, easily as tall as Greg. He shifted so he could see Janine. Greg felt her press against his back.

"It's a whole goddamn brood, here." The gunman jabbed Greg in the chest. "What the hell are you looking at?"

"No. No, I didn't see anything." Greg's voice sounded amazingly calm to himself. "Look, please leave us alone. You can have what money I've got. You can take my car. But just leave us alone."

The gunman jabbed the barrel into Greg's mouth, splitting his lip. "Shut up! I know what I can have, and what I can't. All of you, up front. Take your wallets out and put them on the counter."

He backed up the aisle and Beth and Greg followed, Janine between them. Greg looked down at her once they got to the front of the store and saw she was looking at his split lip, at the blood on his shirt. A rage swept through him. How dare they scare his daughter like that?

She was trying not to make any noise. He patted her head. "We'll be all right, sweetheart." Greg laid his wallet on the counter and Beth did the same. He laid his keys beside them, and as a final gesture, he slid off his watch, a gift from Beth.

The gunman held the sawed-off on his hip, then picked up the car keys. He glanced outside. "So that BMW is yours, huh?" He turned toward the woman. "I always wanted a BMW. How about you?"

"I always wanted a BMW," she repeated, her voice dead.

The man ran through Greg's wallet with one hand quickly and pulled out the cash and the driver's license. He whistled as he slid the license into his back pocket. "You live in Lincoln, huh? Nice town. Nice-looking wife there. Nice kid. You must be rich, huh?"

"No."

"Oh, yeah, you must be. You must be so rich, you forgot." He placed the gun back against Greg's chest and leaned into it, looking down at Janine. "How about you, little girl? Do you know what rich is?"

Greg felt himself grow cold. He said, "Take the stuff and go."

The man ignored him, and continued on with Janine. "Maybe you can show me. Maybe you can help me."

Greg could feel her pressing up against him more tightly, and could feel his wife's eyes. He pushed Janine back gently and tried to catch the man's eyes through that mask. "Leave her alone."

The man took his time, cocking his head slightly, so he could see Janine cowering behind Greg. Then he looked back up, slowly. "I don't want to."

Greg went for the gun.

He didn't think he was a hero. He didn't think he was brave. He didn't think at all. Down to his very fiber, Greg simply knew he needed to get that gun away.

But Janine had grabbed at his legs again, and he stumbled. The gunman delivered two powerful blows with the shortened stock, one to Greg's mouth, the other right over his ear. And then the gunman whirled and shot the store owner in the face.

Beth screamed as Greg fell onto his back. And though he fought to get to his feet, to drag himself up against the counter, the floor felt as if it were moving. His arms and legs seemed without bone. He was distantly aware that the woman had sagged against the counter, too, her gun turned away from them. The gunman stepped over and hit Beth as she tried to help her husband.

Janine was left standing. She couldn't get her breath in to cry; she was too shocked.

"Take her," the gunman said, and the woman came back to life. She scooped Janine up and started for the door.

"No!" Beth grabbed at her daughter's foot. The woman kicked Beth away, and the gunman bent down and punched her in the stomach, knocking the breath out of her. He turned to Greg and cracked him across the face. "Pay attention, you. This is all you're gonna get, so you better listen."

"Please—"

"Shut up! I've got your address. I've got your daughter. You try to follow us, I'll kill her. You call the police, I'll kill her. You do what I say, I'll return her safe. So, what you do now is you count to fifteen after I leave, and then walk out of the store, and drive home. There's no witnesses to screw you up. I'll call some-time soon with a nice round number."

Greg shook his head, trying to clear the momentary paraly-sis, get past the horror of the words coming through the gap in the black cloth, the moving yellow teeth. The man tossed Greg's keys and wallet onto the countertop. "This has been my lucky day. Tomorrow can be your little girl's if you do what I tell you."

CHAPTER 2

Ross figured he would spend the night inside the house for a change. He'd passed the last couple on the beach, wrapped in an old blanket. The sand in his hair and the stiffness of his back was a small price to pay for the ability to look up anytime, two, three in the morning, and see the stars.

Not that he saw his destiny there, or even spent much time contemplating his personal significance in the scheme of things, or lack thereof. He was just happy not to see Crockett's leg hanging out of the top bunk, his sock half off his foot. Happy not to breathe the humid, pent-up air of too many people in too small a space. Not to wake up to the reality of being a screwup of the worst kind . . . a prison inmate.

No, as Ross tacked the top rail of the deck with a couple of finishing nails, he figured he was ready for the old place, and it was reasonably ready for him. Under the glow of his battery-powered work light, he put the level on the railing and was pleased to see the bubble neatly between the lines.

It was a small accomplishment, but it made him smile. Perhaps it was the location, too, standing on the deck again, smelling the salt air. He switched off the work light. Fifty feet below, the crashing waves reflected white in the moonlight. The house was positioned on the northern tip of the deepwater cove. The moon was big and fat that night, making the cove alive with light.

Two months out, Ross still wasn't used to having this kind of view available to him alone. He felt drunk on it, more so than he had on the bottle of cognac he'd found in the cupboard the night before. He'd downed almost half the bottle just for the sake of being able to do it.

He saw the open bottle on the living room table next to the kerosene lantern, and made a mental note to put the liquor away. He didn't want Beth looking at him with that slightly worried expression he seemed to inspire.

He looked around the beach house critically. She and Greg would be pleased. Ross had freshly painted the interior and almost finished rewiring the house. The smoke-damaged furniture hadn't been salvageable, and he'd tossed it all. And he'd finished shingling the roof, had the blisters to prove it. The deck floorboards were entirely new—that's where the fire had started.

Apparently some beach kids must've found the stone fireplace inside the house too inconvenient or constraining. The fire marshal had told Greg they were lucky the whole place hadn't been gutted.

Ross thought back to when he was a teenager and tried to remember if he would have done that. Certainly he'd had more than his share of late-night races with a series of fast cars. He hadn't been what he'd call a responsible kid. But he had never set a house on fire for fun.

Ross shivered suddenly. The night was still warm, but, unaccountably, some of his euphoria began to tick away. He looked down the water crashing against the rocks below and found himself thinking about the changes since those days, the wrong turns. Married and divorced by twenty-four, imprisoned a year after that. Hell of a record by his thirtieth birthday. There was a core of melancholy always beneath the surface, knowing that five years had been permanently stripped out of his life. The stigma of being seen as a drug smuggler.

And now he and Greg were thinking about breaking at least half the cove into four smaller parcels to sell off for private homes. Ross looked back in the direction of the beach and inhaled deeply. He told himself the tang of the salt air would still be as sharp. That they were committed to doing the job right, to not overselling the place. That they would still be retaining the best of the place for Janine . . . and his own kids, if he ever got his life together enough to get married again and have them.

Still, it didn't feel entirely right.

The house was a smallish Victorian. It had a widow's walk and a beautiful view of their cove. The cove itself was a deep cut into the mainland; high, rocky walls rose out of the water and led back to a pristine sandy beach. And it was for that beach he and his brother had named the place, simply enough, the Sands. The house had been set where Ross's great-grandfather could watch his fleet come in. The old man had made his money on shipping, and the cove had been his private working port. Back when the name Stearns had meant something.

Now the family was down to two brothers who loved each other but had to work at getting along. And the cove, ten acres in all, was still beautiful and gave the appearance of privacy. But it was surrounded by encroaching industrial sites on every side.

Ross figured replacing the dock and doing the remaining work on the house would take him through the summer, and then he'd have to get a real job right after Labor Day. He intended to live there until the other parcels sold. Then, after he paid Greg back for the legal fees, Ross figured he'd get himself another boat. Get his life fully back on track.

Ross put the level on the lower rail and found that it, too, was fine. Some of the satisfaction returned, and he smiled, thinking once again that just being out on his own meant his life was already back on track. Thoughts of the upcoming vacation with his brother's family suffused him with a steady pulse right under his breastbone that he recognized as happiness.

He was telling himself that he'd even indulge Greg and listen to his advice when the cellular phone rang. Ross jogged out to the truck to get the bad news about his godchild.

CHAPTER 3

Greg's BMW and a Volkswagen with roof racks were in the driveway of his house. Allie Pearson's car.

Ross let himself in.

Beth made it into the foyer first. Her face was pale, and he could read the disappointment on her face; he read instantly that the very sound of the door opening must've given her the hope that somehow, some way, her daughter would be walking through. She'd clearly been crying.

Greg was right behind her. "You told no one, right?"

"That's right." Ross held Beth briefly, felt the rigidness of her back.

She pulled away to look at him, her dark blue eyes intent. "Please. Anything you can tell us about someone who'd do this, anything. . . ."

Ross simply nodded, masking the sense of resignation her comment engendered—the automatic assumption that he knew more about people who robbed stores than they did. Because, of course, he now did. And he knew there had been stories at Concord Prison about families of inmates who were followed home. Sometimes they were just hassled for money, sometimes worse.

Ross squeezed Greg's arm. He had a large bruise over his left eye and his lip was puffed and split. Greg was trembling slightly. He said, "Allie called me tonight, and I told her what had happened, and to come right away. We're going to have to raise some money fast."

Allie joined them and waited impatiently. She was their attorney, a striking woman with dark auburn hair and green eyes. And a month ago, she'd been Ross's lover for all of about two weeks. Ross was dismayed at the jolt he still felt just upon seeing her. He'd thought he was past that.

"I'm glad you're here, Ross," she said. "Tell them this is crazy. Tell them we need the police."

"No," Greg said. "We want Janine back fast, and I don't want to screw around with experts who've got their own ax to grind. This guy wants money, and he's going to get it."

"Have you heard from them yet?" Ross asked.

"No."

"How long has it been?"

"Four and a half hours." Beth's voice was barely audible.

Ross walked them back into the dining room. The telephone rested at the head of the table, and Ross found himself looking at it as Greg talked, as if it were a fifth person.

Greg went through the robbery and abduction quickly, starting with when the gunman walked through the door.

"You didn't see anyone following you in the car beforehand?" Ross asked. "Any strange phone calls the week before? Or anybody you didn't know show up at your door?"

"No. Nothing like that."

"Beth?"

She looked off to the side, then turned back. "No one out of the ordinary. The mailman, the boy who cuts the grass, the pool guy. All people we know."

"Describe how the guy behaved again."

"Excited," Greg said. "Not quite angry, but pumped up. Seemed to be enjoying himself." Greg touched the bruise on his temple.

"Not scared? A lot of guys go in there shaking as bad as the people behind the counter."

"Not that I could tell. But he had a mask on."

"But what's your impression? Was he in control? Or totally off?"

"Somewhere in between."

"Was he skinny or heavy?"

"Skinny."

Ross found himself relax slightly. A guy he'd had problems with got paroled around the same time he had. But no one would have ever described Teague as skinny. Teague was a moon-faced biker, with a scraggly goatee and shaved head. Ross asked, "How did this guy smell, like he hadn't bathed recently?"

"Smell?" Beth asked.

"He's trying to figure out if the guy was a junkie," Allie said.

"I didn't notice a bad smell particularly," Greg said. "But the guy certainly seemed wired enough. He could be a junkie."

"Why'd you jump him?"

Ross asked the question without accusation, but Greg flushed angrily. "Goddamn it, Ross. He was going to take her."

"He said that? 'I'm going to take her'?"

Allie raked her hair back angrily. "Look, Ross, if we were crossing the Atlantic, I'd listen to your advice. But being an ex-con doesn't make you an expert on criminal behavior. We *need* the police."

Out in the open, Ross thought.

Allie had broken up with him after it became apparent his long-range plans involved a sailboat and a distant destination. Not that different from his ex-wife's disenchantment with him, he'd realized. But Allie had come from an entirely different angle. Whereas Cynthia had been drifting herself in many ways, Allie was an extremely motivated woman. Maybe it was because she had been an assistant district attorney, or maybe it was her tough upbringing in upstate Maine, or maybe it was just a fundamental difference between her and Ross, as deep as their blood cells. She had no patience with drifting. And that's the way she saw his sailing to the Caribbean.

"I think you're right," Ross said.

Allie looked surprised but said nothing.

"The two of you, listen to me," Greg said. "I don't need arguments. I need your help getting me a buyer, getting me that cash."

Allie's tone with Greg was gentler. "Greg, the odds are slightly better if you involve the police, the FBI actually. It'd be the FBI that'd run it, being a kidnapping. They know so much more about it. They can put wiretaps in, bring all sorts of trained personnel."

"Greg?" Beth leaned forward.

Greg rubbed his face, then abruptly shoved away from the table. "Don't talk statistics at me. Don't tell me what on average should be done, and how federal personnel are going to make it all better. I don't need some guy in a nice suit telling me, 'sorry, we found your daughter's body with our dogs and "personnel."' I had the kidnapper tell me to my face that he would let her go if I did what he said. He was wearing a mask; she shouldn't be able to identify him. Beth and I sure can't identify him. What's he got to lose? I give him the cash; he gives me my girl. . . . I'm wishing the guy well. I'm wishing the guy a goddamn vacation for the rest of his life, on me. I want Janine back, and I will play ball with this bastard to get it. So if either of you decide you know what's best and trip me up on this, I will break you in half."

"Greg, I—" Ross started to say.

"I mean it!" Greg hit the table with his fist. "You owe me, Ross. I need you to stand behind me."

Ross's blood quickened, but he kept his mouth shut. He was willing to argue with his brother—if he knew the right answer. But he really didn't. When it was all said and done, Greg had listened to the guy, and he hadn't.

Finally, he said, "Whatever you want."

"I only want to do the right thing by Janine," Allie said. "You know that."

"So get us a buyer," Beth said quietly.

Allie turned to Ross. "It's your land, too. You'll sign, won't you?"

"Sure, we already made that decision. But that's not going to be the quickest way."

"Hell of a time to be cash-poor," Greg said hoarsely. "I could scrape up five, maybe ten thousand in cash. Maybe up to fifty if I throw myself on some friends . . . but they'd end up talking to the cops, someone would."

"Your business is that bad?"

"It's that bad. We're staving off bankruptcy. There's simply no lump for me to get my hands on, not if this guy comes back looking for any sizable amount of money. I've got the house mortgaged to the hilt, and you know we've had no luck selling it. I'd never get a loan of any size."

"How about if we just put the Sands up as collateral on a loan?" Ross asked. "That might be faster."

"I can't imagine a banker not calling the police on this," Greg said. "What do you think, Allie?"

She nodded reluctantly. "It would be the rare banker who could leave the police out of it."

Greg continued. "Maybe I could raise another twenty if I can sell the car fast, but it's got over fifty thousand on the clock. I won't get that much."

"Jesus." Ross knew the business hadn't been doing that well, but nothing like this. Greg had based his computer reseller business on two manufacturers who were both having serious problems. Consequently, his own sales had gone south. And Ross still owed him over fifty thousand dollars for legal fees. "You think we can find a buyer to move that fast?" Ross asked.

"You know how many offers we've had."

"Yes, but to move so fast? And what if the kidnapper insists on more than the parcels we had in mind? Total, it's assessed at, what, a little over a million?"

"What if the guy calls insisting on a million-five?" Beth interjected. "What if he asks for more than we can do?"

Greg shook his head. "I don't know. I don't know."

CHAPTER 4

The night before, the woman had put her coat over Janine's head and told to her stay on the floor of the car.

Janine had buried her face in the dirty carpet and squeezed her eyes shut. Without quite thinking it through, she'd known it would be bad to see the man, to really see his face.

He talked fast. Swearing. "Goddamn, *goddamn.* We're making it big with this one, babe."

He yelled things to the woman. "Don't use my name. Got it?" Or, "We're gonna be cold on this, babe. Fucking ice water."

"Did you have to shoot that man?" the woman said, once, quietly.

"Hey, I did what I had to do. I can do it with the little chick, too."

Then he talked to Janine. "Tell me about your house. How big is it? How many rooms? You got a swimming pool? Huh? You're a smart kid, how much money does your daddy make?"

Janine didn't answer.

She didn't think he really wanted her to. Sometimes adults did that, asked questions but didn't really expect her to talk.

But this time, the woman nudged her. "Tell him, sweetie. You got a pool?"

Janine nodded her head.

"Yes, she's got a pool," the woman said. "Now, sweetie, how about your dad? You know how much money he makes?" The woman rested her hand on Janine's head, and, after a second, Janine shook it no.

"No, she doesn't."

"Bullshit!" The front seat thumped near where Janine's head was and she cried out. "You want me to stop this car?" The man's voice had kind of a laugh in it that terrified Janine all the more. She tried to dig deeper into the floor. "You want me to stop this car and come back there?"

The woman said, "I don't think she knows, really. Did you know what your dad made when you were a kid?" Her voice then got closer to Janine's ear. "How old are you, kid?"

Janine didn't said anything. Couldn't speak.

The woman rested her hand on Janine's head again. "Seven? Eight? Nine?"

Janine nodded.

"Nine," the woman said. Her hand remained on Janine's head for a second longer. "Nine," she repeated, and then said to the man, "Did you know what your dad made when you were nine?"

"Yeah. Diddly-shit. And that he drank and pissed away." The seat thumped near Janine's ear again. "Better hope your daddy didn't piss it all away on pools and BMWs. Better hope he's got some left over for you."

After a while, the car stopped and Janine could hear the man get out for a second. Then the car moved again, and she could hear a slamming sound. Like a garage door being closed. They shoved her up a lot of stairs and finally into a room, with the coat still over her head. Janine wondered if they were still wearing the masks and shuddered. Black-and-red faces. She could only see the floor; that's all, a wooden gray floor.

Janine kept seeing her mom being kicked. Her dad on the floor, his face bleeding.

She kept coming back to him patting her on the head before, telling her, "We'll be all right, sweetheart."

That man hitting them. Talking to Daddy in such an ugly way. The storekeeper.

That was a scene of noise, and red, and that just couldn't be looked at directly. She hadn't been friends with the storekeeper, or anything. But she and her mom had gone there before.

One time, he had been whistling as she and her mother walked up to the counter. He had said, "Hi, beautiful." Talking to her. Janine had remembered turning her head away, embarrassed. Her mother had smiled for her. That had been early in the year. March, maybe.

She wondered immediately if he had a little girl, too. He was old. But the way he had smiled at Janine, she bet he did. And what if that little girl had seen him that way . . . ?

Janine let out a low keening sound.

"Shut her up! Here, I've got a roll of that duct tape."

"Get me some of those paper towels," the woman had said.

"Why?"

"Put the paper over her eyes, then do the tape."

"Fuck that. Just do the tape."

"It'll be easier on her later, taking it off."

"Who cares?"

"Look, I'll do it. Just get yourself a beer."

"Little mama, you can't keep her. Hell, I may have to put her in a bag and drown her if her old man doesn't come through."

The woman didn't say anything.

Janine started to cry again. She couldn't keep the sounds from coming out. She had to pee, too, but couldn't imagine asking if she could go to the bathroom.

The woman had reached under the coat with paper towel and pressed it against Janine's eyes. Janine felt the coat pulled away and the ripping sound of tape being pulled off the roll. The woman put it on quickly and tightly; the tape pulled at Janine's hair. "Shssh," the woman said into her ear. "Don't make a fuss. It'll go bad for you if you do."

Janine nodded.

"You gotta pee?" the woman asked. "I'll walk you into the bathroom."

Janine heard the man talking. It didn't sound like it was to her, and then she heard her dad's name, and she realized the man was on the phone.

"Yeah, a Greg Stearns. Ridge Road, Lincoln."

The phone clattered.

"OK, got his number," the man said. There was the sound of paper rustling, and she heard him chuckle. "What'd I tell you? Look at the prices of these houses in Lincoln. Six hundred thousand. Four-fifty . . . a million-three, for Christ's sake. . . ."

The floorboards creaked in front of Janine, and she pressed back against the woman's body.

Janine felt a hard finger under her chin. "I'm going to think up a nice number, then me and your dad are going to talk. Now tell me something—let's see; how does it go—tell me something that just you and your mom and dad know."

Janine couldn't speak. She felt herself trembling so hard:

"Come on, come on."

She couldn't. Her mind had gone blank. Couldn't think of what he wanted. She said, "Mama."

He shoved her. "Goddamn it! Tell me something only you and

your mama know. Just *saying,* 'Mama,' doesn't do shit for me!

"Oh, Christ, she peed on the floor!" the man yelled, and Janine realized with terror that she had. Her leg was warm.

Suddenly she felt herself lifted up and she cried out before realizing it was the woman. The woman called out in a loud voice, "Drink your beer! I'll clean up in a second. And I'll get what you want out of her." The woman's voice was hard and not very friendly, but Janine hugged her with all of her strength.

She heard the door close behind them, and then the woman said in a mean voice, "Listen, I'm not always going to be able to get in between him and you like I just did. So when he asks you something, you answer him fast. You got that? Now talk to me. You got any brothers or sisters?"

Janine shook her head.

"OK, let's see. . . . What did you have for breakfast this morning?"

Janine tried to think, but her mind was jammed with only what had happened in the past few hours, and she'd have been hard pressed to say her name in that moment.

The woman's voice was impatient. "Well, what do you usually like? Pancakes? Cereal?"

"Bagel," Janine said softly.

"What?"

"Bagel. I like a bagel with peanut butter and banana mashed up on top of it."

The woman laughed. "Kids," she said. Janine didn't know why what she said was funny and didn't like it that the woman could laugh when all she felt like doing was crying and being held by her mama, and having her dad sitting beside them, his hand on her back. . . .

"OK, bagel with peanut butter and banana. Let's see if that and your old man can get you out of here."

The woman brushed Janine's hair with her hand for a mo-

ment. That made Janine feel a little better, and she worked up
her courage to say, "Take me home, please?"

"Shut up." The woman had taken her hand away abruptly. Janine heard the sound of the tape being pulled off the roll again,
and the woman taped Janine's mouth and tied her hands and feet
to the bed.

And left her.

CHAPTER 5

The phone finally rang at 3:43 in the morning.

Greg and Beth reached for it at the same time, and then Beth pulled her hand away. "You do it."

Ross sat beside Greg and nodded over at Allie, who quickly rolled off the couch and pushed back her tousled hair. Beth shoved the pad and pen over to Greg as he picked up the phone.

Ross put his ear beside his brother's and held his hand lightly over his mouth so whoever was on the phone would only hear one man breathing.

"Yes?" Greg said.

"Guess who, Mr. Lincoln," a rough voice said. Ross closed his eyes, listening hard.

"Let me speak to my daughter, please."

"Shut up. She's not with me. I'm in a phone booth, and I'm gonna say this once. Five hundred thousand. Tonight. I'll get back to you on when and where."

Greg said, carefully, "Please listen to me. You've *got* to understand that I don't have that kind of cash sitting in the bank."

The man hung up.

"Jesus." Greg looked up wonderingly at Beth. "Oh my God, that's it?"

"He's probably just thinking about a trace," Ross said. "He doesn't want to talk that long, that's all."

"You're right," Allie said. "That's probably all it is."

Beth's lower lip trembled, and she stared at Greg. "Why'd you tell him it would be hard?" A flush swept up her face and she suddenly shouted, "Why did you say that? Why didn't you'd tell him we'd do anything to get her back?"

"Honey, he didn't give me—"

The phone rang again, and Greg snatched it up.

"I don't *got* to understand anything," the man said. "Your girl is crying for her mama. Ma-ma. It's up to you to get her back. Now, I'm a big reader of the real estate pages, the *Globe,* the *Herald,* the *Phoenix.* Guy like me learns things, like who's getting ready to move, who's gonna let me walk through on an open house and shop for my next hit, you know what I mean? So when I see Lincoln, I know your house costs somewhere around five, six hundred thousand and up. And I've got to ask myself, Is this guy's kid worth a house? I bet she is."

"The bank owns the place!" Greg cried. "We don't have that—"

"She's safe until tonight," the man interrupted. "And then she's dead. You've already seen the last of your girl if you're planning on fucking with me."

"Please take care of her." Greg fought to keep his voice calm. "We'll do anything to get her back. We don't care about the money—it's just a matter of raising it. Give me something to know she's alive."

"Yeah, yeah. She likes bagels and bananas, she says. With peanut butter."

Greg's laugh was just a short bark. "That's true. She does. But how . . ." He licked his lips.

"But how do you know I didn't ask her that right before killing her? You don't. But let's see what I can do. . . . How about I call you tonight around eight? That's sixteen hours from now. You have the money, and I'll have her on the phone. And if you're sitting there with the cash, you can ask her what she wants for dinner and then I'll tell you where to go pick her up. You'll have her back in time to make the little doll whatever she wants."

The man's voice continued. "But if you've got some lame story for me about how you couldn't raise the cash, how you need me to give you a few days, then I'm gonna figure you're jerking me around. I'm gonna figure you're sitting there with the FBI. And then I'm gonna treat you to the sound of me blowing her away, right while you're talking to her. You *got* that?"

He hung up.

Beth's hands shook as she fished through the top kitchen drawer for a pack of cigarettes. Her voice was bright and high, on the verge of hysteria. "Here's a deep dark secret, Greg. I still smoke." She fumbled with the little propane lighter, lit the cigarette, and said, "How in God's name are we going to raise that much in a day?"

"Half a million dollars." Greg's expression was blank, stunned. "Doesn't he understand no one has that kind of money lying around?"

"No," said Ross. "Guys who're willing to go into stores with guns have a very simple view of the world."

"He's right," Allie said. "Don't assume this guy is operating from anything you know. He's from another planet." She switched tacks. "We need to get somebody to buy the whole property, the whole cove. Someone with a business."

Greg nodded. "There was that developer. Geiler. He was pretty interested. Even sent somebody to talk to you inside, didn't he?"

Ross nodded, remembering the meeting through the glass with Geiler's attorney, a man by the name of Bradford. The attorney had pushed hard.

"You didn't burn any bridges with them, did you?" Greg asked worriedly.

"Nothing irreparable. I just told the guy we definitely weren't selling the whole thing. Nothing worse than that."

"That's what I said." Greg turned his attention back to Allie. Just talking over the specifics of selling the Sands had focused him. "We're going to need a letter of agreement, because we'd never be able to actually close in one day. We'll start with Geiler, and let's work out whoever else is a possibility. Let's go for Cabletech Systems, that wire-extruding company that's right up against our property line. And any other company in the industrial park. Let's do a list. Maybe one of them needs to expand. Let's get going."

The three of them began making calls at 7:30 A.M.

Ross wandered about the house as they did. Five years of being inside prison had left him feeling clumsy and out of place with even normal business practices. Greg was in control now, and approaching the sale of the land as logically as could be expected under the circumstances.

Ross hesitated outside Greg and Beth's bedroom, then went in.

Sure enough, he found his father's gun along with the cleaning kit and bullets on the top shelf of Greg's bedroom closet. Right where their father had kept it.

Ross felt a hand squeeze his heart, just taking the thing out of the box. His parole officer, Bernise Liotta, and the judge would be myopic about it. Ex-con with a gun, that's a violation, don't tell me about your niece, don't tell me how hard it is to sell real estate in one day, next case file, please.

Ross took the revolver up to the attic and pulled up a chair to a rickety table and started cleaning the thing. It was an old Smith & Wesson .38 with a black handle grip. The gun hadn't been oiled in a long time. Ross wondered if it would blow up in his hand.

To his knowledge, the gun had never been fired. His father had just thought a man needed a gun in his house. Or more likely, he had thought that was how a man *should* think.

It had been the hardest lesson of Ross's life to accept that his father was a weak man. But he'd done it one afternoon not long after his thirteenth birthday, when his father had cracked him across the face for flushing a vial of cocaine down the toilet.

Greg hadn't wanted to hear it. "Shut up," he'd said. "God-damn it, Ross, he's got a problem. He misses Mom. You're too young to understand."

"Brody is an addict," Ross had said.

Greg had shoved him into the bedroom. "Don't call him by his name. He's Dad to you and me."

Ross hadn't pushed his brother back, even though he was already faster and almost as strong. After all, Greg was older. Greg remembered better days. He would talk about how much fun it had all been when their mother was alive, going to concerts, traveling the country in an old Volkswagen van. That they had been lucky to have parents who weren't boring.

She'd died in a car crash when Ross had been eight, and Greg, ten. Their father had been driving.

Ross remembered the days before only vaguely, and that had troubled him a lot at first. He remembered his mother as warm, and her hair blond. That she smelled good, and held him and

Greg easily, and she kept things OK even when their dad was tense and angry. That she'd call impromptu picnics, just her and the two boys, up overlooking the cove. She'd make light of their father's "grumpiness."

Ross shared his father's dark hair and regular features. Greg had their mother's coloring, high cheekbones, and fair skin.

There had been a time when Ross had hung on his father's every word, a time when he'd swelled with pride when people said he looked just like his father. Maybe it was that earlier bond that let Ross see even more clearly what his father had become—a man who couldn't leave the house without taking *something* before going off to work. Pills, sometimes. Coke, if he could get it. Something to make him preen, check his mustache in the mirror, smooth his long hair. Apparently oblivious to the fact that alcohol had bloated his features.

For years, he had had a series of declining jobs after he lost his antique store in Marblehead. Nothing was ever his fault. Someone was always out to screw him. He always had a plan to get them first, but the plan inevitably backfired and Ross and Greg would come home to his petty rage. He had acquired hundreds of blues records, and when he was in a good mood he'd pull Ross and Greg in to listen while he held forth on one musician after another . . . and then become furious, down to smashing the record itself, if he didn't get the reaction from his sons that he wanted.

Months would pass before he'd get another job and the whole process would start all over again.

He'd talk about how he didn't *need* to work, as if he'd earned a fortune himself. Instead, he dipped into the principal of an ever-shrinking inheritance and cursed his father and grandfather. "Greedy bastards, the both of them," he'd say. "Ripped the guts out of me."

Weekends and evenings, he'd go from near catatonic to hyperactive depending upon what he was taking.

Ross and Greg would escape into the cove and the woods surrounding it. They'd sail, go rowing, diving . . . just hang out in the woods for hours at a time. Greg came home with a tent one day, announced with a false cheerfulness that he wanted to do some camping. The two of them slept out in the tent overlooking the cove many a night when their father was really in bad shape. Without discussing it, they covered for their father, letting no one in school know what was going on.

At age forty-eight Brody had declared himself retired, that there were no jobs equal to his creativity. Ross had been just under fifteen.

Greg had taken everything onto his own shoulders. Getting Ross off to school, keeping the house reasonably clean, helping the old man up to his bedroom when he couldn't make it himself. He had eventually started losing weight, turning into a gray shell of a man with watery blue eyes and a red flush of broken blood vessels across his nose and cheeks.

And he'd begun hitting more and more often.

Greg was no coward. He was strong and would take care of himself in schoolyard fights. But when the old man had started swinging over the coffee being too cold or that Ross was out too late, Greg would take the blows, pleading for the old man to come to his senses.

One night when Ross was fifteen, he threw himself at the old man. He woke up minutes later with one of his teeth chipped. Greg was pushing his father back, shouting, "Look what you did, for Christ's sake!"

His father had looked at Greg and touched the blood on his own mouth and said, "Shut up, you little shit. He understands me. He and I are just alike."

That had chilled Ross then, and he'd thought of it often behind prison bars.

When Greg had decided to commute to a local community college even though he'd been offered a scholarship at Cornell, Ross had objected. "Go, for God's sake."

"I can't leave you here."

"The hell you can't. Go."

Finally, they had compromised, with Greg going two hours away to Amherst College and planning to come home on weekends.

Ross had watched his brother's car roll away with the blackest despair. He'd tried to keep the peace for almost a month, making the meals, taking care of the old man.

But one night after a trip to Laconia Speedway in New Hampshire, Ross came home to find the old man waiting with the very gun Ross was now oiling. He'd raged that Ross had damn well better learn to behave—whatever specific infraction Ross had committed was unclear.

Ross had simply turned on his heel and walked out.

He'd gotten back into the car, and on the way out of the Sands, he'd done a quick assessment. Saw that he'd grown up in a place that he loved, with a father he'd learned to hate. That with Greg in school, his family life was on hold. That he might as well do what he most wanted to do—learn to race a car so fast there was room for nothing else in his head but the speed, the upcoming turns, the win ahead.

For if he stayed at home, he and his father would very likely kill each other. It took Ross a few days to land a job on a pit crew for a stock car driver named Bill Cobb. Ross had quit school on his sixteenth birthday and hit the road.

Six years later, Greg had walked into Ross's hospital room and told him their father had overdosed on cocaine and died of heart failure.

Already Greg looked older than his twenty-four years, wearing a trench coat and a sport jacket underneath. Ross was recovering from a crash during a rally race in Washington's Capitol State Forest. His knee was in a cast; they said the surgery had been successful. But his knee still hurt like hell, and his sponsor had just informed him that they wouldn't be renewing their contract. "Are *you* going to live?" Greg had asked.

Ross had nodded, unable to speak. He was shocked at how much it hurt to hear his father was gone, even though they hadn't even talked since Greg and Beth's wedding two years before. "Yeah," he'd said, finally.

"Good. You finish the high school equivalency?"

Ross nodded.

"Then come back and help me start something. A business I want to tell you about. You can make some money, go back to college nights, maybe." Greg had put his hand out. "Come on back home. Stay alive."

Ross wiped the gun off with a cloth. It was clean now, but he still wasn't sure of how well it would shoot. And while there was no doubt in his mind that he owed his brother, Ross still had no idea how far he was willing to go with that gun.

CHAPTER 6

Ross watched Greg talk on the phone, trying to make the deal happen. Sweat beaded his forehead, and Ross wished he could close his ears to the edge of panic that was coming through.

He asked Allie if they'd had any success.

"Not really. Geiler's out of town and won't be back in the office until early afternoon. They won't give us his number. The general manager of Cabletech Systems is on vacation; ditto with him. We've gotten through to only three of the other people who'd made offers in the past, and none of them were in a position to commit so fast."

"Not surprising."

Greg slammed the phone down. "No one can comprehend the idea of moving so quickly! And who can blame them? This isn't how it's done." Greg began pacing. "Maybe we can give this guy something down. Get the ten thousand and tell him it'll just take some more time; give him that tonight."

"And let him keep her?" Beth said.

"What's the choice!" Greg rubbed the back of his neck. "The guy can't understand what he's asking! Can't he understand people just don't have that kind of money lying around? Maybe it'll appease him."

Ross went out to the truck and got the postcard Crockett had sent him months before, when he first got out on parole. Ross sat on the open tailgate and dialed Crockett's number. The receiver was picked up at the other end, but no one said anything.

"It's Ross," he said.

"You finally getting around to answering your mail?" Crockett said.

Ross thumbnailed the situation quickly, and asked Crockett for an introduction.

Crockett sighed, hearing what Ross had to say. "That sucks. It really does." He hung up, and then it was Ross's turn to wait for the phone. Crockett got back after a long ten minutes and said, "Yuh. He'll see you. Bring the deed, pictures of the place, but don't get your hopes up. Guys like him don't make their money on vacation homes." He gave Ross an address on Hanover Street in the North End of Boston.

Tommy Datano looked at the pictures. He looked at the deed, the property assessment, the property lines. He listened to Ross's story about the previous offers.

He listened to why they were selling the property now and shook his head sadly. "Ugly business. No wonder you're so desperate." He was a small, dark man, with wire-rimmed glasses. "Believe me, with your being a friend of Crockett's I'd help you recover your niece directly, I would. Crockett did a couple of things for us that've made us appreciative. You know that. But none of my associates are involved, this sounds like someone just taking a chance. An opportunist." Behind Ross, there were half a dozen people waiting in chairs, waiting as Ross had done, agonizing over the hour he'd wasted so far.

Datano called over his accountant, a white-haired man with a suit covered with cigarette ash. The accountant wheezed slightly as he went through the documents, his blunt finger sliding over each of them carefully. Finally, he said, "You already got a nice summer place, Tommy."

"But this gentleman's got trouble. I'd like to help him out."

The man shrugged. "So help him out. Two hundred and fifty."

"That won't do me any good," Ross said.

Datano looked up. "You got no other money?"

"We need the whole thing."

The white-haired man laughed. "You think this is Century Twenty-one?"

Datano said, "Let me be honest. This isn't our type of margin. We'd expect to pay twenty-five, thirty percent of the legit value. That's what we'd be looking for if we were to purchase. Or, if you were to take out a loan, and put your land down as collateral, through the vig we'd very quickly own the place anyhow . . . and I just don't know, with the terrible state of the market, if this land is still worth anything near what it was a year ago." He smiled regretfully. "Maybe if we had some time, we could assess it better. But I realize you have none. So either take the two-fifty and go make the balance some other way . . . or go try to make it, and come back to see me before it's too late." He reached out and touched Ross on the shoulder. "Good luck with your little niece."

The interview was over.

Ross had never been to Crockett's apartment in South Boston. Although Crockett had been Ross's best friend inside, he'd never planned to be looking for anyone from Concord again. And he felt a little guilty about that, standing outside Crockett's building.

The place was an old brownstone that had been renovated years ago; the foyer walls were cheap wooden paneling, the floor littered with takeout-food paper bags and cigarette butts. There was no answer when Ross sounded the buzzer. But a moment later, he saw Crockett standing on top of the landing looking down through the glass.

Crockett opened the door. "Any luck?"

"Not enough."

Crockett grunted. "Little bastard." They went up to Crockett's apartment, a spartan clean room overlooking the street. Crockett went right to the stove. "I was just fixing myself a late breakfast. You want some?"

Ross said no.

Crockett nodded at the phone in Ross's hand. "Any word?"

Ross shook his head.

"So tell me what happened to her, in detail." Crockett shifted his false teeth as he listened. He was in his midforties, with prematurely white hair. He showed no emotion throughout the story, but when Ross mentioned the eight o'clock deadline, Crockett checked his watch. He served himself breakfast, and before he began to eat, he said, "So what do you want from me?"

"First, do you have any ideas . . . do you think someone we knew in Concord might've coming looking for my family?"

Crockett chewed his toast. "I dunno. It happens sometimes, extortion. You knew about that guy, Gilchrist?"

Ross frowned. "Vaguely."

"This was over in Walpole, not Concord. About a year ago, a guy was telling me about it. Gilchrist's wife was a looker. Used to show up to visit him wearing tank tops, tight jeans. Guess they sent her away a few times, not wanting her going in like that.

But she came back, dressed a little quieter, but still, she couldn't hide herself that much, you know? Real pretty—blond hair, blue eyes, right out of a magazine. Gilchrist was in for embezzlement, and they started hitting him up, saying they'd hurt her."

"Who's 'they'?"

"Got me. Just the word around. Gilchrist went around whining that he was broke; he didn't have anything to give. He'd tell that to whoever listened. He didn't know for sure who else was in on it. Word was they got to her. Rape, battery acid. She didn't come around no more."

Ross shook his head, trying to clear the image. "I keep thinking about Teague."

"Yuh. I got a note a while back from Reece. He said you had some problems. And that was for the way Teague was running on and on about your niece, right?"

"That's right."

"How big was the guy, did your brother say?"

"He was taller and thinner than Teague."

Crockett shrugged. "Guess he could've sent someone else in if you want to look at it that way. But this snatch you described, it sounds random, right?"

"It does. But like you said, things like this do happen sometimes. And Teague and I got into that fight over what he'd said about Janine. That's enough for a conversation with him now, I figure."

Crockett snorted. "A conversation, yeah. Well, he and I don't exactly work the same circles, you understand." Crockett grinned. "Guys like him are dog shit to guys like me. He *does* do stores, liquor and milk stores. I'll ask around, but there's no guarantee I'll be able to find out today."

Ross sighed. "I've got no time. Janine's got no time. What do you think about Datano's offer, the two-fifty? What if we gave that to the guy? Have you got any sense as to how he might react? That's still a hell of a lot of money for a guy used to robbing stores."

Crockett shrugged. "What do I look like, a psychic?"

"I know. I'm grasping at anything."

Crockett looked at Ross consideringly. "Giving him the two-fifty *could* buy some time. A few days, maybe. Then you could come up with the balance."

"Once the land's gone, we're tapped."

"Not necessarily." Crockett paused, then said, "I never would've approached you on this before. You were different than the others inside. I know you figured that sentence as a one-shot fluke, that you'd probably die without a jaywalking ticket. . . ."

"You've got a job planned?"

"Armored car. Kenmore Square. Right about one-thirty. Driver likes his onion bagel with lots of chives, every day about now. Two coffees in his hands. Walks them back to the passenger door, guy opens up. Sloppy, the both of them. I need someone who's a hell of a driver, who could hop a truck or four-wheel drive onto the sidewalk while me and one other guy make the snatch. Then get us out of there and to a clean car within three, maybe four minutes."

"There's enough in there?"

"My info, your cut would be right around three hundred thousand."

"What about today?" Ross felt disassociated from himself, hearing the words. Thinking about going back to prison. Thinking that there were no guarantees the guards wouldn't put up a fight, that innocent men wouldn't be killed.

"No." Crockett shook his head firmly. "We need another guy. And I don't intend to get caught, so it has to be the right one. You, I know, won't shoot me in the back."

Ross felt a dull flush of resentment well up inside him. Greg wouldn't be able to do this, Ross knew. But it could well be the only way to get the money in time. "I'll think about it."

Crockett checked his watch. "Just after one now. Why don't you check it out?"

Ross pulled up in front of the restaurant and waited. College students milled around the square, looking far younger than Ross remembered himself looking at that age. He glanced at himself in the rearview mirror. His black hair was already salted with gray. Ross was only thirty, but he could pass for forty.

He thought about what the first day back in would be like. Walking in with the bars behind clanging shut, the bars in front waiting to open and take him in deeper.

He thought of Janine, of holding her when she was just three hours old.

Logically, he knew the kidnapper may have just been trying to throw a bluff into Greg. But Ross had believed the man himself. He'd known enough people at Concord who could kill a person, a child even, and look at you with incredulity if you suggested *they'd* done something wrong. Could imagine this guy saying, "I *told* the kid's old man what I'd do."

Ross had always considered himself different from the rest of the inmates. He had been certain he'd never be putting himself in the way of the law again. Yet here he was. Ross couldn't help but be angry and resentful of Greg. He should've been here, not Ross.

The armored car pulled up. As Crockett said, the driver went into the restaurant. He was a middle-aged man with sunburned skin and a bristling gray crew cut. A little on the heavy side, not too fat. Ross tried to divine by looking at him if the man would resist.

Sweat beaded Ross's forehead. *This is wrong,* he thought abruptly. *It's wrong, it's stupid, and I just can't do it.*

He felt ashamed, knowing that he was letting Janine down. Knowing that the gun was right under his seat and, if he'd been willing, he could've tried to pull off the robbery himself right then.

Ross picked up the phone and tapped in his brother's phone number.

Greg answered guardedly, presumably ready for the kidnapper.

"It's me," Ross said.

"Where are you?" Greg was clearly excited. "We just got through to Geiler and have an appointment in thirty minutes."

Ross sagged back into his seat. "That's great news. Better than you can believe."

"Take down these directions, and Allie and I'll meet you there."

Ross smiled as the armored car driver came out with a bag in one hand and two coffees balanced in the other. He laughed at something the other guard said.

Alone in his truck, Ross said, "Great news for both of us."

CHAPTER 7

Greg felt that he might well be going insane.

Hope and despair battled inside his head, and both seemed to be equally strong. Both delivered solid blows that made Greg's knees weak one moment and filled him with a rage that he could barely contain the next.

Like seeing Ross waiting for them in the lobby, his face drawn and worried. Greg knew Ross had been out trying to sell the place to the shylock, knew that Ross would stand behind him all the way. He knew that Ross would do whatever was necessary to get Janine back.

Yet it infuriated Greg that Ross wasn't wearing a tie, that his beard was untrimmed, that he'd left the business years ago and was out of practice with negotiating. Geiler's office was in a recently renovated waterfront building. The view of the harbor was spectacular, with millions of dollars on display in the form of a few beautiful sailboats bobbing gently at the dock. The very bricks of the old building had been sandblasted to a rosy glow. All of it said money, and Ross, Greg, and Allie needed to work together to pry it free.

Greg found himself thinking that if Ross hadn't left the business years ago, maybe it wouldn't be on the brink of bankruptcy now. Maybe Greg would've been able to pay this kind of ransom without trying to convince someone to hand him $500,000 within two hours, didn't that fucking bastard who held his daughter have the slightest idea how the world turned? That it was crazy, goddamn crazy, you could be a millionaire five times over and not have that kind of cash sitting around liquid. . . .

Greg closed his eyes briefly as they stepped into the elevator. He told himself to calm down. He told himself that none of this was Ross's fault. "How'd it go with Datano?" he heard himself ask.

"Datano?" Allie looked at him sharply. "You let him go to Tommy Datano on this? Are you crazy?"

"Yes, Allie, I am."

"Two-fifty," Ross said. "If Geiler doesn't work out, we should take the offer and give the kidnappers that. Two-fifty is a lot of money to a guy who robs milk stores." Ross's tone was reassuring, but his eyes didn't meet Greg's.

"Geiler's got to work out," Greg said, as the elevator reached the floor. "He's got to."

Geiler's secretary escorted them into his office right away. Greg had met Geiler just a few times before, first at a party at the Watersons' beach house and again when Geiler made the offers back in May and June. A million-one had been the last offer.

That had been tempting back then, especially the way the business had been going. But Greg and Ross had both agreed they didn't want to sell more than the four parcels. It had pained Greg to even think about doing that, and he knew Ross felt the same way. Greg would think of their father, draining the inheritance to feed his habit. It was easy to think they were being just as irresponsible, that they were cutting the land in pieces because they couldn't manage their own lives.

But seeing my girl safe is my job, Greg thought abruptly. *All else is secondary.*

This was the first time Greg had been to Geiler's office. He took in that the place had a nautical touch: an original Winslow Homer over the desk, a model ocean tanker, and a brass telescope overlooking Boston Harbor.

Geiler was on the phone when they entered, and he smiled genially and waved them to chairs across from his desk. A tall man with dark curly hair and an affable manner, he was known for being a gentleman who got exactly what he wanted at the price he wanted. He put his hand over the mouthpiece and politely asked his secretary to bring them all coffee.

Greg wondered for a moment if he and Ross were going to be subjected to hearing a one-sided business call, the kind where the goal was to impress the listeners. But Geiler terminated the call quickly, saying only, "We need to discuss this further, Al, but I have an appointment right now. I'll call you back within the hour."

He set the receiver down and reached across the desk to shake each of their hands. Greg noticed Ross seemed a little stiff. Greg felt the same. He and Geiler were both in their early thirties. There had been a time when the two them would've been perceived by most people as cut from the same cloth: both vigorous young men with their own businesses, agendas of their own creation. But now when Greg measured himself automatically against Geiler, he felt older and softer. His business was failing, and now he was approaching hat in hand, absolutely desperate. He could imagine how Ross, fresh from prison, must've felt even more insecure. Particularly with Allie there.

Geiler said, "I can see you're impatient to get started, so let's get to it."

Allie started in. She began on the story that she and Greg had discussed earlier, about how he and Ross needed to sell their inheritance to give Greg's business an infusion of cash. That they would become full partners. She smiled disarmingly. "Of course, none of this is terribly important from your standpoint, Bob, other than you realize that speed is of the essence for us." She paused. "We need to close today."

Geiler frowned, looked at his watch. "Today? You can't be serious. I haven't even seen the place in three months. We need to do a title search. I'll need to have the house inspected. I'd made the previous offers with the idea of investment, but I also intended to use the place as a vacation home myself."

"Do you want the house?" Greg's voice seemed to come from deep inside him.

Geiler shrugged. "I did. Probably still do. But this afternoon?" His brow wrinkled. "Greg, you must understand, that's not how it works." He began shaking his head. "I'll be happy to take a hard look at the property, and if all goes well, I very likely would make an offer. But not in this time frame."

"Do you have the money?" Ross said abruptly.

Allie put her hand on his arm. "Ross—"

"We need to know," Ross said. "If you get the right price, do you have the kind of cash to move ahead?"

Geiler smiled. "I've swung deals many times this size."

"I know you've swung deals. I asked if you have the kind of cash we're talking about in the bank. Today."

"One step at a time, Ross," Allie said tightly.

"This is the first step," Ross snapped.

"This is going nowhere fast," Geiler said coolly.

Greg put his hands up. "Stop. I'll tell you what's going on.

But only if you can keep it to yourself, that you don't go to the police no matter what you decide."

"Police?"

Greg told him about the kidnapping.

Geiler listened quietly, and when Greg was done, he said, "My God." He seemed to be lost in thought for a moment, then said, "Of course I'll help. I'm afraid I can't match the offer I made earlier this year, but I can come close. I just sold a small building in Waltham that I'd bought years ago, and have about seven hundred that I can turn over for this investment." He frowned as he looked at his watch. "Do you have a purchase and sale agreement?"

"We do." Allie placed the document on his desk.

He said to Ross and Greg apologetically, "It's a rather hefty cut, I realize. In the normal course of business I would've tried to get the lowest price, of course. But I hope you don't think I'm taking advantage of your terrible situation. It's simply all I can put my hands on now."

Greg felt his eyes well up slightly as hope landed a staggering blow. He believed Geiler *was* taking advantage of the situation, but it didn't matter. It was a good two hundred thousand more than they needed for Janine's ransom. And almost three times what Datano would've given them. "We accept your offer," he said. "Right?"

"Absolutely," Ross said. "We've had worse."

CHAPTER 8

Time had stopped.

Ross watched the clock. Two more hours to go. He imagined things he wished he couldn't.

He drank cup after cup of coffee and kept an eye on the big suitcase. That was a lot of weight. Five hundred thousand dollars. Geiler had arranged for two private security guards to deliver it to their home. Ross and Greg had agreed with Geiler that the remaining two hundred thousand balance should remain with him until after the closing.

"Your hand's trembling." Allie joined him at the kitchen table. "Mine, too. Adrenaline and caffeine."

He nodded.

"I owe you an apology."

"Maybe." He knew she meant for apologizing to Geiler for him.

"You pushed things along."

Ross lifted his shoulders. Geiler had struck him as just the kind of man Allie had in mind for herself, and Ross knew that had been a factor in his snapping at him. So he felt uncomfortable with her apology. "Greg had to trust somebody to get the money in one day."

"One hurdle passed, anyhow. The whole thing could be over in hours, don't you think?"

He could see the tension in her face. "You know as well as I do what a crapshoot this is. If Greg and the kidnapper both keep their cool, and if we all get lucky, that's the way it'll turn out."

"You're a big believer in luck, aren't you? Good and bad."

"I admit to my mistakes along the way."

"That's true," Allie said, putting her hand on the back of his neck. It was a touch of casual intimacy that brought back the first time they'd met, months ago. "That was one of the things I first liked about you."

Greg had thrown a party soon after Ross's parole began. It had been just a casual barbecue, and while some of the guests had known Ross from before, many of them didn't know about his prison record. Ross had pointed out to Greg that by the end of the party most of them would. "Having an ex-con work the gas grill is just a little too interesting a tidbit to pass over when people are talking around the pool. I don't have to be here, you know."

"Screw them," Greg said. "You're my brother, it's my house, and it's none of their business."

Once it started, Ross forced himself through it, even though he hated small talk and was lousy at faking it. He chatted with a couple of guys he had remembered as Greg's friends in high school and talked with Greg's neighbors and clients. For the most part, these were successful people like Greg, owners of small businesses, doctors, a dentist, a couple of software developers. Ross could see the nervousness in the eyes of some of them and the curiosity in others. He didn't like it, but he could understand it. Just what do you say to an ex-con?

Two of Ross's buddies had made it. Bill Cobb and Jimmy Miller. Cobb was the driver who'd hired Ross for his pit crew when Ross was a kid. He was looking gray and a good deal heavier than he had before. But he seemed genuinely glad to see Ross, and thumped him hard on the shoulder and invited him out to the offices of the speed equipment distributorship he'd started. Jimmy had grinned at him in his cynical way and said quietly, "So, you passing muster?" Jimmy had been starting a boat brokerage when Ross was selling for Greg's company after he'd come back from Washington State. Jimmy had also introduced Ross to a friend of his cousin's, a young woman by the name of Cynthia Bowen, who later became Ross's wife.

"Did you call her when you got out?" Jimmy had asked.

"Sure. Seemed like the thing to do."

"How'd it go?"

"She said, 'Glad to hear you're out, but I've closed that page of my life,' or something damn close to that."

Jimmy had raised his eyebrows. "I always felt bad about that introduction. She was so pretty and interesting, I thought I was doing you a favor."

"So did I."

"Come see me when you've got your feet under you. I've something in mind for you, a salvaged Hinckley forty-two. Needs just about everything. But it's floating, and you could live aboard it while fixing it up. Interested?"

"Definitely."

Bill and Jimmy knew each other slightly, and after a while, they had drifted away, talking. Ross had taken over the grill from Greg, and other than the occasional guest who came along to comment on the cooking, he had been free to his own thoughts, free to think about his ex-wife.

Cynthia had been an artist living in Newport, Rhode Island, when Ross had met her. He had just bought the *Bon Vivant* from Jimmy, a beautiful forty-foot wooden ketch, painted a deep sea green. Cynthia had seemed fascinated with the way Ross was re-creating his life: with the image of the two boys growing up in a seemingly wealthy but dysfunctional home; of the auto racing; of his new directions helping Greg start his business.

"You're a born winner," she had told him. "Both you and your brother got it from your grandfather; it must've skipped a generation."

Ross had been flattered. Her words soothed that part of him that kept him awake at nights, the image of his father saying, "He and I are just alike."

In short order, Ross had taken a significant bite out of the credits needed for a bachelor's degree in computer science from Northeastern University, and he was making money as the primary salesman for Greg's computer distributorship. Lots of money, in fact.

He and Cynthia were married after six short months. They talked of sailing the world; Cynthia talked of capturing new images and experiences that would translate into her work.

The marriage, however, had proved a disaster. Ross was dismayed to see Cynthia's commitment to her art fade off soon after they bought their first house in northern Rhode Island. She let the studio lease run out. She didn't want to go out sailing for more than an occasional day trip on the bay. No other interest seemed to replace her artwork, other than seeing Ross's own career grow.

"Doesn't it bother you?" Ross had asked.

"Kid stuff." She had shrugged. And then told him about a new house she wanted him to look at.

Two years into Ross's new job and marriage, he realized that he could cut the work, he could make the money—and none of it was what he wanted for himself. He respected the life Greg had built and would be forever thankful for Greg's support, helping him learn he was capable of more than driving a car fast. Ross loved Beth and little Janine, and he was pleased Greg was earning his dream.

But that was Greg's life, not Ross's.

The idea of generating more commissions year after year to buy ever-bigger houses filled Ross with an essential boredom that he couldn't ignore. And Cynthia, meanwhile, had shed much of the persona of the woman he had married the way some might shed a hat. He didn't believe she had purposely deceived him, but rather once she was married the things that interested her simply changed. She wanted a more traditional lifestyle, and she wanted it immediately. Her ambitions for him were narrow and clear: Earn more. Settle down. Have children, now.

He suggested a compromise. That they take their round-the-world cruise while they could. Afterward, base themselves down in the Virgin Islands for two years and charter the *Bon Vivant*. If they didn't like it, even if they took several years trying it out, they'd still be only in their late twenties. Still plenty of time for children, for everything, he'd said.

"Grow up," she'd said.

They were divorced, and he sailed off to the Virgin Islands on the *Bon Vivant* within the year. The divorce had left him one boat payment behind, so he had to throw himself into the char-ter business right away. And that suited him; he wanted to prove to himself he could make money on the charters, that he could attract the guests and make the whole dream work in reality.

As Ross seasoned the steaks and kabobs, he was pleased to find the dream was just as powerful as it had been then. The Hinckley Jimmy had mentioned was probably still out of his price range, but he figured he might go down and take a look at it. Give himself something to shoot for. His reverie had been bro-

ken when Greg interrupted him to introduce his attorney, Allie
Pearson. She had shaken his hand and said coolly, "Welcome
back."

And then she moved on.

Ross had seen the assessment in her eyes, without any of the
curiosity or nervousness of the others. Greg had told him before
that she had been an assistant district attorney before going into
private practice. In spite of that—or maybe because of it—Ross
had found himself wanting to talk with her.

Maybe he wanted her acceptance, he thought.

Or maybe he was just analyzing himself too much. Because
the fact of the matter was that Allie Pearson took his breath away.
Not just because of the glow of her skin, her fine cheekbones
and lithe movements. It was the way she handled herself with
the others. She laughed well and to all appearances seemed
friendly and outgoing. But he could sense a reserve in her, a self-
awareness that he liked.

Toward the end of the evening, he noticed her wineglass was
empty and joined her near the pool and offered a refill.

"I've been watching you," she said, smiling. "You've been a
major disappointment."

"You mean because I didn't try to cut my steak with a shiv?"

"You told no stories about men in showers," she offered. "No
prison riots, no revelations about God, and . . . you didn't tell
everyone you were innocent and railroaded. I particularly appreciate that one."

He'd laughed. "Give me time." Early on, he'd learned that the
idea of an innocent man being sent to prison was considered a
myth in the court system. "I'm innocent, I'm innocent," people
in the business heard every day, and only the hopelessly naive
were supposed to believe it.

"You *were* guilty, right? Cocaine, was it?"

"It was. Unfortunately, what I was mainly guilty of was stupidity."

"For getting caught?" She gestured for him to sit beside her.

"For being there." Ross had found himself telling her about it. She was a good listener, and it had been so long—five years, in fact—since he'd held a conversation of any length with such an attractive woman. As the rest of the party continued around them, he began by telling her how he'd been taking the *Bon Vivant* up the coast on a Florida to Maine charter with a newly-wed couple and his first mate, Giselle.

Giselle had been with him for just a month. She was a small, pretty woman who'd answered his ad for a mate and cook by showing up at his boat with a picnic basket and the best meal he'd eaten in months. The two of them had established a good working relationship quickly. She was an excellent sailor, pulled her time at the wheel without flagging, and maintained an outward cheerfulness, with even the most obnoxious guest. She'd laid her ground rules early: she had a fiancé, Dermott, who was traveling through Australia at the time, and when both of them finished their six months of wandering they were moving to Boston, where he was going back for his MBA. From Ross she wanted a job and, she hoped, a friend.

Ross had been fine with that. He'd been divorced for almost a year at that point, and though he'd had a few quick affairs since then, he wasn't looking for anything like that with an employee. But he found he liked Giselle enormously.

All had gone well until they were docked in Miami for a week. A short series of phone calls changed Giselle's demeanor: Dermott wasn't sure he wanted to go to Boston. Wasn't sure he wanted the MBA. Couldn't see how he could afford it. No, she shouldn't catch a flight. He needed time alone to figure out exactly what he wanted out of life.

Giselle did her work, but late at night she wanted Ross's advice. "Is he just trying to say good-bye to me? Is that it? Or is it really the money? Oh, God, if it's just the money, I'd find a way to help, I really would."

In Charlestown, her gloom seemed to lift, and by the time they reached New York, she was cheerfully working harder than ever. Everything was fine . . . with the exception of a nasty summer cold.

Ross had acted on the sinking feeling that had been building in him for days. He left Chet, the husband, at the wheel as they were leaving Long Island Sound. Ross had followed Giselle straight into her little cabin in the bow. "Skipper, it's a little late for this," she'd said, but her voice sounded more scared than kidding. She'd tossed her duffel bag back into the locker, and that's when he noticed the razor blade on the cabin sole. He'd picked it up. White flakes clung to the razor, and her face flushed angrily. "Get the hell out of here."

It took him just minutes to find the packages. Altogether there were eight kilos of cocaine. Trafficking weight. Apparently worth about two hundred thousand dollars.

On his boat.

With guests, witnesses, aboard.

It was all he could do not to throw her off right there in the sound.

Giselle had followed Ross on deck that night when he went to throw it overboard. And though he had told Allie an abbreviated version that night, he could still remember it all.

"You can't," Giselle had whispered. "The guy said he'd find us. That maybe I might get away with stealing the coke for a short time, but I'd better give up on living in Boston with Dermott, or sailing on this boat. He said it like it was a joke, but he meant it. He let me know he'd kill us. Look, let me tell you what happened. I went to a bar, and this guy saw my shirt, you know, with the *Bon Vivant* name on it, and we started talking about your boat, and then where we were going. I told him about Dermott, because I thought he was trying to hit on me. Then he offered this wedding present, he called it, a way to make $10,000. That'd take care of our rent for a year! And I knew what the guy was about, but it seemed to simple then, to take this coke up the coast. Very low-key, he said at first, that everyone involved was cool. But the day he dropped it off—you were out getting supplies—he came on knowing your name, and I guess I'd said Dermott's full name, and mine. And then I got so scared coming up the coast thinking about actually making the delivery. So I started dipping into just a little, to keep my confidence up. I'm scared, Ross. I'm supposed to call this number when we get into Boston and then meet them wherever they tell me. What if they decide to hurt me, or worse? What's to stop them?"

"Let me guess," Allie had said. "This is where the criminal stupidity comes in. She was so scared, and you liked her, maybe loved her a little . . . and you walked the coke in for her? Or did she go along?"

"She went along. Introduced me as the skipper. Two guys in a hotel room. One was a big guy, acted like he was bored, kind of pissed off. The other one was cold, wiry."

"Which one was the cop?"

"The wiry one. I was starting my little speech about how this would be my one and only time when cops with guns burst into the room."

"They could've given you a break on that."

Ross had been silent for a moment and then said, "Not the way it turned out. The dealer had a gun and he went for it. The cops yelled for him to put it down, but he wouldn't. I'd grabbed Giselle and put my back to the guy, to the dealer, but I felt this tearing along my side. Then the undercover cop fired. I remember looking back at the dealer and seeing that he was dead, and then realizing that Giselle was hanging in my arms. She was dead, too. The dealer had gotten one shot off, and the bullet that had grazed my side had gone on to her heart."

"Oh, Jesus."

"And it was eight kilos of coke, and this was the year that Jackie Kale overdosed. You know, the Boston College athlete?"

"Who was the cop?"

"Detective Byrne."

She shook her head. "I don't know him. How about the judge?"

"Palmer."

She winced. "And the ADA?"

"Guy by the name of Ryan."

"Bad luck. He's good."

She'd checked the bottle of wine then. "This one's gone. If I have another, I won't be able to drive home."

Ross had realized he'd talked way too much. "I'll shut up."

"Don't." She'd put her hand on the back of his neck. Her fingers were cool on the surface, but he could feel her heat beneath the skin. "I still haven't heard about that ex-wife of yours yet."

Just as she had those two months ago, Allie withdrew her hand as Greg joined them.

He didn't seem to notice, saying, "Beth's asleep. First time since this started." He poured himself some coffee and sat with them at the table and said, simply enough, "Did you take the gun, Ross?"

Ross pulled it from his belt and laid it on the table.

Allie paled. "How long have you had that on you?"

"All day."

"Jesus Christ. That's a parole violation right there, enough to send you back."

The connection Allie and Ross had made was gone. Her armor

was up, and Ross could see he had returned to the dangerously unreliable status.

"This situation's a little different," Greg said.

"Explain that to a judge," she said.

Greg met Ross's eyes. "You didn't do anything extreme, did you? Anything we need to know about now?"

"Not a thing."

Greg held his gaze for a moment, then shook his head. "You must be slipping. The brother I grew up with would've robbed a bank by now."

CHAPTER 9

Beth found him in the garage.

Greg was at the workbench, Janine's bicycle locked into the vise. The socket wrench set was laid out, glittering and clean on the well-swept bench.

"What are you doing?" she asked.

He started slightly before turning back to the bicycle. "I can't believe I let it get like this," he said. "The back brakes are gone, the fronts are grabbing, the cables are way out of adjustment. It looks like she tried to fix it herself: The nuts are all stripped."

Beth rubbed his shoulders. The tension in his back made his muscles hard as bone. "The two of us tried to fix it with a pair of pliers," she said. "Switched the pads."

"Could've asked me."

"You've had a bit on your mind, lately."

He turned around. Put his arms around her. She held herself against him, felt that the beating of his heart was faster than usual. She could also feel his trembling, and knew he must feel the same in her. She pressed her face against his chest, trying to close out the light. She was buzzing. She felt as if her life had turned into some kind of documentary, as if she were following the view of some handheld camera showing how the mother of a kidnap victim made it through the day. Going through the house, straightening, doing the equivalent of tuning the bicycle. Seeing her daughter in every room: Janine, looking up from the dinner table, Janine with her new beret, talking in a silly French accent, "Bon-jour, monsieur." Saying it, "Miss-sure."

Beth kept envisioning the end of the documentary, where, with Janine in her arms, she could say into the camera how awful it had been. That she'd been terrified, but always had faith her daughter would make it home alive.

She'd be lying at that part.

Truth was, at one moment she'd believe this whole thing would be over soon. Swap the money for her daughter, simple. The next, she'd imagine how it could go wrong, how that man could make what was simple complicated, and her daughter would be dead.

And that image would just freeze her, stop her at whatever she was doing, leave her in a blind panic. Then she'd kick herself back into the logic; she'd think if only the man knew how she felt about her daughter, if only she could explain so he really understood what Janine meant to her.

If only she could explain to him that she didn't always know she wanted to be a mother. That at first she'd thought she and Greg were enough. Two years into their marriage, she'd just sold her first short story, her first real sale. During the celebratory champagne that night, she'd pushed her glass aside reluctantly; it had tasted terrible. The next morning she had been sick. Another day passed before the doctor confirmed what she already knew—she was pregnant.

And then it had been a difficult delivery. Afterward, Beth had gone through a period of depression. It was just the body drugs, the doctor had told her, the hormones. And Beth had believed him, largely. But what she'd thought about during those depressions was how tired she was, and how she just didn't have the energy to sit down at the keyboard.

Even during the time when Janine had started to smile and become a beautiful child that her friends wanted to hold and kiss, Beth had felt a distance toward her. And that distance was Beth's personal shame; she'd felt guilty and disgusted with herself. Could she really be so shallow as to resent her baby? She'd tortured herself with the idea that her daughter would grow up to see herself as not loved. Greg had pitched in every way he could and lavished more affection than ever on Janine. Even that had made Beth feel guilty.

Beth still remembered the day it had changed for her. It was a nothing-special day, just one morning at home after Greg had gone to work. Janine had taken Beth's forefinger in her pudgy little fist and grinned delightedly as she pulled herself up to stand. She'd squealed, "Mama, mama, mama!"

Beth's eyes had filled with the kind of joy of which she'd thought herself incapable. *I got away with it,* she'd thought, scooping Janine up into her arms. *Thank God, I got away with it.*

And now she was thinking maybe she hadn't. Maybe this was some awful atonement that she'd brought down on all of them.

She looked up at Greg. "Make him understand what she means to us."

"It's all I think about," Greg said. "But the more desperate we are for her, the more it strengthens his position."

Beth looked away from her husband's face. She knew he was right, intellectually. But the talk of position, of negotiation, made her want to scream. She had come down to find him and Ross in the kitchen talking things through. Her fair husband and his dark brother, heads close together, trying to make it all fit into some game plan. Greg was concerned that the man might not be willing to turn Janine over directly, that the kidnapper would expect them to leave the money someplace and then just hope Janine would be set free.

And Ross was different than he had been before. He was more sober. On one level, Beth felt he was even more frightened than they. She could see the doubt in his eyes, and that sickened her. Because he knew the kind of person who'd do this. She'd found it hard to be around him for the past day; she'd leave the room when he came in.

She felt bad about that but couldn't help it. He was doing everything he could, and Beth knew he loved all of them dearly. But he'd said it himself: The kidnapper was from what had become his kind of world.

She closed her eyes now and pulled Greg tight.

The man just didn't understand.

And that's what they needed to let him know. This was her daughter, and she'd come to love her daughter more than any words could explain. And she would pay, no matter what the cost.

She looked up at her husband and saw the man she loved. Saw what was good and solid and right about him and wondered if he had what they needed. She let her fingernails sink into his back. "You let that man know what she means to us. There's got to be a way to make it count to him, too. So he's got a reason to let her come home."

CHAPTER 10

Janine bit back her question because the man started talking again.

"We're going to do it in the cash," he said to the woman. "You and me, right on a big pile of it."

"I like that," the woman said, laughing. Then she must've turned to Janine, because her voice became clearer. "Hey, close your ears, honey."

The tape around Janine's eyes kept her sightless.

"It'll be compliments of your daddy, girl," the man said. To the woman, he said, "Here, these two lines are yours."

In Janine's direction, again, he said, "Now, if your daddy doesn't come through, maybe we'll just do it on top of you."

"Stop!" The woman's voice was sharp and then she laughed again, but Janine could tell she was scared, too.

Janine didn't say anything. She just sat on the hard chair and kept very still. She'd think sometimes if she just didn't move, they'd forget about her and walk away. And so the longer she sat silent, the better her chances. Her back, arms, and legs were stiff from the night and day she'd passed tied down first on the bed and then in the chair.

Time had passed more slowly than anything she could ever remember, worse than any day home sick, any math class, any morning in church. She thought of those times, those boring hours that she had thought would kill her, and wished she could be there now, kicking her feet against the pew on Sunday, her mom and dad telling her to hush.

But she didn't complain. She thought how funny that was, in a way. That she could just tell herself to shut up, don't be a sissy, and she could.

They'd fed her. She'd had a doughnut ages ago, then a hamburger a long time later, and just now they'd given her another. McDonald's or Burger King's.

So she'd been through the day.

The woman had said they'd let her go that night.

The question had been building.

She licked her lips. Thought about it and started to form the words, then waited. She let a long time pass, and finally said it. "Is it time yet? Is it time for my daddy to pick me up?"

"Is it time yet?" the man immediately copied her, making his voice ugly and screeching. "Is it time?"

She heard him stand up, and the woman said, "Don't."

Suddenly he picked Janine and the chair up. Janine shrieked. He put his hand over her mouth, and she almost bit his hand but stopped herself somehow. She cried out behind his hand and could barely get enough breath in, it was so tight against her mouth and nose. "OK, little girl. You want to rush your daddy, that's OK with me. What the hell, if he doesn't have the money now, he's not going to have it later, right? Let's go call him, find out if he really loves you or not."

"Leave her alone," the woman snapped.

"You telling me what to do now?"

Janine felt herself lifted higher, maybe over his head. She said, "No, please, no!"

"Put her down!"

The man dropped the chair.

"Lee!" the woman cried out.

Janine screamed as she fell forward, struggling to get her arms free to protect her face.

But the woman was there. Janine's head hit the woman's body hard, and together they fell to the floor. The woman cried out again, and Janine could feel the dull thud through the woman's body and realized the man was hitting or kicking her. "You said my name!" He was raging. "You stupid bitch, you said my name!"

It was over suddenly.

Janine could hear him walk away, heard him say, "Shit! It's on your head."

"No," the woman said. "Not again."

"Shut up about that! Your head, you got that?"

"I won't take that."

"You will if I say you will. Now get her ready."

The woman said in Janine's ear, "Shush. Just be quiet." The woman cut away the tape binding Janine's arms and legs and led her away. A door closed behind them, and the woman was crying as she got Janine ready. She told Janine she was putting dark glasses over the tape and giving her a hooded sweatshirt to wear. The woman's hands were shaking, and that made Janine cry more, the tears stinging her eyes inside the tape.

The woman said, "Listen to me; listen to me. I don't know if you heard his name, but never say it if you did. If he asks you what it was, just play dumb. Say you don't know what he means,

Cry, do anything, but if you heard it, never say it. Do you understand?"

"Yes," Janine said softly. And the shame of it was, she did.

They put her on the car floor again. The man drove the car hard. Janine could feel it move in a jerky way. The woman's voice was very bright now. "Easy, baby. We don't want any cops, do we?"

"Shut the fuck up." His voice was very clear. "Don't call me 'baby' or anything else. The little chick's got big ears."

"Sure. You're right." The woman patted Janine's head. "Once you get the money, where you want to drop her?"

The man didn't answer.

After a few minutes passed, the woman said, "I just wanted to know."

"I told you to shut up."

"Baby, we don't have to do this." The woman's voice sounded tired.

"I'll decide what we have to do, and then we'll do it. And that's my last word."

After a long time—Janine wasn't sure if it was ten minutes or a half hour—the car stopped. The man said, "This one should do it. I broke the bulb this afternoon, but the phone works fine."

"You've got it all thought out so smooth." The woman led Janine out of the car.

Without being able to see, Janine found even walking was hard. She wanted to have her hands out in front all of the time, sure she was going to walk her face right into something. But the woman said for her to keep her hands by her sides. Janine could hear cars passing.

"Don't get any ideas, honey," the woman said. "This is a busy road. People are driving by too fast to pay you any mind. You're just a kid wearing her hood up, walking to the phone with your dad and mom. You got that?"

"You're gonna tell your old man you're fine and we haven't hurt you," the man said. She heard the sound of a phone being dialed, the little beep-beep-beep of the numbers being punched in, and suddenly the realization that she would be talking to her parents was all she could bear. Her lower lip start to quiver. She'd always hated that, and she forced herself to breathe deep. She found once again she could stop the tears if she really had to.

"Well, hello," the man said, his voice suddenly friendly in a mean way. "I got something for you here. Have you got something for me?"

The phone was shoved against her ear.

And her father was there, saying into her ear, "Janine? Is that you, baby? Are you there?"

"Daddy!" she cried. And then her mother was there, too, on the other line. "Janey, Daddy's going to get you. Hold on, baby."

Her dad said, "Janine, tell me fast. Do you think he's going to hurt you? I don't mean talk badly to you—I mean do you think he's going to hurt you?"

"Yes," she said, softly.

"Speak up, sweetheart. It's important," her dad said.

So she yelled it. "He is! I know he is!"

And then the phone was snatched away, and she lashed out with her fist and hit the man. She was screaming, "No, no, no!" and she hit him again, and then he knocked her down. The woman was dragging her away, saying, "Don't! Are you crazy? Don't do that!"

The woman shoved her in the car and pushed her onto the floor. Janine knew she was in real trouble now, but somehow she was just as angry as she was scared, and she wasn't going to let them hear her cry.

CHAPTER 11

She's a fresh little brat," the man said. "So we put her in the car. Now tell me what I want to hear."

Anger cleared Greg's mind suddenly, swept away the nightmarish cloud of doubt and debilitating fear.

In the past day, he'd forgotten everything he'd ever learned about negotiating, about balancing power. The money had become just a hurdle, the appeasement to the violent little god who'd stormed into his life. He'd almost forgotten how much $500,000 would mean to a man whose last robbery had been a convenience store.

But with what Janine had just said, and with Beth coming into the room, her face stricken, Greg put that into the forefront of his mind. He threw the suitcase onto the kitchen table and opened it.

"I'm looking at $500,000," Greg said. "It's in a big tan Samsonite."

"Listen tight and I'll tell you where to leave it. You do that, and after I've picked it up, I'll leave your girl right beside a telephone with a quarter and your number."

"No, sir," Greg said without hesitation.

"What?"

"I've done my part. I moved heaven and earth selling a piece of property in one day to get the cash you want. I don't care about the money. All that's important to me is Janine. So I can't simply leave this money in the bushes someplace and just hope you'll do the right thing and let her go. But I will hand the money over to you directly, when you hand her to me."

"Just who the hell do you think's calling the shots here?"

"Both of us." Greg kept his tone respectful, even though his insides were churning. His hand dropped to the tabletop, and he picked up Beth's lighter and flicked the flame on and off absently. "I want my daughter back. You want the cash. So the way I see it, my only way of making sure I get her back alive is to hand it off to you at once."

"You'll drop it where I tell you, or I'll put her on the phone and shoot her right now. You saw the storekeeper's head. You know I'll do it."

Ross and Allie were looking at Greg, their faces worried. "Make him understand," Beth said, her voice low.

Greg locked his eyes on hers. "You can do that."

"You cheap bastard," the man said. "Your own daughter."

"But you'll never have the money."

"I'll *have* it, one way or the other." The man's pretense of control was gone. "If you won't come through for your daughter, then maybe you'll do it for your wife. It may not be this week, this month, but I'll pick her up some time, and I'll make it last with her before I drop a dime."

The man's voice cracked with his rage, and Greg leaned briefly against the table, his knees weak.

"No, sir. You'll never have a chance at my wife or me. If I hear you kill my daughter, I'll douse this cash with gasoline and light it." He touched the flame to a packet of cash and watched it curl the top bill. "The money means nothing to us. I'll shoot my wife in the head, and then I'll shoot myself."

"Yes," Beth said. "Make him see."

Greg could see Allie and Ross were alarmed, but he kept his voice steady and hard. "Because none of it counts without Janine. If you want this money, I'll trade you for her directly. And that's my offer."

Greg could hear the man breathing. Greg forced himself to say nothing more, to watch his wife's eyes.

"Merry fucking Christmas," the man said, finally. "Let's do it."

CHAPTER 12

Sit her up here," the man said. "She can help me play a game."

They had driven for another long time. Janine was sick to her stomach, her face shoved into that dirty carpet that smelled of grease and cigarettes.

But the idea of being up there with him made her stomach flutter even worse. She shoved deeper against the carpet, burrowing her shoulder under the front seat.

"What're you thinking about?" the woman said. "What kind of game?"

Janine's rage had seeped away by the time he'd returned to the car. She'd been ready for him to start hitting her. But when he hadn't, when he hadn't said *anything,* she'd found herself becoming even more frightened.

All Janine wanted was to be home. Wanted nothing of what might happen in between.

Just home.

"I didn't ask for a conversation," the man said. "I told you, the little chick's got big ears. Get her up here in the front with me and see if she's got big eyes."

"Hon—"

The woman's breath drew in sharply. Her legs shifted away from Janine. "Don't! Put it down, please. You're scaring me."

"That's the idea," he said softly. "I don't want any more advice tonight, *hon.* Just take off that blindfold, and get her up here. I want her to pick out her daddy's car for me, see if she can help."

"That's it?"

"And what if it's not? Now, move."

The woman got Janine by the elbow and pulled. Once they were outside, the woman peeled off the tape. It hurt the side of Janine's face, but she didn't make a sound.

Janine looked at the sky. It was a bright starlit night. The moon was full, and even that hurt her eyes. She looked at the woman and felt startled, seeing the ski mask where her face should be. She'd gotten an image in her head of the woman, for no reason in particular, of a woman with black hair and very white skin. This woman was wearing dark clothes, but Janine could see she was a little smaller than she had imagined. She looked at the woman's eyes now, and at the woods behind them.

She knew she should run, do something to get away. But the thought of being alone among the dark trees with him chasing after her was more than she could bear.

She looked over at him. He was wearing his mask, too, and that made her feel better. She didn't want to see his face. He was big. Bigger than her dad, even. He leaned over, opened the door, and said, "Get in."

"Go ahead," the woman whispered.

The seat was wide and slippery. Janine sat as close to the door as she could. She could see a gun sticking out of his belt. He was wearing white gloves, the kind her father bought at the hardware store.

"Fasten that seat belt."

She did. She could barely see over the dashboard, but if she strained she could see the hood of the car was wide and long. They were backed into a little rest area. The lights were off, and the road curved to the right in front of them.

He grasped her by the back of her head and forced her to look left and then right. "From there to there. We'll see the cars coming up; they'll swing through the curve in front of us and then pass that streetlight and follow the curve around. You know what your daddy's car looks like?"

"Yes."

"Well, I do, too, but I figure four eyes are better than two. So you're going to help me point it out. Now, I told him to meet us a few miles down the road. But I want to make sure he's alone. And when the car passes that streetlight, we're gonna be able to look right in for a second and see who's driving, and if there's anybody else in the car. Now, if it's your daddy alone, that's fine. Then I'm going to get his attention, and we'll pull over and make the swap. You're gonna tell him that everything's OK as long as he does what I say, you got that?"

"Thank God," the woman said behind her quietly. Then the woman said in her ear, "You do what he says, you hear?"

"Yes."

"All right. Now, if you see his car, but if somebody else is driving it—like a cop—you say it. Or if you see your dad with somebody else in the car, front seat or back, you say that, too. Because then I'll just let them go, call your dad tomorrow, and tell him to try again, no screwing around. But if I get there, and there's somebody else waiting . . . baby, I'll have to shoot your dad. You hear me?"

"Yes, sir," she whispered.

"Sir," he repeated. "Real smooth, just like your dad."

There weren't many cars. She found that he was right—the way the streetlight was, she could see drivers as they went by. She hunched forward, sure that she would miss her dad's car.

She thought about what the man had said. Part of her wanted to make him happy, wanted to show him she was doing a good job looking. She felt bad about that, too, felt it was wrong to be helping him see her dad when her dad didn't know they were watching.

But she wanted so much to see her father. Wanted so much for it to be over.

Every set of headlights started her heart thumping.

After six cars, she felt her lip begin to quiver, and she bit down.

After the tenth, her bite became painful.

When the twelfth first came into view, she turned to the man.

"BMW," the man said, the mask turning in her direction.

She couldn't help herself. There was no stopping her cry of relief as the car swept around the corner and she saw her father's face in the light. She said, "Daddy."

The man started the car. The engine noise was loud, scary. The tires spun in the gravel, and she was pressed back into the seat. The tires made a squealing noise as they went around the corner and the man didn't say a word as they came sweeping up to her father's car.

It looked so small in the big car's headlights, and suddenly they were very close, and she could see her dad's head as he looked up into the mirror. Janine was looking at the man's leg, waiting for him to put on the brake. But when he jammed his foot down hard, the car seemed to gather itself and leap.

Janine screamed as the woman grabbed at the man and said, "Lee, watch it!"

He rammed the BMW. Janine's seat belt held onto her as she snapped forward. She saw her dad's car swerve off to the side, and she cried out to him. He came back onto the road, the back light broken.

"You think that's bad?" the man screamed at the window. "You think that ruins your day?" His right foot shoved down again, and he pulled alongside her father's car. He snapped on the interior light. The electric window slid down beside her, and she could just make out her dad's face.

He called her name.

"Pull it over up there!" the man yelled past her. "Down the dirt road!" He had the gun jammed under her ear, and he pressed hard.

Janine cried out as he stepped on the brake, and moments later they jostled over rough road. Her father stopped the car up ahead, and the man let the car roll into the BMW again. "Move it!" he yelled out his own window now. "Inside the trees, get away from the road. Kill the headlights and turn on the interiors. And pop that trunk. Do it now!"

Her father moved the car ahead.

The man reached down to the floor and pulled up the shotgun he'd used in the store.

"No!" Janine cried. She grabbed at his arm. "Don't hurt him. Please, don't hurt him!"

The man snapped at the woman, "Hold her right there." He got out of the car and moved his hand on the gun, and it made a loud clacking sound. Janine threw herself at the window. "Daddy, run, Daddy!"

"Sssh." The woman held her shoulders from behind. "Let them work it out, baby. Let them work it out."

CHAPTER 13

Greg steadied himself against the door as he got out.

The man was on him in an instant, grabbing his right arm and spinning him around against the side of the car. "I didn't tell you to get out, fucker." The man patted Greg down quickly, then looked in the backseat. "That's it?"

"Yes. That's the money. It's all there."

"All right, open the trunk."

Greg said, "Show me she's OK."

The man punched Greg in the side. It brought him right to his knees. "You don't listen, man. I'm not an easygoing guy, and that's the second time you've been in my face tonight."

The man hit him again.

Greg cried out. There was a sharp pain in his side, and he figured a rib was broken.

He also figured maybe Ross had been right, too. That forcing the face-to-face meeting might've made things more dangerous for everyone.

"Now, open the trunk," the man said.

Greg stood, breathing harshly. "There's nothing in there." He pointed again to the suitcase.

"Open the goddamn trunk!"

Greg tried, but the trunk was wedged shut because of the collision. He couldn't get the key to turn. He said, "I'm telling you, there's nothing in there."

"Yeah?" The man leveled the shotgun and Greg moved aside just as the gun spoke, blowing a hole through the trunk lock. The shot ricocheted through the back window and out the front. The gunman pumped the shotgun fast as the lid swung open and looked in . . . to find it empty.

"Good for you. No cops. Now open that suitcase."

Greg quickly pulled it out of the backseat. He turned on the flashlight. "I just want to show you, right?"

"Go ahead."

Greg opened the suitcase and flashed the beam across the stack of cash. He picked up the packets quickly, to show that it was all money, no tricks, no stacks of cut paper. "It's all there," he said. "Please, let me see her now."

The man bent down beside Greg to run his left hand through the money. "Jesus Christ."

The gun was pointed roughly in Greg's direction, and for a moment, he considered trying to take it away. But the gunman seemed to regain himself, and he closed the lid and snapped the lock shut. He yelled over to the car, "Bring her over here!"

The car door opened.

Janine came running to Greg. "Daddy, oh, Daddy!"

He was grinning so hard it hurt. He thanked God he'd kept his head, that he hadn't pulled a stupid stunt, going for the gun. He swung Janine up to his chest, the lancing pain in his side nothing compared to the pleasure in his heart. He whispered, "Sssh, Janey. I love you, baby, but be quiet now."

Toward the gunman he felt an absurd kind of gratitude. Even though he still hated the man, there was a sense of their having gone through an ordeal together.

The woman stood a few feet away. "She's all right," the woman said. "Your girl's a good kid. She'll be all right."

Greg turned to the man, who was looking in at the front seat of Greg's car. "Are we through here?"

The man turned on him. "You motherfucker."

"What?" Greg was bewildered.

"You've got a car phone. You were going to call the cops, what, thirty seconds after I left?"

"No." Greg felt a hollowness in his belly. He slid Janine down to her feet as the man stepped up to him. "The car has always had a phone. Look, it's not on."

The woman said, "Come on, babe, let's go. We got the cash."

The man was shaking his head. "It's not that easy." He pointed the shotgun at Janine. "She knows my name. You've said it twice, now."

Greg stepped in front of Janine. "For Christ sake, we did what you said. You've got the money."

"And *you* . . ." The man raised the gun to Greg's chest. "You've gotten in my face—"

"I didn't hear your name!" Janine cried, her voice high in the night air. "I didn't!"

"Oh, yeah, you did, little chick." The man put some heat into the words. "You sure did."

He's building himself up, Greg realized dully. Just like his own father had done, building up into a rage over some trifle. Cold coffee, waking him up too early. It didn't matter.

"No, baby, don't." The woman stood beside Greg, in front of Janine. "She doesn't know. I asked her."

"Nat, get out of the way."

"She doesn't know!"

"It doesn't matter! Get the fuck out of the way!"

There was a cracking noise off to the left. A flash of yellow in the darkness, and in the faint light from the BMW's interior lights Greg could see the man's shirt move on his left shoulder. Greg grabbed the shotgun barrel and tried to yank it away. He cried. "Run, Janey!"

The man was too strong. Greg could see Ross running from the trees. "Shoot!" Greg cried. But even as he said it, he knew it was a bind, that Ross couldn't fire with him so close to the gunman.

"Daddy!" Janine screamed. The woman was pushing her into the car.

Greg shoved the man hard, trying to knock him off balance so he could snatch the weapon away. But the man just went with the motion and was still there. The barrel of the gun began to move toward Greg's face. His breath was rushing in and out and he was thinking too many things. He was thinking that all those years in the office sitting behind the desk had left him in no kind of shape to fight this man. He was thinking that everything he'd hoped and planned for Janine was coming down to a few pounds of muscle strength.

"Get her, Ross!" Greg's voice was strangled by his lack of wind.

The gun was almost in his face, one huge barrel.

Greg tried to knee the man in the balls.

But the guy twisted and took the blow on his thigh. "Nice try," he said, putting his foot behind Greg's standing leg. He knocked him to the ground.

Greg was on his way back up when the man shot him.

CHAPTER 14

The gunman went for Ross next.

He spun fast, pumped the shotgun, and let loose.

Ross jumped off to the left into a shallow ditch and rolled. The grass and weeds above him whispered, as if a scythe had swept through.

He sat up and snapped off two rounds. He called his brother's name, but there was no answer. Only the gunman's silhouette was visible in front of the BMW.

Greg was still on the ground.

The man bent down, apparently going for the money, and Ross steadied his hand and squeezed the trigger.

The man cursed. There was the ratcheting noise again and a flash of yellow flame. "Start the car, Nat!" the man yelled. "Start the frigging car!"

The engine roared to life, and the headlights washed over the man and then settled on Ross, as she swung the car around in reverse. Ross hit the ground again as the shotgun blasted. Shredded leaves drifted into the light from the branch over his head.

Ross fired again, forcing the man away from the case of money. The car's tires spun in the dirt, and the man gave up on the money and dove into the open passenger window. Ross got to his feet and ran alongside the car, and he almost fired his last shot into the man's back—but then he saw Janine.

She was reaching over the backseat, screaming, "Uncle Ross, Uncle Ross!" as the man shoved his way in.

Ross steadied his hand.

Told himself this might be her only chance.

The car hit a pothole and bounced. The gun sight covered what he could see of Janine's face in the moonlight.

Ross pulled back the gun, knowing how close he'd come to killing his niece, as the car disappeared through the trees.

Seconds later, he heard another shotgun blast.

The car took off around the corner just as he got there.

It took him a few seconds to understand what had happened. Janine wasn't there, on the road. Dead or alive. They still had her. It was Ross's truck the man had shot. It was tilted to one side, the front tire blown.

Behind him, the BMW's horn wailed.

Ross shouted with relief as he sprinted back. Part of him had already believed, if not accepted, that Greg was dead. Ross had seen how close the man had been, could imagine the damage the shotgun could inflict. As he ran down the dirt road, he saw that the BMW's headlights were back on.

But the car hadn't moved, and the horn was still blaring.

When Ross opened the door, his brother began to slide out. Blood covered his legs and the door. Greg's head was resting on the wheel.

Ross pulled him back gently, saying, "Oh, Jesus, Greg." Tears blurred his vision. His brother's torso was a bloody ruin. Much of his shirt had been blown away, and his lower ribs were exposed. When his head lolled back, he coughed blood and began to choke. "Drive," he gasped. "Go."

"Hold on, Greggie," Ross said. "I'm going to get you to the hospital, man. We're not too far away." He lifted his brother over the gearshift, all 180 pounds, without being aware of the weight at all.

Greg shook his head. Turned to the side and coughed up blood. "Go for her. Now."

Ross turned the car around and took off between the trees.

"Which way?" Greg asked.

"Hospital's down there to the right. We're not that far from the Sands. They'll have your records going back to that broken arm." Ross found himself talking fast, knowing what his brother really wanted. But he also knew his brother would die soon if he didn't get medical attention.

"Damn it." Greg coughed. "Which way did they go?"

"Greg, you can't make it."

"Don't . . . have the strength to argue," Greg managed. "If you do . . . anything right in your whole life . . . you get her back right now. Go."

"You'll die, Greg!"

Greg cracked Ross across the face. "Go! Do it now!" Greg cried out with the effort the movement had cost him. His voice was barely a whisper. "Please, Ross, do what I'm telling you."

Ross turned left.

He glanced at his watch and saw that less than five minutes had passed since Greg had told him over the car phone that his car had been rammed. All told, the man probably had a full minute lead in the car.

But the road was long and winding, and while there were housing developments along the way, there weren't any major connecting roads off it in that direction for a half-dozen miles, until the highway, Route 128. There was a slight chance he could catch up.

After that, the kidnapper could take Janine north or south and drop off at any number of exits to lose him and steal a new car. Be gone for good.

The speed limit was forty-five, and Ross wound the BMW up to a hundred and ten in the first straightaway.

The wind through the shattered front window made it hard to see, and the safety glass rattled over the dashboard.

"We need the police," he shouted over the wind noise and reached down to the car phone.

It took him three tries, between the wind and his concentration on the road, to realize he had dialed correctly, but no one was answering 911. The phone wasn't working. He looked in the rearview mirror, through the broken back window, and remembered the antenna had been on the trunk.

"Goddamn it!" He raked his fingers through his hair. He could've taken the cellular phone in the truck, if he'd only thought it through. Ross was scared, and it had nothing to do with the speed at which he was traveling. If anything, that settled him. He glanced at his brother and saw how pale his face was, how much blood he was losing sitting there.

The worst of it for Ross was thinking maybe he could've averted it all. He should've made Greg listen. He'd known down to his marrow that Greg had made a mistake by challenging the man without being ready to back it up.

Greg hadn't been willing to take the gun, and he hadn't even been willing for Ross to follow him out. Ross had simply done so and called him on the car phone to say he was keeping a mile back, to let him know when anything happened.

They should've been ready, he should've brought a rifle and scope. . . .

Should've, should've, should've. Ross made the car scream around the next corner. Ross watched the odometer. Four miles gone. He'd been averaging around ninety, but if the kidnapper had been able to make even close to that in the big Plymouth . . .

Ross downshifted to third around the next corner and floored the car, letting the back end knock out in a power skid.

Mile five passed.

"Ross, listen. . . ." Greg's voice was barely audible over the wind.

Ross didn't want to hear what his brother was saying.

He told Greg to shut up again, said he needed to concentrate on the driving.

But his brother talked anyway.

By the time they reached the ramp for Route 128 Ross had to decide if he would do what Greg had asked. And do it without any further discussion, without a chance to work out what came next, without any possibility of convincing Greg that he was asking the impossible.

Because, by then, Greg had died.

CHAPTER 15

Janine was cold.

They had the windows down in the car, and she was between the man and woman. The man had yelled at the woman for a while to keep going faster, and once Janine thought they were going to crash, but the man had reached over and grabbed the wheel. Then they'd reached the highway, and he'd told the woman to get on and off twice.

Once they were on a back road again, the man had pulled his mask off. The woman said, "Why are you doing that? Put it on!"

"It doesn't matter anymore," he said.

"Put it on!" The woman tried to cover Janine's eyes, but the man slapped her hand away.

"I said it doesn't matter anymore." The man's face was sharp and mean-looking.

Janine stared at him directly. And though he was close, she felt as if she were far away.

Not that she wasn't scared. A part of her could feel how her body was still shaking, that her shoulders would hitch as she tried to get in air.

That she tasted her own tears.

When she closed her eyes, there was the flash of gunfire. The flash showing her father making a face she'd never seen.

She opened her eyes and stared again at the man.

He noticed. "What're you looking at?"

"Did you kill my daddy?"

"He went for the gun, little chick. That's the way it goes." He snapped his fingers at the woman. "Pull over at that phone booth over there."

He took Janine by the hand. "Let's go talk to Mommy."

Janine had lost count of the various turns, stops, and starts. But she knew she was in Boston. They walked her up the stairs of an old factory building. The stairs looked the same as the place they'd taken her before.

In the apartment, Janine recognized the old linoleum floor, saw the hamburger bags in the big plastic trash can in the kitchen. The place was bigger than she'd imagined, with wide green shades pulled down in front of the windows. It didn't look like any apartment she'd ever been to. More like a place to do work.

"Go ahead, take off that idiot mask," the man said to the woman.

Janine could see the woman looking between the man and her, and finally she, too, pulled off the ski mask. Her hair was different than Janine had imagined, sort of blond. She glanced at Janine quickly, then turned away.

The place stunk of a smell Janine remembered, a chemical smell for cockroaches. The stuff didn't seem to be working; bugs scattered across the table when the man put the shotgun and the pistol down.

The two of them were silent now. The woman finally looked over at Janine and put her finger to her lips. Janine remembered her mother doing that in the store, back when all of this started. She closed her eyes. She tried to bring back her mother's voice, but there was no comfort there, because less than an hour ago she'd had to tell her mother that her father was dead.

Her mother had been so happy to hear Janine's voice at first that she hadn't seemed to hear it when Janine told her that Daddy was dead. She'd kept saying, "Put Daddy on, put Daddy on," and then the man had yanked the phone away and said the words again.

Janine couldn't shake the feeling it was her fault. She thought about how she'd helped the man pick out her father's car. The idea of it scared her so bad she couldn't breathe.

She saw the flash of yellow fire again, her father's face.

That's the way it goes.

She opened her eyes. Stared at the man, then at the woman. The man kicked the big armchair suddenly, spun it so it faced the center of the room. He grabbed Janine by the arm, and before she knew it, he'd flung her into the chair. She bounced half out but grabbed the arms and pulled herself back.

She didn't make a sound.

"Please," the woman said. "Leave Leanne—"

"This isn't Leanne," the man said. He bent down so his face was inches from Janine's. "All right, little chick. Who was he? The guy in the bushes, the guy who did this?" The man pointed to the blood on his shirt.

For the first time she realized he was bleeding. There was a tear in his shirt, soaked in red.

Good, she thought. She didn't say anything. Just stared back at him.

Behind him, the woman was trying to get her attention. Janine ignored her, felt mad at the woman. Janine knew she was getting in worse trouble, but she just didn't care.

"Who?" The man hit her on the side of the head, jarred her vision. "You think it's bad now, kid, it can get worse. Now who was he?"

The woman turned away. Janine felt her face get all hot, knew she was about to cry. She thought again of her father driving by in the car and her telling the man, and suddenly the tears started pouring out, scalding hot. The smash of the big car into her dad's . . . she knew she hadn't wanted it to happen, but somehow it seemed like she'd been on the man's side, she'd been helping him hurt her father.

That's the way it goes.

The man chucked her under the chin. "Cut the shit. Or I'll give you reason to cry. C'mon. Who was he?"

She drew herself up and screamed it in his face. "Uncle Ross is going to kill you!"

"Yeah?" He hit her with two fingers again. "Your uncle, huh? He thinks he's some sort of tough guy?"

Janine bit him. She grabbed his hand and got her teeth into his thumb.

"Shit!" The man half dragged her out of the chair and hit her so hard that she relaxed her bite. But she bore back down and tried to tear his thumb right off.

He hit her again, in the side. It knocked the breath out of her, and she fell away from him. Her head hit the floor, and from the great distance up, she saw the man draw his boot up.

And she knew from the look on his face he wasn't going to stop.

CHAPTER 16

Ross left the hand brake down and stepped away from the car. The BMW rolled down the hill, going maybe twenty or so, then disappeared. He got to the edge of the cliff just as the car sank from view in the moonlight.

He knew the cove was deep enough to hide the car well. The entire cove was exceptionally deep. Right up against the cliff wall it was over eighty feet.

Even though the Sands was no longer theirs, it had seemed like the best place to go to hide the car, and to bury his brother. To keep the police out of it like he'd insisted, right up until he died.

When Ross had driven back to the truck with Greg's body, the cellular phone had been ringing. Beth had been on the line, hysterical. She'd just heard from Janine and the kidnapper, and was it true? Was it true Greg was dead? Ross had told her it was. He had her put Allie on the phone.

Allie said, "How did it go so wrong?" Her own voice was shaking, but she seemed in control of herself. "Ross, how?"

"What'd he say?"

"He told her he was going to give us another chance, and to not call the police."

"We're going to take that chance. That's what Greg told me he wanted."

She had wanted to talk further, but he had closed the conversation, knowing that if he was to do as Greg had asked, he would have to move fast, or he would never do it at all.

When it came right down to it, Ross thought maybe he had waited too long after all. He was sitting on the knoll overlooking the cove. His brother was wrapped in the tarp he'd taken from the garage. The knoll was where they'd set the tent, the nights they needed to keep away from their father. Their mother had taken them there for picnics before that. The oak tree behind him still held the weathered frame of their tree house.

Ross started digging. As the shovel sank into the soft dirt, Ross could almost hear their voices coming from the tree house, from days when their mother was alive. Greg's voice good-natured, a little on the bossy side. His own a bit cocky, but still looking for his older brother's approval. Other scenes and times came to life inside his head in a random shuffle. Greg's wedding reception held there overlooking the cove; Greg and Beth taking vows they'd written themselves; Janine, as a toddler, standing at the foot of the tree with her father, excitedly babbling up as her Uncle Ross walked along a tree limb.

And Ross thought about five years ago, the day before he was to hear his verdict on the drug charge. He had been out on bail. He and Greg had sat under the tree and shared a beer. Greg had reminded him that the place had been in their family for over a hundred years and that it and the people who cared about Ross would still be there even if the jury came in against him. "It'll all be here for you when you get back," Greg had said. "All of us."

Afterward, Ross went back to the garage and strapped the case of money onto Greg's old Honda motorcycle. It took almost a dozen kicks to get the bike running.

But, out on the road, the bike revved easily, and Ross had to fight the urge to use screaming power of the engine to chase away the images of what he'd just done.

Back at the truck, he changed the front tire and ran the bike up on the plank he kept in the bed. He threw the case of money alongside.

He checked his watch and he saw it was just after midnight. Nothing to hold him from going back to Greg's house now. He'd kept himself locked into the logistics, the horrific steps involved in burying his brother. Somehow he'd managed that, but he didn't know how he was going to do with the words, with the explanation to Beth why he'd come home with the money, but not her husband or daughter.

CHAPTER 17

Ross told them everything from the moment he began following Greg.

"You started the shooting?" Allie said. "Are you crazy?"

Beth tuned out. The enormity of it was too much. Her mind could barely touch it. Greg dead, buried up at the Sands.

Insanity. Her life, in little more than a day, everything gone. Yesterday, she and Greg had been discussing things like how they could save money. Discussing possibility of bankruptcy. That'd kept both of them awake nights, and oh God, for one of those nights now. To think losing your house was the worst thing that could happen to you.

Beth bit her the knuckle of her forefinger, sank her teeth down so she tasted blood. Trying to wake herself up from the nightmare.

Janine, her little girl, still gone.

Her husband dead. Buried by his own brother. She had a sudden image of Greg, the day they'd met at Amherst, the day he knocked on her door holding one of the cards her former roommate had put up around campus. He needed a tutor in French. She remembered his double take, and the way her shyness suddenly just didn't exist. And she'd lied and told him she'd taken over from the roommate, and she'd be delighted to take him on as a student. Thinking that with a little time, she could convince him he needed an art history tutor. But it hadn't felt like a lie; it'd felt like they'd always known each other and her lie was just a dance step she had to take for them to be together.

Could the two of them have known somehow it could end like this?

Allie was still hammering hard at Ross. Her face was flushed, and Beth was dreamily aware that this was what they paid Allie for. She was their advocate, their fighter. She was saying, "What did he look like?"

"Both of them were wearing ski masks."

"License number?"

"I didn't see it. The bulb was gone over the plates. And there was too much going on for me to get a closer look."

"Too much going on? Christ!" Allie was pacing back in forth across the kitchen. "I begged you not to go. What was it? Some sort of macho convict bullshit? You couldn't let him rip you off?"

"He was going to kill them both. He was working himself up to it."

"Why would he do that?" Beth could see Allie was near tears herself. "Greg was going to give him the money!"

"Apparently the woman said his name in front of Janine."

Allie hesitated. "You know his name?"

"No. Janine said she hadn't heard it. But he said the woman's name: Nat."

"Like 'Natalie'?"

"I suppose." Beth realized that Ross was looking at her. His tone with Allie was weary. Beth recognized he was in the same place she was, a kind of drugged state. Where her heart, her whole chest, had turned into wood. She knew that it wouldn't last long, that anesthesia.

When Allie started to ask another question, Ross put up his hand. "Just a minute. We need to agree on where we go from here. Greg was clear that he wanted no police. That's why I did what I did."

"What you did was—"

"—was what Greg wanted," Beth interrupted. She realized she needed to make some decisions fast, before Allie decided to make them for her.

"Greg felt this was the only way," Ross said. "I think he's right. The kidnapper will figure he's been burned once, and if he has any sense that the police are involved, I think he'll just kill her." He turned to Beth. "Let me help."

"Help?" Allie gestured to Beth. "Don't you think you've helped her enough? She didn't want the cash back. She wanted her husband and daughter—"

"Stop it, Allie." Beth stood up, aware that the pain in her chest was already burning through, that she had only a little time before it would overwhelm her.

"Beth, you can't see it—"

"I said *stop it.*" Beth put her hand out and Ross took it. "Allie, I know you're fighting for me, but that's not what I need right now. Ross did what Greg asked. He's doing that now."

"You don't know that!"

"Shush. I do." She looked down at his hand, and saw how much it was shaped like Greg's, only more callused. "He's family. He's been Janine's godfather and guardian ever since Greg dragged him back from Washington State. We never changed it during the time he was in prison." She squeezed his hand hard.

"Greg always had a lot of faith in his younger brother. He always said you were the fighter of the family." She turned back to Allie. "And he's going to earn that faith now. He'll do anything to get her back. No police, Allie. That's what I want."

Allie looked from one to the other, and finally she agreed. "I won't get in your way. No police."

CHAPTER 18

Ross was back in the hole. Back in isolation. Where the air was thick from his own rebreathing, the walls an institutional beige, laden with many coats of old paint. Where the lightbulb, safe behind heavy mesh, was left constantly on.

The loneliness was physically painful. He rubbed at his chest in his sleep.

As the sunlight filled Greg's office, Ross swung off the couch, his mind fumbling with the hope that it had all been a dream. He stepped into the hall, and pushed open Janine's door.

Her bed was empty.

He sighed, too fully awake now to indulge in the idea any longer. He went back up to the office and turned on Greg's personal computer. As it warmed up, he dressed and formed the words he had in mind. It took a few minutes for him to open the file, and familiarize himself with the system, but soon he had the ad composed:

MASKED MAN, YOUR SECRET IS SAFE FOR 48 HOURS

BURIED, BUT NOT FORGOTTEN

UNCLE R LOVES J

CALL, HE'S BUYING.

Using the mouse, he created a line drawing of the ski mask, as best he could remember it in the brief flash of car light. It didn't have to be perfect, he figured. The man had said he read the classifieds every day, including the *Phoenix,* so he should know how to read the personals.

Ross did another version as a flier, and then simply typed up the copy as a straight classified listing, without the mask or border. He printed those out, and put the poster onto the photocopier. By the time he had a hundred fliers finished, he could hear Allie talking with Beth downstairs, and he went down to join them.

Beth nodded at the poster in his hand. "So what do you have in mind?" Her voice was husky.

Allie stood beside her and they looked at the ad. Beth said, "What makes you think that he'll see it?"

Ross told her about the man's comment about classified ads. He held up the stack of posters. "And making the assumption that he chose the store in Watertown because he knows something about the area, we'll start there with these posters."

"That's quite an assumption," Allie said.

Ross nodded. "True. So I'm going to hit some of the main streets in Boston, like Boylston, Mass. Ave., Commonwealth. And I'm going to blanket here, Lincoln."

"Lincoln?" Allie said. "You can't think he's from here?"

"No. But I wouldn't be surprised if he's scoped this area out, driven through at night, maybe even looked at the house."

Beth glanced out the window. "I'd love to see him," she said, her voice remote.

Ross kept his tone mild. "That's not out of the realm of possibility. I think it's unlikely today. He'll probably just lie low and try to figure out how he'll know if the police are involved. But he knows we have the money. He could assume accurately we have it here in the house—so he may try to just come in and take it."

"Could you get us another gun?" Beth met his eyes.

"How about yours?" Ross said to Allie.

"You have a gun?" Beth asked, surprised.

Allie smiled thinly. "I keep one in the nightstand drawer. The people I used to put away made threats from time to time and it helped me sleep, having it there."

"Could you get it for us this morning?"

She hesitated, then nodded. She said she would be back in a few hours. "I've got a ton of calls to make. But then I'll pick up some clothes, and plan to stay here tonight."

Beth thanked her, and Allie gave her a hug. "Whatever I can do."

After she left, Beth turned back to Ross and said, "What next?" Clearly trying to keep moving, trying to keep something in front of herself.

"OK. Does Greg keep his appointment calendar at home?"

Beth covered her face briefly and then stood. "I'll get it."

Ultimately, they decided Beth would call Greg's business and say that the whole family had caught a virus and Greg was particularly sick and probably wouldn't be in for several days. They'd leave his secretary to cancel his appointments. Janine was on summer break, so she wouldn't be missed until a birthday party later in the week.

In the middle of their plans, there was a noise at the front door. Ross ran across the living room with the handgun drawn. He looked out the window and felt like an idiot.

For there was a teenage boy walking away with a big bag slung over his shoulder. The paperboy.

"Jesus." Beth stood beside him. "This is what we do now."

Ross opened the door and picked up the paper. He was about to throw it down on the table when a small item at the bottom of the front page caught his eye. A late breaking story, just a few column inches. The second convenience store killing in as many days had occurred early that morning in Cambridge.

And the store owner had been shot in the face with a shotgun.

CHAPTER 19

Ross told him about Greg.

"Ah shit," Crockett sighed. "Knew you'd throw me off my food. Buried your own brother." He rubbed his hands over his face, his stubbly beard rasping. He said, "You got any reason to think the girl is still alive?"

Ross lifted his shoulders. "He said we had one more chance. The way I look at it, the man had his hands on the money, he saw that it was real . . . and he lost it. I'm hoping that'll eat at him enough that he'll give it another try." Ross slid a poster across the table.

Crockett looked at it, grunted. "So maybe he'll call. What do you want with me?"

Ross passed the newspaper over and pointed to the article.

"Convenience store, shotgun."

"Yeah? Your pal's not the only one who sticks up grocery

stores. We've got a thriving metropolis here, you know what I mean?"

"Shot the owner in the face. Same as with the store owner when he kidnapped Janine. And this store's just a few miles away. Both cases, he took off in a car, though in this case the witness said he drove away alone." Ross circled the name of the witness, Muriel Gray, age thirty-three.

"That's a little different." Crockett nodded. "Guys hitting stores in cities usually take off on foot, blend into the crowd."

"And I saw him last night put his gun in Greg's face."

"Still means shit," Crockett said. "Blowing a guy's head off is part of the appeal of that particular weapon."

"Maybe," Ross said.

"Definitely." Crockett showed no sign of recognizing what images might be going through Ross's head right that moment, given how Greg had died.

Ross's first night in the cell, Crockett had let him know how it was. "You're gonna be passed around this block like a doll, young guy like you. Unless you know something about how to fight. It which case, you better be ready to hurt the first guy who tests you, and it's gonna come soon. You hurt him bad, you break a bone, you make him bleed, and you make sure everyone sees it. And then do your time in the hole without crying about it."

Now, Crockett stood and scratched his belly as he went over to the refrigerator and pulled out eggs and bacon and turned on the gas under the frying pan.

"So you want to do something," he said. "You sure there's anything to do except for wait by the phone? You said the kidnapper's skinnier than Teague."

"But Teague could have friends. Extortion is a pretty common piece of business for bikers, like that story you were telling about Gilchrist. And I hurt Teague pretty bad. That's enough motive for a guy like that."

"What if the kidnapper calls and you're out dancing with Teague?"

"Beth's by the phone, she can get to me on the cellular."

Crockett shook his head as he cracked three eggs into a bowl. "Bad business, Ross. Really bad. Seems to me you want to get some exercise, maybe ease your conscience? Show yourself that your Concord time had nothing to do with your niece getting kidnapped."

"Psychology never was your strong suit, Crockett."

Crockett snorted. "Like hell."

"Besides, there's one thing that's kind of strange about what happened in the store."

"What's that?"

"The way Greg told it, he jumped the gunman before the guy actually told the woman to take Janine. Greg felt the guy was working up to kidnapping her."

"Yeah?"

"Well, the guy knocked Greg down with the gun, but he shot the owner. I mean, in the instant before he even committed himself to taking Janine, he knew to leave Greg alive and kill the owner, so there were no other witnesses."

"Guys like that make up their minds fast. Not much thinking involved, but they jump to a conclusion and then they follow it. Besides, maybe he figured the store owner had a gun."

"He didn't. I asked Greg that, and he said he didn't see a gun."

"Yeah, but the guy wouldn't have known that. He would've figured the store owner moving behind him might've had a piece behind the counter. Lot of them do."

Ross nodded. "Yeah, that's a point. But I still want to talk with Teague. Have that conversation."

"Yeah, yeah. I made some calls, and got his address. You gotta promise me not to mention my name when you go see him. He's stupid, but he's too mean to let that slow him down much."

Ross smiled as Crockett wrote down the address and said, "On to the next topic—how'd you like to try a completely different line of work?"

"Holy Christ," Crockett said an hour later as they parked in front of the house. "I've broken into nicer homes, but I've never been invited into one as nice."

"Are you going to be able to do this?" Ross asked. In truth, he doubted Crockett had ever broken into a house, or at least not for many years. The man prided himself on being a professional, and for him that meant stealing from other professionals—bankers, armored car drivers—not widows.

Crockett said, "I can keep my hands off the cash and the silverware, yeah." He blinked, and looked smaller and older than he ever had before. Ross looked at him more closely, and realized that Crockett was embarrassed, maybe. Shy.

"C'mon." Ross cuffed him lightly on the shoulder. "You'll be doing us a favor."

"Like hell," Crockett snapped. "You'll be paying me."

Ross grinned. "Wait in the truck a minute, OK?"

"A bank robber?" Allie said. "You're asking a bank robber to guard us and the money?"

"He's smart, and he's steady, and I've known him a long time."

"Five years, right?"

Ross ignored that. "And he knows guys like the one we're dealing with. He won't hesitate to do what's necessary if the kidnapper breaks in." Ross paused. "And frankly, we can use all the help we can get."

"Help doing what?" Allie said. "Just where will you be?"

"I've got to go out. Will you be staying here?"

"I've got some calls to make down the street. But after that I'll come back. I can't see leaving Beth alone with a bank robber and my gun. But you can?"

Ross nodded. "He'll be fine. I trust him."

Beth had gone over to the doorway and was looking out at Crockett in the truck. She said, "If he can help us hurt that man, I want him, Allie. I want him in here."

CHAPTER 20

Teague lived in Brighton, just across the Charles River from Cambridge. The area was a general mix of run-down buildings with occasional blocks where gentrification was under way: brownstones sandblasted clean, flowers in the window boxes, freshly washed steps.

Teague's block was not one of those.

Garbage cans were stacked along the sidewalk, and a plywood sheet replaced what should have been a full-length glass pane in the outer doorway of Teague's building. A Harley was chained to the streetlight post, a big bike with extended front forks and swastika rearview mirrors. Teague's kind of bike.

Crockett had said Teague lived in apartment eight. In the foyer, there was no name on the mailbox, just the number. The name for apartment six was Hernández. Ross pushed the button for eight, held the button down for the count of ten.

He looked up the stairway, ready to take off if he saw anyone coming down.

Nothing.

He waited and did it again.

This time the speaker crackled, and Teague's voice filled the little foyer. "What?"

Ross pitched his voice a bit high. "Pizza for Hernández."

"You fucking dink, this is eight."

Ross simply buzzed six quickly, figuring that Teague could hear it through walls, and then he walked out the door and to the back of the building. There was a small parking lot surrounded by a high fence. There was just one driveway in and out, and there were no other bikes. The big Plymouth wasn't there, not that Ross really expected to get that lucky. He kept close to the building, figuring that it'd be hard for Teague to see him that way unless he had his head out the window. And Ross didn't see anyone doing that.

So he got back into his truck and positioned himself where he could see both the driveway and the front door.

And he waited.

The first hour was manageable, but the second was excruciating.

Ross couldn't get into the Quiet Place, as he had called it back when he was doing time for a living.

He'd found essentially two ways to manage time. One, to throw himself into the routine, the four roll calls, standing in line for chow, the work details, painting under bridges, working in the furniture shop.

The other was the Quiet Place. Thinking at first of nothing but a gray fog. He'd wrap himself in a blanket so his body was warm while he floated . . . until he eventually landed in the place he wanted to be, on the deck of *Bon Vivant,* or swimming in the cove, sometimes even with Giselle, throwing that coke over-board and watching his troubles dissolve.

He could pass hours there.

But the Quiet Place wasn't available today. He needed to keep his attention focused. And when his eyes just blinked, the sight of Greg's ruined chest came into lurid view. And Janine. Her face in that back window, crying out for him.

It was all too easy to envision that the kidnapper had been scared and angry, that he might've already killed her and left the state.

As the second hour closed, Ross called Beth.

"Anything?" he asked.

"Not a word. Where are you?"

"The last poster is up," he said, truthfully enough. He told her he'd get back as soon as he could. He told himself he didn't want to raise her hopes, thinking he had something solid in looking after Teague. More to the point, he realized, was he didn't want her looking at him as if it was all his fault.

Not any more than she had been already. Even though she had supported him with Allie, Ross could feel the undercurrent of hostility from Beth. *Who could blame her?* he figured.

He was a changed man from her husband's kid brother she'd known before he went away. That first night in his cell, after listening to Crockett's advice, Ross hadn't slept at all. The power in his arms and legs had surged and faded as his fear would boil into rage and then cool again. Leaving him a frightened man, facing five to ten years without any idea how he'd pass the next twenty-four hours.

So when the test had come, as it had the middle of the next day, Ross had let himself go. A con named Cridler had looked Ross right in the eye and reached across the lunch table for the apple on Ross's tray, and said, "I'm starting with a bite of that, sweetmeat." The frightened man inside Ross had driven the angry man. Together they left Cridler with a broken cheekbone, cracked ribs, two missing front teeth, and a broken knee.

Ross had to do that kind of thing just a few times more in his term, once to Teague. The frightened man always went with him on those battles.

And as Teague came swaggering down the front stairs of his apartment building, Ross was glad to find the frightened man was with him again.

Teague kick-started his bike and took off, and Ross followed in the truck.

Ross let his breath out when Teague came out of the store. There was no shotgun in his hand, no bag of money. Just a pack of cigarettes. Marlboros, of course. Ross watched him rip open the package and tap one out. Except for a slight limp, the biker moved with a heavy kind of grace, as if he knew he was being watched. Not that Ross thought Teague had noticed him. Rather, it was the overt mannerisms that became second nature inside the wall, the body language to tell everyone, *Don't mess with me.* The way Teague hunched his shoulders when he lit the cigarette, even though there was no breeze. The way he squinted at the mild sunlight. Ross would've found it kind of funny, if he didn't know Teague was equally willing to prove his brutality in a more direct manner.

The trouble with Teague had started a few days after Ross had received a letter from Greg and Beth that held a few snapshots of Janine. Ross had taped the photos to the wall beside his bunk. As Teague was walking by, he'd slowed to look through the bars at the pictures.

"Looks good enough to eat," he said, grinning right into Ross's face.

Ross had told him to fuck off.

That's all it had taken.

Teague had slammed his weight against the bars once, then moved on, saying only, "You're gonna pay for that one."

Ross hadn't thought that much about it—until he saw the way Teague began watching him. Ross would be at dinner, and he'd see Teague turning away just as he looked up. Teague was novor far away during the free time. And they ended up on the same work crews cutting grass along the highway. A wariness that prison time had ingrained in Ross took over. Crockett had been paroled for almost six months at that time, so Ross had asked Reece to watch his back.

"We've got to watch to see if he's grouping up," Reece had said one night after chow. "He's not the brightest guy, not the sort who moves on his own. You know how it'd be, him and three other guys on you. One holding the pillow over your face, the other two sticking you about fifty times."

Luckily, Teague had been arrogant.

One evening just as Ross was breaking down from chipping paint on an overpass, Reece had brushed close and said quietly, "Behind you." Ross had turned to see Teague coming his way fast, his hand inside his shirt. The nearest guard was two dozen feet away, and his view was momentarily blocked as he stood alongside the truck watching the men stack the ladders.

Apparently Teague had figured he could do it himself, figured his fifty or so pounds of weight advantage could overcome Ross. Ross had raised his hands, as if to box it out. Teague pulled out the blade and came in fast, his left arm out, ready to pull Ross onto the knife.

Ross had kicked him right in the balls, and followed that up with a solid right and left into Teague's face.

Teague had shaken his head, confused for a second, and then he'd charged, both arms wide, apparently ready to take the punishment so he could pin Ross against the rail.

Ross didn't stand his ground. He'd backed up until Teague

was almost on him, then grabbed the man's wrist, ducked down, and spun, letting Teague's 250 pounds roll over his back and, with a little lift, over the rail.

Luckily for both of them, Ross had been standing near the end of the bridge, and Teague only fell eight or ten feet alongside the road. The men below had dropped the knife down into the storm sewer before the guards could get down to Teague. And Teague had denied everything, simply covered all their questions with a string of curses about his damaged knee.

And that's why Teague had a limp now.

Ross followed the man to his next stop, a bar on Harvard Avenue, and saw through the dirty smoked glass that Teague was set up with a beer and a shot. And he figured that it was as good a time as any to go back to Teague's place and see if there was any evidence that Teague had decided Janine should help pay for his limp.

CHAPTER 21

Back at Teague's building, Ross sounded the buzzer for several apartments again. After a few minutes, a young woman with a crying little boy at her leg opened her door and looked at Ross through the glass. Ross lifted his toolbox up and smiled, thinking that here was his chance to see if there was any truth to Reece's adage about how you could go anywhere and steal anything as long as you carried a toolbox.

She opened the door. "You for the sink? Apartment two?"

"No, ma'am," he'd said cheerfully. "Cable company, got to go up to the roof for a minute."

"That's great," she said, her back already turned. "TV but no water, that's what I need."

He continued up to Teague's apartment, which was in the back of the building, top floor. He knocked, and then waited quietly. Nothing. He continued up the back stairway to the roof.

Ross squinted in the bright sunlight as he walked casually

over to the tar-covered roof and onto the roof of Teague's small deck overlooking the parking lot. In case anyone was looking, he pulled out a tape measure and a pocketknife and played the part of a building super, picking at the rot in the frame. After a few minutes, Ross took a coil of rope out of the toolbox, and while he whistled tunelessly, he used it to swing the toolbox onto the deck below. He looped the line around the chimney, and before he gave himself too much time to think about it, he slid over the side, and walked down the brick wall a few feet until he could step onto the rail, and then down onto the deck.

From there it got really easy. Teague's window was open. Maybe the weather was too hot for Teague, or maybe he counted on his own personality to keep the place safe. Inside, Ross could smell the man: a mix of sweat, stale beer, pot, and cigarette smoke. Ross moved through the rooms quickly, the gun in his hand. No one was there.

He came back to the living room. To his left were a big-screen television and a stack of porno tapes. Ross glanced through them quickly and saw several featuring titles like "Barbie Dolls" and "Daddy's Girl."

Kiddie porn.

Ross felt the pressure right behind his eyes, felt the tightness of his jaw. And he decided against trying to keep the search of Teague's apartment a secret.

He went through all the drawers, ripped open the couch, pushed through the kitchen cabinets, through the bedclothes. In the closet, he pushed aside work clothes that were stiff with sweat, dried dirt, concrete dust. Teague apparently worked in construction. Ross looked through the bathroom. He didn't know exactly what to look for, other than some sign of Janine, anything to suggest she'd been there.

But he found nothing more than a bag of marijuana, a lot of

cockroaches, a box filled with a stack of porno magazines . . . and, at the bottom of them, a box of shotgun shells.

Buckshot.

Ross pulled up a chair facing the door, put the gun on the coffee table beside him, and settled in for the wait.

Almost two hours passed before Ross heard the sound of heavy footsteps outside the door. Ross moved quietly into the bathroom, directly across from the entrance. He could hear Teague's breathing and figured the guy probably had knocked back more than a couple of drinks. That could be bad. Ross didn't imagine Teague was the type to turn into a friendly drunk.

Ross waited until he heard the front door open and close. The smell of beer filled the room, and Ross tensed himself, figuring the first stop Teague would make after all that beer and a jolting ride on the Harley would be the bathroom.

Through the crack in the door, Ross saw Teague coming straight in, his hands fumbling with his zipper. Ross stepped around the door, put the gun in the biker's face, and cocked it. "Right there, Teague. Now tell me what I want to know."

Ross kept his eyes on Teague's, looking for something beyond the initial surprise, some flicker of recognition.

For an instant, maybe there was something there, maybe not. Teague's face went slack.

"What?" he said stupidly, then shook his head as the color began to rise in his face. "Stearns. Little Rossie Stearns. What the fuck're you doing?"

Ross hit him, two fast left jabs in the nose that drew blood and set Teague back on his heels. Ross grabbed Teague's shirt and ran him backward into the hallway and slammed him against the front door. Teague's breath gusted out, and Ross tapped him hard on the bridge of his nose with the gun butt, making the man cry out. Ross cupped Teague's jaw, shoved his head against the wall, and put the barrel to Teague's temple. "Where is she?"

"Who?" Teague said between gritted teeth.

Ross buried his left fist in Teague's stomach, and when the biker reflexively went to cover himself up, Ross grabbed him by the chin again and bounced his head against the door. "Where?"

"If you didn't have the gun, man—"

"But I *do* have the gun. Tell me about the shotgun shells."

"What?"

Ross hit him again. "Come on! The shotgun shells under your baby pictures. Where's the gun?"

"Gone."

Ross drew his hand back, and the big man said, "No, I'm telling you, I dropped it in the river after I did a job."

"With who?"

"Huh?"

"Who'd you do the job with?"

"Nobody."

"You send him in? You get your friend to go after her? C'mon, Teague, you've got the brains of a gnat. You didn't set this up. Who're you working for?"

"Nobody, I told you."

"What about the shotgun? You shoot somebody? That why you got rid of it?"

Teague shrugged. "Gas station. Broke some glass. Guy pulled a gun and I missed. He took a coupla pellets, but he was in the paper next day, big hero."

"Where?"

"Dorchester."

"Now where is she?"

"Who?"

"My niece."

"That's done business, man. You fucking dropped me. I

can't walk good, now. What more do you want?"

"Where is she now?"

"How the fuck do I know?" Teague's voice rose. "Do I look like a goddamn school monitor?"

"You look like a short-eyes pig, and your leg drags behind you because of what you said about my niece," Ross said evenly. "And now she's gone. I'm going to kill you unless you tell me who you sent into that store and where I can find Janine." Ross kneed Teague in the balls, and when the big man crumpled, Ross shoved him into the corner and stepped back two steps. He held the gun in both hands.

"What're you doing, man?" Teague's face was white under the splash of red from his nose. His hands were up. "I don't know anything—"

"Teague, look at my face," Ross said gently. "You know I'm going to do it if you don't tell me."

The thing of it was, at that moment, Ross meant it. The adrenaline was singing through his veins, and all the fear and anger was free, and he was no longer on the defense.

"Me and you are done, man. You should see me walk."

"We're not done."

"Then you might as well pull it. 'Cause I know jack shit about your niece." Teague stared up at him.

There was no way to tell if it was the truth or not.

Ross let the hammer down with his thumb and swiftly stepped in and cracked Teague behind the ear with the gun butt.

The big man slumped down, unconscious. Ross had to drag him away from the door before he could leave. Before he could walk down the stairs with his tool kit and get into his truck and drive away, his hands trembling on the steering wheel.

CHAPTER 22

The next morning Beth and Allie pressed Ross for where he had been the day before. Crockett simply listened quietly.

"What did you find out?" Allie said. "What did you do?"

"Nothing good," Ross told them.

He waited with them until midafternoon, and then said he would be back in a while.

Allie followed him out. "What are you up to?"

Ross almost snapped back at her to mind her own damned business. The way she seemed to think his own family needed protection from him was infuriating. But when he turned, he could see by the rigid set of her shoulders and tightness about her mouth the strain she was under.

"I can go home when I want to, but Beth has to just wait. The least you could do is tell her what you're doing."

He opened the door of the truck. "Why don't you get in for a second?"

She slid across to the passenger side and turned to face him.

He said, "Look, I've just been checking out whether or not my being in prison brought this down on them."

"Is there any evidence of that?"

Ross told her about how Teague had tried to kill him, and about Gilchrist's wife. "And Teague's a biker who does armed robberies. That's why he was in prison in the first place. And extortion is a pretty common piece of business for bikers. So he could've sent somebody in after Janine. He had the motive, probably the contacts."

Allie listened carefully, apparently weighing everything he had to say. Finally, she shook her head. "That logic wouldn't fly in court, believe me. It sounds like Teague had motive to hurt *you,* but nothing else."

"Maybe. But it was worth the time to find out."

"So what'd you do?"

"Applied a little pressure."

"Meaning you beat him up?"

Ross simply nodded.

"Did you find anything out?"

"Nothing useful."

"Jesus Christ." Allie laughed shortly and looked away. "Maybe I can just put it down to experience. I've slept with a guy who beats people up to get information. You realize it used to be my job to put people like you away."

"I'd never be doing anything like this except for the circumstance with Janine."

She shook her head. "You just don't get it. No 'circumstance' makes it OK for you to go around beating people. That's the kind of faulty thinking that got you in prison in the first place, and it's going to land you back there sooner or later. That's the kind of shortcut thinking that lets you figure on sailing away as soon as you sell a little land."

"You mean if I was rich, I'd have made sense. Otherwise, I was just an interesting experience for a few weeks."

"I *meant* think ahead! I could've understood if you'd planned on selling the entire place and using the money to throw in with Greg, or start a business of your own. But just sail away? There's no future in that."

"Look, this isn't the time," Ross said abruptly. "The only future I'm working toward now is getting Janine home."

"It *is* the time. I'm telling you you're crazy to be mixing into this any further. Let's just let the man call again, and try to get Janine back. No shortcuts. No circumstances." She touched his cheek, her voice softening slightly. "No more prison terms. Please, Ross."

He bit back his response. He was angry, and it would be easy for him to dismiss her as approaching him the same way Cynthia had, with her prescribed formula for success. But he knew Allie thought for herself, that, whereas Cynthia had wanted him to deliver success, Allie drove herself fiercely to achieve her own ambitions. He still didn't know her well enough to know exactly what they were. Allie had grown up in the backwoods of Maine, where most of the roads were owned by the logging companies. She had told him one night as they lay in her bed how it had been like growing up in the Deep South except for the snow. "Pickup trucks with gunracks, lots of mud, blackflies, snow, and stupidity. Living with people whose dreams consisted of a bigger satellite dish to catch more television." She had done everything for herself, forcing her family to recognize she was smart and unwilling to stick around and marry another logger. She had won scholarships and scraped her way financially through law school. Ross respected her self-sufficiency and drive. He was even a bit envious. But that didn't change the fact that he had no interest in a future that was centered on how well he did with an office desk, a suit and tie.

He reached across and opened her door. "I've got to go."

"Don't ignore me," she said flatly.

"I'm doing what I think is right. And I don't have anymore time to talk about it."

She slipped out of the truck and went into the house without another word.

Ross stopped at the store in Watertown first. The name over the door said: "Jacob Family Spa."

He'd never been there before, but from what Greg had told him about the night Janine had been kidnapped, Ross had a strong sense of déjà vu. He looked down the aisle to the ice-cream freezer and then back up to the front counter. The wall behind the counter was bare. There had clearly been shelves there in the past—racks were still screwed into the walls.

An older woman was at the counter. She was probably in her midfifties, with gray hair and a scared, hurt look on her face. He bought a newspaper, giving her a dollar.

Her eyes never left the cash register during the whole transaction.

"I read about the robbery," he said, picking up a business card from the small bulletin board beside the register. "I'm sorry to hear what happened."

She simply nodded.

The name on the card was Bobby Jacob, a piano tuner. "A family member?"

"Louis's boy," she said abruptly.

"Louis wasn't your husband?" Ross said.

Her eyes were wet when she looked up at him, shook her head. "Brother."

"It's a terrible thing." Ross knew how inadequate the words were. "I lost my brother not long ago, too."

"You're young for that." She looked at him directly now. "But it doesn't make any difference when you get older. It hurts just as bad. Both of us were alone. My husband died eight years ago. Louis was divorced. His boy, Bobby, had moved on. We opened the store, bought a house. It wasn't so lonely that way."

"Did the police find out anything?"

Her face twisted. "Nothing. No one saw anything. No one heard anything, except one of the boys up the street at the sub shop says maybe there were two cars parked in front around the time of the robbery. The police said one most likely was the killer's. Maybe the driver of the other one saw something. But no one has come forward."

"So there's no clue who did it?"

"Not unless whoever was in that car saw something," she said bitterly. "And I guess they can't be bothered."

He got even less at the Store 24 in Cambridge.

There was a young man at the counter with a long ponytail who had no time for small talk. His books were open beside him. About the robbery and murder all he had to say was, "You won't catch me working the night shift. There are monsters out at night, and they come here to shop."

It took him just a few minutes to find the apartment of Muriel Gray, the witness to the Cambridge robbery. There were two M. Grays in the phone book, but according to the street map he bought at the Store 24, one of them lived just a few blocks away.

When he buzzed her apartment, no one answered at first. He tried once more, and just as he was about to leave, a woman's voice said, "Who is it?"

"Ms. Gray? Could I talk to you a minute about the robbery?"

He could hear her sigh. "I'm on my way out."

"It'll just take a moment."

She asked him to wait there. After a few minutes, she came

downstairs, a dark-haired woman with a thin face and an impatient manner. "I don't know what more you want me to say. . . . Hey, are you a cop?"

"No, ma'am." Ross gave her the business card he'd taken from the bulletin board at the Watertown store. She looked at it curiously and handed it back. "Pianos?"

"My father was killed in a robbery just a few days ago."

She put her hand to her mouth. "Oh, I'm so sorry."

"Thank you. But when I read about the robbery you saw, what with it being so close and all, I wondered if they might be related."

"Well, I'm sure the police are looking into that."

He shrugged. "Maybe. But it doesn't seem like it. It seems like the two different departments aren't talking . . . and I guess maybe I just feel I need to do *something.*"

She nodded. "I can imagine. But listen, I didn't see that much. I wish I never talked to that reporter. He made it sound like I'm some kind of star witness."

"What did you see?"

"Just about what you read, probably. A man running out of the store, holding a gun. Driving off. And then I looked into the store, and—" She dropped her eyes. "Well, you know, it was awful."

"Yes, I know." He paused. "Did the man drive himself away? Or was there someone else in the car?"

"He drove himself."

"What kind of car was it?"

"I don't know cars. It was big and old."

"Color?"

"Light. Light brown or gray. It's hard to say at night."

"And was he wearing a mask?"

She nodded. "That I saw clearly. I saw him just under the light in the doorway."

"What kind was it?"

"A ski mask. You know, with a pattern on it."

Ross flipped over the business card and gave her a pen. "Could you draw the pattern?"

She shrugged. "Not very well."

But she was more skillful than she gave herself credit. The pattern was close to the same that he'd drawn for the ads, a screaming face.

"And the colors?" he asked.

"Red on black. Scary as hell."

CHAPTER 23

The call came late the next morning.

Beth answered the phone, and Ross could see her face go pale. "Talk to me," she said.

But apparently he refused. "He said he wants Uncle R."

Ross took the phone. "I'm her uncle."

"You're the guy who shot me?"

"That's right. Let me speak to Janine."

"In a minute." The man's voice sounded amused. "Bad news for you. Your bullet just scraped me, and if I read that ad right, you buried your brother?"

"Yes."

The man whistled. "Cold. You must not have liked him much, huh?"

The man hung up.

The next call came about ten minutes later. "Got plenty of quarters. Don't try to trace this."

"If we'd involved the police, you think you would've gotten away in the first place?"

"So why haven't you now?" The man sniffed.

"Same exact reason. We want Janine. We don't give a damn about the money."

"Yeah, talk to me about that. Tell me why I shouldn't waste the little chick."

"Because you saw the cash. You know it's real and that we're willing to give it to you."

"Yeah?"

"Yes. And we'll meet again, the only difference being that I'm bringing a gun, and I will have it on you the whole time."

The man paused, and Ross heard him sniff again.

"You ought to take one of those courses," the man said. "On *persuasion.* You seem to forget who I've got my hands on. You should be worrying about my health, telling me not to take any risks, telling me to take it easy on the coke, sleep good at night . . . you get what I'm saying? Her life and mine, all tied together. So don't go threatening *me.*"

"You'd expect the gun, anyhow. And I'm sure you'll have one on me."

"On *her.*"

Ross let that go. "Let me speak to her."

"She's not with me."

Ross closed his eyes. He could feel Beth looking at him, and his mind went blank momentarily as the man's words washed over him, words saying the man didn't want to take Janine out in daylight, words saying that everything would be fine if Ross just dropped the money off where he was told.

Words that sounded just like lies to Ross.

The guy was talking too much, telling more than he had to. Ross opened his eyes. And said, "No. You get her on the phone.

Sometime today, you call back with her on the phone, and we'll make plans to meet then."

"Hey, fuckhead," the man snapped. "You ask your brother what happens when you start giving me instructions. You go pull the dirt and worms out of his mouth, hear what he has to tell you."

"I need to know she's alive," Ross said. "I'll make you rich, but you've got to prove that to me."

The man slammed the phone down.

They waited for the call all afternoon, but it never came.

Ross went to see Tommy Datano that night.

Datano saw him as he entered the restaurant and waved him to his booth ahead of three other people. "How's your little niece?" he said. "Good news, I hope."

Ross shook his head.

"You didn't find a buyer?" Datano's look of dismay appeared well practiced.

"No," Ross said. He'd decided that telling Datano they had the money would only leave them open to being ripped off. "We've lost all contact with the kidnappers."

Datano shook his head. "Such a shame. So are you looking for the two-fifty? I'm afraid I've committed those funds, but perhaps we can do something for you."

"No. Although I appreciate the offer." Ross kept his tone level, professional. The man's whole manner encouraged him to talk, to spill his rage. To tell him about the hours he'd spent with Beth, about how she needed something, anything, to believe her daughter was still alive.

But Ross kept all of that to himself. He knew Datano's sympathy would cost them. Instead, he showed the clippings about both convenience store robberies, the one in Watertown where

Janine was abducted as well as the one in Cambridge. "I'm willing to pay to find out who did these."

Datano shrugged. "You don't think we get involved in this kind of thing, do you? This kind of thing is very random. It'd be nice to think the punk who did this knows whose territory he's stepping on, but this kinda punk is usually fried out of his brains."

"I understand. But there are a lot of people you know who have their eyes and ears open, and they can learn things . . . say when a guy like this wants to buy a gun, buy some dope, brags in a bar, or sells or hocks something he stole . . . there are people you know who can find things out."

"But you don't know if the same man did these robberies."

"Not definitely, no. But if it'd be worth ten thousand dollars to find out . . . and introduce me when the time comes, with whatever name I give you. I should tell you the man may have a girlfriend or wife named 'Nat.' Probably Natalie."

"We're not in the detective business, Mr. Stearns."

"You are in the money and information business. And that's all this is."

Datano sipped his wine and shrugged his shoulders slightly. "I suppose I can introduce you to some people." He leaned forward, adopting a confidential tone. "Perhaps we should discuss a more direct relationship. If you have some success selling your property, or perhaps if we can complete a sale ourselves, that might free up enough cash for you to make it worth our while to really do a job for you."

"Meaning?"

"Meaning, find this man . . . and do whatever is appropriate." Datano smiled gently. "We'd look to your guidance on exactly what that would be."

Ross was tempted. But he wasn't ready to accept that Janine was dead yet, and until he was, he couldn't put a contract out on her kidnapper. It could go wrong so easily; the hit man might even find it expedient to kill Janine if she saw too much.

"That's a kind offer," Ross said. "But that introduction is all I'm able to afford."

Datano sat back. "Don't be so sure."

"I'm sure," Ross said. He passed an envelope under the table.

Datano took the envelope but didn't look in it.

"That's ten," Ross said. "For now, finding who did this is all I ask of you."

Datano finished his wine. "All right, I think I know someone who might be able to help you. His name is T.S. He's crazy and he appreciates other crazies. You can trust him about as far as you can lift him over your head with one hand, and you'll understand when you see him just how impossible that would be."

"Can you make him talk to me?"

"I can introduce you. *Do not* tell him why you're looking for the guy. He'd rather brush his teeth than help an average citizen in trouble." Datano touched the clippings. "You can't even be specific about looking for the person doing these robberies. He'd figure you for a cop. But he knows the low-level nuts better than me, and he runs some guns, sells some dope. If your kidnapper's black, or really any color except mean and white, T.S. isn't going to be much good to you. But that still leaves a lot of people he knows, and sometimes he pulls them together for jobs."

Datano put the envelope in his inside jacket pocket. "And that's as far as this takes you."

Chapter 24

The blue Caprice pulled up to the corner of Boylston and Massachusetts Avenue, and the man inside yelled, "You Blackie?"

Ross bent down. "Keep your voice down." He got inside the car. "The name's Black."

"Yeah, yeah, hardass," the man said. "I'll call you whatever I want, however loud I want." Ross took a good look at the man. He was fat, easily over 250 pounds. He wore a leather vest, blue jeans, leather gloves, and bathroom slippers, and he smelled very bad. A silver earring glinted under long graying hair. He was smoking a joint.

"Datano tell you what I want?" Ross asked.

The man said, "Let me explain one or two things to you: I do not work for Datano. I do not take orders from him. I got a certain amount of respect, 'cause I know he could kill me anytime this afternoon that he wanted. . . ." Here he took a deep toke of the joint and blew the smoke in Ross's face.

". . . On the other hand, I just happen to not give that much of a shit about things like living and dying, and he knows that, and since we both get some things off the other, we pretty much leave each other alone."

"That's about what Datano said."

"So what do you want?" T.S. drew on the joint until the tip glowed. He leaned forward and ran the burning ember down the dashboard a couple of inches. The vinyl melted in a small line, and T.S.'s attention was clearly off Ross and the road.

"Watch it," Ross said, as a flower van pulled in front of them.

T.S. swerved around the van in the right lane, snapped the wheel back hard to the left, and the van driver must've stood on the brakes, the way the tires screamed. T.S. laughed. "Smell the fertilizer in among those flowers?" He drew deep on the joint again and laid the tip across the top of the line on the dashboard and started on the second bar, making an *F*.

"Aren't you a little old for this?"

T.S. said, "Shit, no. Never too old to write dirty words in a stolen car. So why you wasting my time, Blackie?"

Ross was wearing black jeans and a black leather jacket. He'd cropped his hair short with a razor the night before, cutting it off in purposely sloppy hunks. And he'd shaved off his beard. He'd checked himself out in the mirror just before he left. At a minimum, he looked quite different from the man the kidnapper had seen in the brief flash of car light. What was more important, the paleness of his skin and the signs of stress around his mouth and eyes gave him a desperate look that fit just fine with his cover story about being part of a two-man team in from New York looking for some jobs. Fit the way he was feeling pretty damn well, too.

"I need some work."

"Burger King's hiring."

"I need a shooter who can help me scare up some money right

now, and then maybe help me and my partner out with something else."

"What kind of jobs you got in mind?"

"Something tonight, to help me build a war chest. Then I'm gonna be coming back to you for guns on a bigger job."

"What, you talking banks and shit?"

"I'm not ready to talk about it now. Consider it a test. You get me a guy who can help line me up with some fast cash, I'll come back and spend it with you on the other job. He'll get himself some work, if he's any good. You'll get a cut on the whole thing."

T.S. grunted. "Why'd Datano pass you along? He know you?"

"I've got references."

"Who?"

"That's none of your business," Ross said mildly. "Datano sent me to you."

T.S. gave him a hard look.

Ross stared back at him, not putting too much into it, just letting the big man know he wasn't scared of the steely gaze.

"I've got a tough guy," T.S. said finally. "Sitting right beside me."

"Just like to keep my business my own."

T.S. apparently decided to move on. "What else do you do?"

"Driver and shooter."

"So why don't you go take care of business yourself?"

Ross kept looking straight ahead. T.S. had circled the block and was now back on Massachusetts Avenue. There was a police car up ahead of them in the left lane. Ross looked over at the speedometer, saw they were doing about forty. He put on his seat belt. "I told you, I need cash to buy me a few days' time to set this other thing up. I don't have time to set up this low-level shit. That's why I'm coming to you."

T.S. gave him the look for a moment, but Ross ignored him.

Finally the man said, "Tell me about your partner."

"Name's Mr. Gray."

"Gray and Black, huh?"

"That's right.

"How good you know him?"

"Very well."

"Huh. What're you going to do *if* I set something up for you tonight?"

"Check out your man's game plan, do the driving. Get him home, no cops."

"Yeah? There's people around. Why do you need me?"

Ross shook his head. "I don't want just anyone. Someone good with a shotgun who isn't afraid to use it. Someone who's active right now. I want someone hot and loose, and ready to move fast."

T.S. glanced at him, shrugged. "How the fuck do I know you're not a cop?"

Ross let his eyes settle on T.S. now. "You think Datano would send a cop?"

T.S. yawned. "If it was convenient for him. I don't think I want to find out."

"You think he sent *them?*" Ross pointed to the police car in the left lane just ahead of them.

T.S. had already put his right turn signal on, getting ready to pull over. But his grip on the wheel was light, just his fingertips. Ross grabbed the wheel and stepped on top of T.S.'s slippered foot. The big car kicked into low gear and lunged up to the right side of the police car's rear quarter.

Ross pulled the wheel hard over, planting the front left of the Caprice against the side of the squad car trunk, and shoved his foot all the way down. The engine roared, and so did T.S.

"What the fuck're you doing? What the hell?"

The cop car spun directly in front of them, but Ross kept his foot down, and they knocked the rear end all the way around. T.S. bounced off the steering wheel; Ross's belt held him. Ross reached over with his left foot, stomped on the brake to kill the last bit of forward momentum, and threw the car into reverse. "Give me room, and I'll get us out of this," he said, quietly, to T.S.

T.S. took his hands from the wheel as the rear tires burned rubber in reverse. Ross spun the front end around and dropped the gearshift down into forward. He rammed the side doors of the squad car and shoved the gas down and let the squealing tires drive the police car sideways into the line of parked cars.

He could see the two cops inside, both looking shaken but unhurt, one fumbling for the shotgun, the other reaching down, presumably for his handgun. "Leave your door open and crouch as you run," Ross said. "They'll be stuck in there for a few more minutes."

T.S. did what he was told, running surprisingly fast for his size, and keeping himself behind the Caprice as he crossed the street. Ross waved down a cab at the corner of Commonwealth Avenue. T.S. was laughing as he slid his bulk into the backseat. "You are one crazy bastard," he said. "One crazy bastard."

T.S. was still chuckling as he hot-wired a Lincoln Continental. "This baby has some weight. You want to drive?"

He lit another joint and cranked up the stereo on the way over the MIT Bridge. "You got to teach me that someday. What's it called?"

"Spin and pin."

He offered Ross a hit, but Ross shook his head.

T.S. looked at him suspiciously, and Ross snapped, "This isn't a social call. I want some work."

"Be cool. Come on back to my crib. I'll make some calls. You want, if we get something on, you can use this car." He floored it and the car surged forward. "It's got balls."

T.S. parked in East Cambridge, and they walked a few blocks to his building, in a redbrick apartment complex that had probably been built in the early sixties: Pastel panels decorated the face of the building, covering the rusting frames of each apartment's deck.

"Pretty as shit, huh?" T.S. said as they walked into the lobby. Brown, musty-smelling carpet and silver foil wallpaper. "But the elevator works."

Upstairs, he scratched his gut as he listened to his answering machine. Ten calls were recorded on the dial, but no one had left a message. "I work with a lot of shy types," he grunted.

T.S. pulled out a pair of reading glasses and began flipping through an address book. "I know two, three guys might be doing this right now that got shotguns, or at least I know I sold them shotguns." He looked up at Ross. "So you want this guy to splatter somebody today? Show you he's got what it takes?"

"Definitely not. Just somebody with the capability."

"Uh-huh. I'll see what I can do. Two hundred for the connection. Twenty percent of whatever you take. You do the bigger job, you come to me for the weapons." T.S. walked over to the hall closet, took a key from his belt, and opened the door. Inside the cheap paneled door was a heavier steel door, which he unlocked. There were several shotguns, a couple of them sawed off, a number of handguns, an Uzi, and a combat-style machine gun. He hefted that, grinned at Ross with pride, and said, "I'm gonna go in on the right score with this thing and make my frigging fortune—or a stack of bodies to say why not. I'm gonna want to hear about this big job of yours after I hear how you do tonight. If it's big enough, you might be able to sign me on, personally."

CHAPTER 25

He had red hair, and he was nineteen, maybe twenty-two at the oldest. Ross picked him up in Kenmore Square, right under the big Citgo sign. It was just before ten o'clock at night. The kid wore a full-length black leather coat, jeans, and basketball sneakers, and he had a shotgun slung on a strap under his arm.

"So you're the hotshot, huh?" the kid said. "You're my ticket to murder and mayhem."

He laughed at his own joke, fast and nervous. Looking to see if Ross knew what *mayhem* meant.

"Show me the place."

"Sure, sure. It's a liquor store, down on the corner of Harvard Street."

Ross kept the Lincoln gliding along at the speed limit while the kid chattered away. His left foot tapped the floorboards, and he talked the whole time down. "BU girls, this is like my goddamn bedroom, this street. Chick who lives there, I nailed. And there, up in that dorm. Would've liked to have done the room-mate, too. And there, see the roof deck up there? Got laid there."

The kid snapped on the radio and cranked up the volume.

"OK, I go in," the kid yelled over the music. "I go in, get the cash, you wait with the engine running, and that's it. Stomp on any cops along the way."

The kid's clothes were all different from what Ross remembered of the kidnapper. And his voice sounded older. When the interior lights were on, Ross had seen the kid's wrists were highly freckled. Greg hadn't said anything about that when he mentioned seeing the kidnapper's wrist in the store. Ross turned the radio off and the kid looked offended. Ross asked, "How much do you expect to get?"

The kid shrugged. "Whatever's there."

"Do they have any security?"

The kid slapped the sawed-off. "Nothing compared to this." It was a double-barrel gun, not a pump-action like the kidnap-per had used.

"I mean do they have video cameras or a guard?"

"Yeah. Couple of cameras and a guard."

"How'd you pick this place?"

The kid laughed. "Damn place picked me. I was in last week, guy got in my face."

Ross looked at the kid more carefully, picking up on his last phrase. "Who?"

"Manager. Old fart. Said I was trying to steal a fifth of scotch." The kid looked for Ross's appreciation. "Course I *was*. Walked up there with a six-pack in my hand and the fifth under my coat. Prick had sharp eyes. He could've just let it go, made me pay for the scotch, but he said he was going to call the cops, make a federal case of it."

"So he knows you?"

"Naw. I had to drop all the shit and screw out of there. The security guy almost got me, this guy on foot. I play some ball, you know; I'm pretty fast for short distances. But the cigarettes, they cut down my wind." The kid hit Ross on the arm. "That's why you're here, man—I want to ride away from trouble this time, get my race car driver to take me away. T.S. tells me you do wild shit with a car, is that right?"

"If I have to." At that point, they were passing the liquor store, and Ross was fairly certain this wasn't the guy. The kid's voice sounded different. He was about the right size, but maybe a little heavier. The shotgun was definitely different. And there were those basketball shoes; the kidnapper had been wearing boots.

Ross said, "Are you wearing a mask in?"

"Hell, yes." The kid grinned as he pulled out a woman's nylon stocking. "Damn, I think it's still warm."

Ross circled the block, then pulled over. He drew out a map and began to look at the exit possibilities along the way. The kid tapped his foot faster. "C'mon, you know what the ad says. Just do it."

"Sorry, I missed that."

"What kind of car you got?"

Ross looked up.

"I mean you being a driver and all, you could tell me some stuff. I'm doing this to save up for a Corvette."

"Have you shot anyone for your Corvette?"

The kid grinned. "You want a demo? T.S. told me you might be setting up something big later." It was too dark to see the kid's eyes very well, but Ross's impression was that he was perhaps a bit nervous, but entirely sincere.

Wacko, Ross thought. *But not the wacko I'm looking for.* Ross said, slowly, "Absolutely not. I want you in, and out, no big deal."

"I don't care. Consider it a freebie."

"I care. I'm not looking for any heat. Just a little cash while I set up this other thing."

"Whatever." The kid was impatient. "So let's do it."

This was the awkward part Ross had anticipated, finding a way to back out of committing a robbery without ruining his connection with T.S.

"What the fuck're we doing?" the kid snapped.

Ross sighed. Shook his head.

"What?"

"What we've been doing," Ross said, "is waiting for you to calm down."

"Huh?"

"You're wired for sound. I told T.S. I needed a pro."

The kid shoved the gun in Ross's face. "Motherfucker, what is this? I've capped three guys. I can do you, too."

"Who've you capped?"

"What are you, my father confessor? Or a cop?"

Ross deadpanned it, though his heart was pounding. "I told T.S. I wanted somebody who had the experience. I figured that he realized I meant someone who wasn't going to land me in prison."

"What're you talking about?"

"How old are you?"

"What's that got to do with it? I capped three store owners, one in Revere, two in Medford."

"I'd say eighteen or nineteen. Right?"

"Twenty-one. So what?"

"So when you went up to the counter with that fifth under your jacket, he asked you for an ID, didn't he?"

"Big deal. I'm legal."

"You showed him your ID, right?"

"So? He's not going to remember. He didn't come after me for stealing the fifth, did he?"

"You're going into the same store, probably against the same guy behind the counter and the same security guard, and you've got bright red hair, and you're wearing a woman's stocking. People can see through that, kid. And you showed the guy your name just a week ago." Ross shook his head disgustedly. "Tell me you didn't wear the same coat and shoes."

The kid faltered and looked down at his coat quickly. "No way."

"Uh-huh. That sounded convincing. How many kids with red hair, black full-length leather coats do you think they have on the video cameras stealing from the store? Maybe he wasn't going to make a federal case out of your pissant shoplifting before, but this is armed robbery."

The young man looked confused, and he let the gun barrel drop from Ross's face. "Well, shit, I can change the coat and shoes—"

Ross snatched the shotgun away with his left hand and popped the kid with a short, hard right. He turned the gun back on the kid. "Get out."

"What the hell's your problem?"

The guy had an adolescent whine to his voice that would've been amusing to Ross under the circumstances, except for the thought of those three store owners. He jabbed the kid with the gun. "If I had to share a prison cell with you, I'd kill you before the week was out. And that's where we were headed with this job of yours. Now, move it."

The kid got out of the car reluctantly, but once he did, he seemed to gain some of his cockiness back. "You're dead, fucker."

Ross answered him by tossing out a handful of change from the coin tray. "Next time, take the subway to murder and mayhem."

CHAPTER 26

Crockett would've laughed if Beth hadn't been within earshot in the living room. He shook his head, marveling. "You won't get that lucky again. Red hair and stocking. What a nitwit."

"I called T.S. right after I dumped the gun. Blasted him for sending me such an idiot."

"Good offense and all that, huh? Did he go for it?"

"Oh, yeah. Apologized."

Ross told Crockett what he had in mind, and Crockett nodded.

"Yeah, we could do that. Do some active recruiting, use my place. Your tab's going up with me, though."

Later that night, Ross saw the light on underneath Beth's door. He realized he thought of it that way, too, that it was her room now, not his brother's, and the realization was like a blow to his chest.

He knocked, and after a moment, she said to come in.

She was sitting on the edge of the bed, fully clothed. She was holding a brush, and tears were running down her cheeks. "Pretty pathetic, huh?" she said. "Sitting here like a faithful dog with his brush. Trying to pull out enough strands to make a lock of hair I guess. . . ."

She rubbed the tears from her face and tapped out a cigarette from the pack on the night table. "Guess I'm trying to kill myself with these. Doing it the slow way." She lit the cigarette and put the lighter in her pocket. "I always was a chicken."

"You'll have to sell me harder on that one."

The cigarette seemed to give her a small purpose, and she gestured for him to come in. "Please, sit with me. Tell me what you've been doing, and how it's helping us get Janine back."

Ross hesitated, then said, "If anyone has a right to know, you do. Just keep it to yourself. I'm worried about Allie going to the police." He picked up a blanket on the chair beside the bed and threw it over her shoulders. The window was open and the night air was cool, but she didn't seem to notice. He told her about his conversation with the witness of the Cambridge robbery and that he'd been trying to trace the kidnapper through Datano's contacts—leaving out that he'd almost participated in a holdup himself that night.

"Why would he still be going on robberies?" She pulled away from him, alarmed. "You're saying he robbed the store that night? The same night he shot Greg, and called us? Why hasn't he just returned her? Why is he taking chances for so little money when all he has to do is give her back and we'll make him rich?"

"I don't know. Maybe he's too frightened from last time. And I think he's got a coke habit, from something he said over the phone and the way he was sniffling, like he had a bad cold."

Beth's eyes met Ross's. "Or maybe she's dead, and he's got

nothing to trade us for our money. That's an explanation, isn't it?"

"That's one." Ross took one of her cigarettes. "I'm counting on there being another."

CHAPTER 27

Beth awoke from a horrible nightmare and shifted automatically to Greg, pulling his warmth close to her.

But something was wrong. He was thinner, and his scent slightly changed. Then she truly awoke.

It was Ross, sleeping beside her. He was fully clothed. The blanket was wrapped around her, and he'd apparently fallen asleep some time after she'd dropped off.

And the nightmare was true.

Beth almost cried out as it all crashed back, what he'd told her about the man continuing with his robberies.

As she had for days, she tried desperately to stretch her mind to touch her daughter's. All that mother's lore she'd always heard growing up, about how a mother who loved her child could feel her child's injury no matter how far they were separated, how that mother would always know if her child was alive or dead . . . well, Beth felt nothing.

Oh, she felt pain. She felt black depression, and she felt mur-
derous rage. But most of all, she hated herself for not being able
to somehow know where her child was. The old feelings came
rushing back, that she had been inadequate and terrible for not
bonding with Janine when she was an infant.

Stop it! she told herself angrily. She loved her daughter so
much it hurt, and both of them knew it.

Beth sat up and covered Ross with the blanket. She looked at
the bed. King-size. Wouldn't need that anymore. After this was
over, she'd get rid of it. The house she couldn't afford, now that
they . . . she . . . would have no money.

Or maybe she would. She would still have half the ransom
money. She didn't want it. Each dollar bill would mock her as
much as each minute she spent safely in her house while her
daughter was with that man.

Absently she picked up a letter opener and pressed the sharp
tip against her palm. She wanted to feel the pain. She wanted to
think that maybe even if she couldn't tell if Janine was alive or
dead, Janine could somehow pick up her mother's pain. That
maybe she could receive the message that her mother loved her
and was right with her through the ordeal.

The ringing of the phone shattered Beth's reverie. Beth was
shocked to see she was standing in front of the mirror, her hand
dripping with blood. She checked her watch. Three in the morning. She picked the receiver up and said hello. Cautiously. Not
daring to think what a call this late could be.

"Mommy," Janine said. "It's me, Mommy."

Nat's asleep," Janine said. "She saved me from that man. . . . She
showed him a gun and said she would kill him if he hurt me."
Janine's speech was slow, as if she was half asleep.

"Janine?"

She continued. "He was going to kick me. In the head, I mean, hurt me bad."

"Oh, baby," Beth breathed. "Oh, baby, where are you?" She put her hand over the phone briefly and cried out, "Ross! She's on the phone."

He awoke and rolled to his feet immediately.

"Where are you, baby?" Beth said again. She could hear a woman in the background, saying, "I said turn the radio off, Lisa."

Janine said, "He's been after us. Twice. We just got away. Nat says she thinks we'll be OK here tonight. . . ." Janine began to cry quietly. "She's nice to me, but she's funny. She calls me Leanne, like she really thinks that's my name. I've been so *sleepy*, Mommy. And my head hurts. I told her I want go home—"

"Well, I know it helps *you* sleep," the woman in the background said, her voice rising. "But it's hell on everyone else's night, and that not the gateway—"

"Who's that?" Beth said.

"Is Daddy all right?"

"Honey, you know—"

"I know what I *said*, but I started thinking maybe I didn't see it right. And the man lies. I know he lies. Is Daddy all right?"

"We'll talk about Daddy when you get home. Where are you now?"

Ross held the phone so he could hear into it, too. "It's Uncle Ross, Janey. Where are you?"

"Leanne?" they heard a woman say. "Does your momma know you're doing that?"

"That's not my name!" Janine cried.

Allie joined them in the room. "I heard the phone," she said.

Ross grasped Beth's arm. "Be quick."

"Where are you?" Beth said, her voice rising. "Please, baby, say where you are."

They heard a second woman's voice in the background. "Leanne! Put that down!"

"Who is this?" the first woman's voice said suddenly into the phone, her tone suspicious.

"I'm her uncle, and this is her mother," Ross said, keeping his voice calm.

"Her mother's right here," the woman snapped.

"Please tell us where you are," Ross said. "We've been looking all over for her—"

They heard the first woman from a distance, as if she'd taken the phone away from her ear. "He says he's her uncle."

"It's her father!" the second woman said. "For Christ's sake, it's him; he's the one that did this to me. Don't tell him where we *are!*"

The line was disconnected.

CHAPTER 28

Allie brought them down to the kitchen table. "Let me get this straight. It sounded like she had gotten Janine away from this man?"

"That's right," Beth said.

"What did she say, exactly?"

Beth went through it, and then Ross. Crockett joined them and quietly began to make some coffee.

"What name did the woman in the background call Janine?"

"Leanne," Beth said. "And Janine called the woman Nat, just like you heard, Ross."

"And this Nat, she told the other woman to put the phone down, saying Ross was Janine's father . . . and what? She said, 'He's the one that did this to me,' right? Like she was showing a wound, or a bruise?"

"That's the way I heard it," Ross said.

"How about the woman you said was already talking, the one in the background?"

"She was telling someone else to turn down the radio," Beth said.

"Something about the 'gateway ' " Ross turned to Beth. "Did you get that?"

She nodded thoughtfully. "Or was it the Gate *way* . . . like, 'That's the *way* we do it here.' "

"So it didn't sound like they were at a friend's house?" Allie said.

"No," Ross said. "The woman who picked up the phone didn't sound like she knew the other woman very well."

"Like at a hotel or motel?"

"It all had sort of an institutional sound to it."

"Maybe a women's shelter." Allie said.

She pulled the yellow-pages directory from the counter and together they all looked through the listings under "Women's Services." There were a number of shelters listed, but none with the word *Gate* in the name.

"Means nothing," Allie said. "Most of the ones for battered women aren't listed for the simple reason they don't want the husbands and boyfriends finding their way there. That's probably why the woman was suspicious of you in the first place, Ross." Allie tightened the belt on her robe and grabbed the phone. "Get me a piece of paper, will you? It's time to wake up a few detective friends of mine."

Ross hesitated and Allie waved her hand at him. "Don't worry. They don't have to know for who or why. I won't give them that much time to think."

Allie started making calls, her manner apologetic for calling so late, yet insistent.

"I know, I know," she said on her third "It's the pro bono ones that keep you working at four in the morning. But this client of mine is hiding out, and it's critical I get hold of her for a court appearance tomorrow. She didn't tell me which shelter she was staying in, but I think the name had the word *Gate* or *Gateway* in it. . . ."

Her eyes brightened and she looked excitedly over at Beth. " 'Open Gate.' Sure, that could've been it."

Beth put her hand to her mouth, and Ross felt his heart quicken.

"Hey, hey," Crockett said, handing him a cup of coffee. "Maybe some luck."

"Gerry!" Allie's face clouded, and then she hung up. "Son of a bitch," she snapped and began flipping through her book.

"What?" Ross said.

"He wouldn't give me the address. Said it was a damn secret, that he'd have to talk to his supervisor in the morning." She patted Beth's hand. "Don't worry. I know the supervisor, Nick Jacobsen. I just need his number."

The information number had him as unlisted. It took her two more calls and fifteen minutes before she found a detective in Boston who'd give her Jacobsen's number, and then she called him. She paced the floor as she talked. "Come *on,* Nick, you're making it hard for me to be a good guy. I told you this was pro bono. . . ."

She nodded abruptly to Beth and repeated the address back. "Four-two-two Saint Botolph Street." After she hung up the phone, she grinned over at Beth and Ross. "We're there."

They all crowded into Allie's car. Crockett put the money in the trunk, saying simply, "Better with us than not."

Ross drove, and Allie gave him directions, her whole body tense, leaning forward in the seat. Ross looked in the rearview mirror at Beth and saw her head was down, her hands clasped. Praying.

A few minutes later, she said, "Ross, why do you think this Nat didn't simply return her? From what you said, she didn't sound violent herself. It sounded more like she was protecting Janine."

"There's different kinds of violent." Crockett's voice was a low rumble from the back. "Maybe she's not willing to hurt your girl, but she's willing to trade her for a stack of money."

"And maybe she's got other reasons we can't guess," Ross said. "What we need to hold onto is that Janine is alive."

"What Ross is saying is don't get your hopes up," Crockett said. "She could've spooked after the phone call. She did go into that store, with a gun, let her boyfriend blow away the storekeeper. We don't know what she's getting out of this, and you're not talking about a nice lady here."

"If she keeps my girl alive, she's nice," Beth said. "She's a saint, if she does that."

When they got to the address, Allie put her hand on Ross's arm. "Why don't you and Crockett wait here."

He nodded, thinking that it wasn't the time or place for a man to be pounding on the door. Reaching back, he clasped Beth's hand and said, "Don't take no for an answer."

"Oh, I won't." She squeezed back hard and stepped out of the car. Ross saw she had pictures in her hand.

"Man, I hope this is a happy ending." Crockett leaned forward.

"Tired of being good?"

"Sucks. Especially being so close to all this money, it makes my back itch having it behind me in the trunk." Crockett thumped Ross on the shoulder. "If the girl is safe, that means

you're rich. . . . How about you treat the two of us to a trip to
Mexico, huh?"

"You've got it."

"First-class?"

"First-class."

"Yeah, you're full of it. Once this is over, your parole breaking's over, your associating with known felons—"

A large black woman came out to the front door. Allie and
Beth began talking, and Beth stepped up beside the woman and
showed her photos of herself and Janine. The woman was wearing a big, loose bathrobe, and she was clearly tired and irritated.
She was shaking her head and pointing down the street and then
inside the house. Becoming more animated as she spoke. She led
them inside, and Ross and Crockett waited silently until they
came out a few minutes later.

The woman was shaking her head. Waving them off.

Ross rolled the passenger side window down and heard her
voice raised. "They're gone. I told you. I told him. Gone."

"Shit." Ross hit the steering wheel. "Shit."

CHAPTER 29

He was after them." Beth got into the front seat, her face stark white. "She said a man pounded on the door just ten minutes after they left, demanding that Natalie come out. He wouldn't leave until the woman said she'd call the cops."

"On foot?" Ross started the car.

"She didn't see a cab. She said she wasn't paying that much attention." Beth wiped her eyes angrily. "Said she didn't hear the little girl say that Nat wasn't her mother. That she was busy, very busy. And that Janine . . . Leanne . . . had slept most of the night she was there."

"Jesus."

"I think that woman drugged Janine." Beth's voice quavered slightly.

Ross held her hand for a moment, and she visibly pulled herself in control. She said, "At least that's what it sounded like to me. Janine said she had a headache, and was awfully sleepy,"

They turned left on Massachusetts Avenue toward Roxbury, back on Columbus. Circled around again and got onto Huntington Avenue past Symphony Hall and down to the Museum of Fine Art. They swung around and drove back into Copley Square. Up and down the streets running parallel to Boylston.

Ross's heart was pounding and a feeling very near panic surged through him, as he thought how the choice of a left turn versus a right might make the difference between whether or not they found Janine before the kidnapper did.

He said, "Allie, how does someone get into a shelter like that? Is there some sort of official channel?"

"There can be," she said. "The police, or a social worker, sometimes the Department of Youth Services. But this woman said that the two of them had showed up on her doorstep, and she had an opening for the night, and she took them in. That she'd had Nat in there once a few weeks ago."

"That must be how he knew where to come looking," Crockett said. "Either that, or maybe he's knocking on the doors of a bunch of those shelters."

"Probably," Allie said. "The woman told us Nat had obviously been scared, and she had a bruise on her cheek. Janine had been asleep in her arms."

"She didn't question her having a daughter?"

"No," Beth said. "She said Nat had talked about having a daughter before."

Beth's back was rigid as she directed them up and down the streets. "There. Try there," she'd say.

Fifteen minutes passed.

Twenty.

Beth used the cellular phone every few minutes, to see if anyone had called their voice mail. "What if she calls?" she said. "Would they really leave a message?"

As they rounded the corner of Berkley Street, Ross said,

"This is crazy. We can't do this alone any longer."

"No." Beth shook her head. "We can't."

Ross pulled over, took the gun out of his waistband, and gave it to Crockett. He gestured to the Boston Police building in the middle of the block. "We need the police out there combing the streets right now. When that man had Janine it made sense to keep them out of it. But there's nothing I've heard about this woman, Nat, that makes me think she wants to hurt Janine. So it's a matter of finding them before Nat gets desperate and takes off, leaves the state maybe. Or before he finds her."

"If the police are in, I'm out." Crockett stepped out of the car. "I'll toss that gun into the river for you." Crockett leaned back in and said to Beth, "Best of luck with your girl." He grasped her hand briefly.

Ross looked at Allie and Beth. "Crockett was never here, right?"

"Fine," Beth said.

Crockett shut the door quietly and walked away.

"Let's get going," Beth said.

Allie checked her watch. "Are we doing the right thing? I know I've been pushing for the police all along, but we're so close. You know it's going to take some time to get them to listen and move. Especially once you tell them about hiding Greg's body and breaking parole with the gun violation. You know what's going to happen."

"You'll be my lawyer, right?"

Allie hesitated, then said, "Technically, I already am. I helped you sell your property."

"All right. I'm going to tell the police what I saw. Including the fact that it was my brother who pulled the revolver when it became obvious that the kidnapper was going to kill him and Janine."

"Don't ask me to perjure myself," Allie said.

"I'm not. That's what happened. I'm asking you to represent me."

"Where's the gun now?"

"I threw it in the cove," Ross said. "Technically, that's pretty close. It's in the water."

Once inside the station, Allie stepped up to the glass window, introduced herself, and asked for the detective who was catching that night.

"What's this about, Counselor?" The desk sergeant was a big man with heavy jowls and dark, patient eyes.

She told him.

"Kidnapping?" He raised his eyebrows and looked over at Beth and Ross. "You the parents?"

"I'm her mother," Beth said. "This is her uncle. Please, she's out on the streets right now."

"How about your husband? Is this a divorce situation? You think there's any chance he has her?"

Ross answered that one.

And when the detective who introduced himself as Olsen came up to the desk, the sergeant relayed what Ross had said. And then they read him his rights.

Have you got someone over at Open Gate yet?" Beth asked Olsen as he rejoined them in the interrogation room. She'd been pacing for about twenty minutes. "The woman there said Natalie had stayed there before. Maybe she has an address or can tell us who Natalie's friends are. Maybe she knows something."

"We are doing that right now," the detective said. He was a small man with watery blue eyes and lank black hair, wearing a sport jacket. "We sent a car out."

"Do the patrol cars have their descriptions? And how about sending men with copies of those photos to the bus and train stations?" Ross asked.

"Thanks for the ideas," the detective said dryly. "We're putting out a description over the radio right now. With your permission, we can have your phone signal switched right into here until we get you home."

"How about the photos?"

The cop sighed. "We'll circulate those photos at roll call in just a few hours. But let's hope the manager of Open Gate comes through. Let's hope you-all didn't push her the wrong way. If she decides to hold onto that information about this Natalie, it's going to take a court order to get it."

"Why would she?" Beth said, raking her hair back. "I'm just trying to find my girl!"

Olsen shrugged. "Some people insist on going through channels." He looked at Ross and said, "Not others." He opened a notebook. "At this moment, you're not in custody. If you want, you, me, and your attorney can do this off-line. Because I do want to know about your brother's murder, and your burying him. I want to know anything you have about the murders of the two storekeepers. But for the purpose of trying to find the girl, I'm willing to take the statement from all of you at once."

Allie said, "If Janine's hurt, or worse, because you couldn't bother to follow up on this in a timely manner, you'd better get the mothballs out of your uniform, Detective."

"Take it easy," Ross said, looking at her. Thinking about how quickly the cops would stonewall if they felt they were being pushed.

Olsen looked her up and down appraisingly. In a bemused tone, he said, "Threats already, and the investigation is so early yet." He took a computer printout from the sleeve of his notebook. "We just ran your name, Stearns. What a surprise to find you are on *parole*. For drug smuggling. And, Ms. Pearson, as a former ADA you should know how much cops love threats."

"My daughter doesn't have any time!" Beth said.

The detective shrugged. "Seems to me you've had a week before bothering to notify us."

"It was a matter of how we thought we could keep her alive," Ross said. "The kidnapper threatened to kill her if we brought in the police, and we had every reason to believe he'd do it."

Olsen sighed. He looked at Beth and said with exaggerated civility, "Look, you came to us for the right reason. If your daughter is still in Boston, we're more likely to find her than anyone else. In the meantime, I've informed the FBI. But the more we know, the better we can do the job. So maybe it seems old hat to you, but go through it again."

"Do you have anyone else going to the other women's shelters?" Ross asked.

"Or how about the known associates file?" Allie said. "Is there anything on a male and female team doing armed robbery? Or a male and female team with the woman named Nat?"

Olsen slammed his hand on the table. "You want to handle the investigation?"

"Detective Olsen—," Allie started, but he cut her off.

"Hey, Counselor, you want to argue this now, go ahead. We can turn this conversation into discussing Ross Stearns's list of parole violations. And we read your client his rights; he can refuse to answer at any time. But me, I'd rather spend it finding out what the hell's been going on so we can find this woman's little girl." He gestured to Beth with his thumb. "What's it going to be?"

Allie looked at Ross, and he nodded his head. He said, "Let's just be quick about it."

Olsen pointed to a mirror at the end of the room. "We're videotaping from behind there. Got any objections?"

"No," Ross said before Allie could answer.

And they all turned to Beth, and she began to tell how it started.

CHAPTER 30

Janine was so sleepy she could hardly walk. Nat kept hustling her along. "Come on, baby. Come on, Leanne."

Janine didn't even bother to say that wasn't her name this time; she was that tired. Nat had kept them in the alley behind the place they'd been staying until it began to rain. Now Janine's legs felt loose, and when she walked, they'd sometimes trip up. And they'd walked so far. Once, she fell, and there was still the sharp, bright pain in her knee to tell her she'd scraped it.

But she didn't care.

This was how things were now. The phone conversation with her mother already seemed far away, and she had to concentrate to know if it had been real or not. She wanted to do that again, put a quarter in the phone and tap out the number, and hear her mother's warmth over the line.

But if she'd had a phone in front of her at that moment, she couldn't imagine being able to remember the number, never mind press all the buttons in the right order. And what would it mean if she did anyhow? Her mother hadn't come before.

She stumbled again.

"Come on, baby. I'm going to find us a place to rest until it's time."

Janine could smell the ocean. There were buildings to her left, and the place to her right looked slightly familiar. She thought she'd been there before. Shopping with her mother last Christmas, she remembered carrying a box with a big wide ribbon. Red. She carried it and they'd taken the subway in. Her mother had said the present was from both of them for her dad. A bathrobe.

Janine began to cry.

She stumbled again.

"We can't get the bus yet, hon," Nat said. "And I don't want to wait in the station. But I'll find us a place out of the rain. I'll find us a car. Remember that big Caddy we stayed in? I'll find us one of those."

The woman had her arms under Janine now, and she kissed Janine on the head. The woman smelled smoky; she had been smoking cigarettes constantly, and even a little pipe once in a while. Janine had never seen a woman do that before, smoke a pipe. But she knew it wasn't good, knew it had something to do with drugs and that it could make you sick.

Janine remembered Nat had made a face the first time Janine had seen her light the pipe. It had been soon after Nat had put the gun to the man's head. To Lee's head—don't say the name, don't think it.

"Do as I say, not as I do, baby," the woman had said. "This stuff's bad, but I like it."

Nat had told the man she'd kill him if he touched Janine again. Stood there with her hand grabbing the cloth of his jacket, the pistol pointed at his head. She'd dragged him away from Janine before he could kick her. Nat had seemed so in charge then. Scared, but mad.

Lee hadn't seemed too scared, but he'd looked even angrier than before. But he'd kept his hands to himself as Nat had shoved Janine down the stairway of the big old building. She'd taken Janine out of there and they'd run down the street. Nat had even shot at him once, the gun making a huge boom, when he'd tried to follow them.

And they'd gone to the house of a woman Nat said was a friend. But the friend didn't smile, and she took Nat's money and gave her a little envelope with stuff for the pipe. The place was dirty, and Nat had lain on a old striped mattress and smoked and started calling Janine by that name, Leanne, like it was a joke. She'd talked a long time, laughing at first about how angry Lee had looked, and then, as it got later and later, she looked scared. She smoked more, and sniffed powder up her nose, and sometimes Janine couldn't tell if the woman was joking anymore when she hugged her and called her Leanne.

And that was bad. Not as scary as when the man had them, but Nat wouldn't take Janine home. And when Janine had started to get mad about that, Nat had gotten all angry right back and kept saying again and again, "Look-what-I-did-for-you." And then Janine had started getting so sleepy. She wondered if it was something she'd eaten. The other woman had brought them burgers and fries and a chocolate shake one time. That was before Lee had shown up, and the other woman was screaming and the gun was going off, and Nat had pushed Janine out the window onto the fire escape, and she was saying, "Go, Leanne, go, go. . . ."

Now Nat was walking faster, pushing her, and when Janine forced herself to concentrate, she saw the woman looking over her shoulder, looking scared, and Janine turned and saw a big man after them, and she got scared, too.

Until she realized it was a policeman. Wearing a uniform and a badge. Walking up to them from what Janine realized was the bus station.

She suddenly remembered that she'd been scared that she might get lost that time she was with her mother at Christmas. And her mother had repeated then what she'd said since Janine was a little girl.

"If you get lost, walk up to a policeman, and tell him that your name is Janine Stearns, 233 Ridge Road, Lincoln."

The policeman whistled. Nat hesitated, and then started to cross the street.

"Hold it, miss. I'd like to talk to you."

Janine stopped, but Nat tugged her on.

"Miss!" The policeman had a radio on his shoulder, and his face was very serious.

"Could I see some identification, ma'am?"

She laughed, but her voice was all shaky. "You're talking to me?"

"Yes, ma'am."

"What is this—Russia? I'm going to meet my husband."

"Is this your daughter, ma'am?"

The woman dug her hands into Janine's shoulder. Janine could see how scared she was, and felt sorry for her. The way the policeman looked at Nat, it was like he was angry at her. Janine felt confused. She started to say what her mother had told her and froze. "She's my girl," Nat said, hugging her close. "This is my little Leanne."

"Awful early to be out," the cop said, putting out his hand. "I'd really like to see that ID, ma'am."

He looked down at Janine and said, "So what's your name again, sweetheart?" To her, his voice was different. He seemed very nice. She saw him looking at her very closely, and then his right hand went to rest on his gun. "She's soaking wet," he said. "Where's that ID?"

"Really," Nat said in a rush, "I'm supposed to be meeting my husband on the corner—"

And then Janine saw a car glide up behind the cop, and it was the man, it was Lee inside, and he opened the door and said, "Honey, *there* you are."

Nat's face turned white.

The policeman looked at the man and woman and said, "Mister, I'd like you to step out of the car." He glanced at Janine and said, "Right now, honey, what's your name?"

The words broke out of Janine: "My name is Janine Stearns! My name is Janine Stearns! My name is Janine Stearns!"

The policeman reached over with his left hand, and before Janine knew what he'd done, she was on the ground, and he stepped between her and the open car door, his gun out.

But from inside the car there was the yellow flash, and the sound that had reverberated in Janine's nightmares sounded again, and the policeman was down on the pavement, too.

Someone was screaming, and Janine looked up at Nat and saw it wasn't her. Janine realized that it was her own voice. The policeman's eyes fluttered open, and she both wanted him to get up and wanted him to stay down on the ground. Because she wanted him to save her, but she also knew Lee would get out of the car and shoot him like he'd shot her father.

Then there was another gun going off. Nat had the pistol out and through the bright flashes Janine could see big, cracking holes in the front window of the car. And over it all, Nat was yelling for Janine to run, to run as fast as she could.

CHAPTER 31

Ross heard Turner, the FBI agent, say to Olsen, "Lucky you." They were standing at the edge of the cliff watching divers go down with hooks for the BMW.

Allie and Ross were standing under the tree while the medical examiner knelt beside Greg's body. Beth was back at the house with the FBI and wiretapped phones.

"Lucky *Babcock,*" Olsen said. "Not all the beat cops wear the vest. Got himself some broken ribs, some pellets in the leg, but he's a hero. He can tell his grandkids someday how he survived a shotgun blast."

"I meant *you're* lucky that he didn't die," Turner said, opening a carton of yogurt. The breeze was blowing in from the cove and Turner's voice was perhaps more audible than he'd intended. "It's bad enough that the kidnapper now knows the police are in on it. You couldn't have a photo of the girl at the bus station. Even after Stearns asked you, and you recorded his request on videotape."

"Babcock had a description over the radio," Olsen said, glancing over at Allie. "And it's not like either of them are going to be able to step foot inside the bus or train station or airport from now on. Cops tend to look out pretty good for guys who shoot cops."

Turner snorted. "You've heard the story about the barn door, right? And who knows what Babcock's going to give us for a description?"

"He's good. He'll come through."

"Turner might just be playing a game," Allie said quietly to Ross. "He probably knows we can hear them." She looked back at Greg's body, and a single tear slipped down her cheek, which she quickly wiped away. "I'm supposed to be tougher than this."

Ross put his arm around her.

"Babcock's good?" Turner was saying. "I don't think he gets the hero prize unless he saves the girl. I'm pretty sure that's how it works." Turner raised his voice to include Ross. "What do you think, Stearns? Is Babcock a hero or a bum?"

Ross didn't answer him. Turner was in his late thirties, impeccably dressed in a blue suit, white shirt, red tie. After a few minutes, he and Olsen drifted over to Ross and Allie. Turner finished the yogurt while he watched the medical examiner go over Greg's body.

Ross watched Turner eat, knowing that it was a conscious display for his benefit.

After a few minutes, Turner put the carton in a paper bag and stood directly in front of Ross. "OK. You and I can both smell your brother from here. You've screwed up fourteen ways to Sunday. What you've got to do now is convince me."

Turner waited.

Neither Allie nor Ross gave him his straight line.

"You've got to convince me that all you are is a screwup," Turner continued. "That you didn't pull this for profit, or maybe to get back at an older brother you never liked."

"You're out of line, Turner," Allie's tears were gone, and the cool professional was back. She stepped forward, and he withdrew slightly. "You've got nothing on Ross except for burying Greg. And he told the desk sergeant that the minute he walked into the station."

Turner gestured down to the house. "Hell, that can be enough. We called the new owner, Geiler."

"Geiler knows the story," she said. "I doubt very much he'll press charges."

"You think so?" Turner grinned. "When we told him Mr. Stearns was dead, it didn't take him too long to start squawking about how he still needed to close on the property."

"All the more reason for him to not press charges against Ross."

"Have you got a sketch yet of the man's face from this officer's description?" Ross asked.

Turner shook his head. "Boston Police are doing that one. It's on the way."

"And Janine looked all right?"

"Yeah," Olsen said. "I told you. Babcock said she was soaked, and she didn't look too steady on her feet. But he saw her run away. We've got no way of knowing whether or not the guy caught up to her five minutes later."

"Anything on the car the kidnapper had been using?" Allie said.

"We found it an hour later in an alley. The owner in Back Bay didn't want it back with all the bullet holes. There was a little bit of blood, and we're having tests run on that." Olsen looked at Ross carefully. "If we're in luck, it's his, not your niece's.

Which will be helpful for identification if we get our hands on the guy later. Prints were wiped clean up front."

"You seem so calm," Turner said to Ross. "Doesn't it bother you? Your brother over there, like that?"

"What'll it take?" Allie said.

"How's that?"

"All my client wants is to get his niece back. What'll it take to get you to believe that?"

Turner raised his eyebrows. "Damned if I know. I'm a suspicious guy. That's why I got in this line of business. I see an ex-con who's about to lose his half of a substantial piece of land to pay for his niece's ransom . . . and I can't help but wonder how he'd feel about that." Turner watched Ross intently as he spoke. "I also find myself thinking, what if that ex-con wasn't just trying to hold onto his half, but what if he had been trying to get his brother to sell? And the brother wouldn't. The brother sang this old song about keeping the land intact for his daughter's grandkids, or some such shit. And what if this ex-con found a friend to help him. And together, by abducting the daughter, they'd force the brother to sell the land, and they'd get *both* the ex-con's half of the cash *and* the brother's half."

"Your math is weak," Ross said. "After splitting it all with my 'friend,' I'd still end up only with what was mine. Besides which, Greg and I had already made up our minds to sell half the land."

"And I've got the correspondence to prove it," Allie said.

Turner waved that way. "Means nothing."

Olsen joined them. "Here he comes."

"Who?" Allie said.

An old Ford pulled off the dirt road and followed the tracks left by the other police vehicles. A tall, dark-haired man with a leather jacket got out of the car and joined them. He held out a manila envelope. "Sketches of the two suspects based on Babcock's descriptions."

Ross reached for them. After a slight hesitation, the man relinquished them. Ross's hands were trembling slightly as he opened the envelope and pulled out the penciled drawings. There were two, of the man and woman. The man's face was just the barest outline: a narrow face, thin slash of a mouth, short hair.

"That could be anyone," Allie said.

The sketch of Natalie showed an attractive woman with wide-spaced eyes and a soft jawline. There were lines about the eyes and a note to the side indicating her age was estimated at about thirty and her hair was blond.

"Recognize them?" the man who'd brought the sketches asked.

Ross glanced up sharply. "I never saw them before." He looked closely at the officer for the first time.

The cop was rangy and hard-looking. Black hair and eyes. He wore a razor blade on a gold chain about his neck. "I met your brother, once," he said. "In court."

Ross recognized him then. The man hadn't had the beard before; that was the difference. And he seemed even thinner than he had five years ago, down to just muscle and bone.

Detective Byrne, the man who'd sent him to prison.

Ross saw Olsen and Turner grinning over to the side, so he kept his expression even. He didn't want to give them the pleasure of seeing the unpleasant shock that was rolling through him. He said, "Did you pass along our thanks?"

"Yeah, I did," Olsen interjected. "How about you, Byrne? Did you do what I said and extend the Stearns family's thanks to Babcock for almost getting himself killed?"

"I did," Byrne said mildly. "He said you're welcome."

Allie took Ross's arm. "This is the officer who testified against you last time?"

"That's right."

"What is this nonsense, gentlemen?" she said. "You're wasting time with my client when you should be looking for Janine."

"Let us figure out what's a waste, Counselor," Turner said.

"What are you up to?" Ross asked Byrne. "Are you looking for a chance to put me away again? Or are you here to help find Janine?"

"That all depends upon what happened before I got here." Byrne gestured to his car. "Let's go for a ride, and you tell me."

"Not a chance," Allie said. "Ross, they're looking for someone to hang this on."

A white van with a small radar dish on the roof pulled up the driveway. "Ah, Christ," Olsen said. "The fourth estate."

Byrne took his jacket off and tossed it to Ross. "Come on. Put that over your head and let's get out of here before your face is all over every television screen in town."

"My client is not under arrest!" Allie snapped.

"Your choice," Byrne said. "I suggest you tell Mrs. Stearns to hold onto any photos of Ross here. And, Turner, you make sure Concord doesn't release a file photo of him either."

"Did the Boston Police get in charge while I wasn't watching?" Turner said.

Byrne looked at him and Turner glanced at the van and shrugged. "All right, get out of here."

Ross took a deep breath. He remembered Byrne's testimony five years ago just fine. But he also remembered that Byrne had been the one to take off the handcuffs so Ross could hold Giselle's body.

He took the coat. "Let's go."

CHAPTER 32

"Turner's a putz and so's Olsen," Byrne said. "But finding your niece would look good for both of them, so they'll try to make it happen."

"Why'd they get you in this?" Ross said.

"They say I'm Boston Police's best undercover officer." Byrne grinned. "They're right."

"So we're going looking?"

Byrne nodded. "Yeah. They figure that the mother back at the house with the FBI will be the most likely to be able to convince the woman to bring Janine in. If the woman calls, which I guess could happen. So their job is to sit tight—mine is to go find her, and the guy who's doing all the shooting." Byrne opened a pack of gum and handed Ross a stick. "Plus Olsen and Turner figured you'd tell me whatever you're holding back because I'd scare the hell out of you. How am I doing so far?"

"Pretty well, actually. Five years is five years."

The detective shrugged. "Look, I felt bad about what happened to you. I talked to that girl's fiancé. . . . Dermott was his name, right? I, for one, bought your testimony about how it was her who put the coke on your sailboat. I know you were just trying to help her out of a jam. But with the mandatory sentencing and some of the shit going down in Boston that year there was no choice."

Ross looked at him carefully. The detective took off straight past the industrial park, toward the highway. He said, "I figure we might as well get out of here. The last we saw your niece was in Boston." Byrne looked back at him appraisingly. "You got any objection to heading back?"

"No."

"So how about you do it again from the top for me?"

Ross told what had happened since Greg's first phone call, leaving out Crockett, T.S., and the liquor store robbery. Byrne's semiapology seemed a bit too pat. Ross did tell the detective about Teague—but not about holding Teague at gunpoint.

"You beat the guy?" Byrne raised his eyebrows. "What's your background with him?"

Ross told him about his fight with Teague at Concord.

"How long ago was this?"

"About three months ago."

"Threw him over the rail, huh? You picked up some nice tricks in there, I guess. What'd you get when you went by his place this time?"

"He didn't break down and confess, if that's what you mean."

"He certainly doesn't fit the description of the guy who abducted Janine," Byrne said. "And you haven't had any contact with anyone else from the good old days at Concord?"

"No."

Byrne's eyes were on him. Ross was sure the police would've made it to Crockett already, what with his being Ross's former cellmate. Ross was certain Crockett had said nothing.

"You're sure?"

"I'm sure."

Byrne waited, and the silence lay heavily upon them until they reached Route 128 South. Byrne said abruptly, "Let's go visit this Teague. I've got my doubts, but he's got a motive to get back at you, and he knows about Janine. That's enough for a talk with an officer of the law."

Byrne had Ross stand behind him, to the side of the door. He took his gun out and held it against his leg and pounded on the door with the heel of his hand. "Teague. Boston Police. We'd like to talk to you."

Ross heard movement in the apartment, a sound like a plate being dropped. Byrne pounded the door again. "Come on, come on. We can hear you in there."

They heard muffled voices, one high, one low. The high voice sounded like a girl's. Ross grasped Byrne's elbow. The cop nodded and put his finger to his lips.

Teague called through the door, "What is this?"

"Open up and find out."

"I didn't do shit."

"Just some questions, Teague."

The door opened. Teague was wearing just a pair of jeans, and his huge white belly hung over his belt. "What is this?" he said again. And then he looked past Byrne and saw Ross.

"Ah, shit. This again."

"This again," Byrne said. "Let us in. I've got some questions."

Teague scratched his belly. "I got nothing to say. And I can tell you that from here."

"Who's with you?" Byrne said, lifting his chin toward the closed bedroom door.

Teague kept his face straight ahead. "Nobody. You must've heard the radio I had on."

"The radio?"

"That's right. Turned it off when you knocked on the door."

"That's a fast answer, Teague."

"Huh?"

"Most people wouldn't figure it out about the radio so fast. Except when they've thought it up as a lie."

"What do you mean?"

Byrne brought the gun from behind his leg. He didn't point it at Teague but let him see it. "I want to meet whoever's in your bedroom."

Teague shook his head. "You can't do this." He pointed a thick finger at Ross. "And this guy, I want you to arrest him. He broke into my place with a gun. Threatened me with it."

Byrne didn't even glance at Ross. "And why did he do that, Teague? What did he want?"

Teague shrugged. "You know."

"No, I don't. Tell me what he wanted."

"The kid. Said his niece had been snatched."

"And why did he come to you?"

Teague waved his hand at Ross. "How the fuck do I know? He's right there. Ask him."

"I'm asking you."

Teague shrugged.

"Get your shirt, Teague. You'll gross everyone out at the station, that gut of yours."

"Prison shit."

"What's that?"

"Some shit I said in Concord. Just a joke, saw her picture, made a little joke. The guy went all nuts."

"That's not the way I hear it. I hear you went all nuts."

"Huh? Well, believe what you want, man. I'm the one that's limping. Tore my tendons all to shit."

"That piss you off?"

"What?"

"Walking funny. That piss you off, give you a reason to get back at him. And at her?"

Teague shook his head. "History, man."

Byrne kept his eyes on Teague. "I want to meet whoever's behind that door. Right now."

"You can't do that."

Byrne sighed. "Teague, I don't know you. So I don't know how stupid or how smart you are. But I'm beginning to lean toward stupid. Because I'm investigating the kidnapping and ransoming of the same little girl you fought with Stearns about in Concord. And I hear a girl's voice behind that door, and I have information you like them young. Whether I take you in for questioning right now or whether you let me in for a chat right now, I don't care. But if I bring you in, I'm also bringing in the FBI. Once they're in, we're talking search warrant, the works. And if you've got so much as an ounce of pot, you're on your way back to prison."

"He assaulted me!"

"Teague, I'm a cop." Byrne shook his head as if he were talking to a rather slow child. "What *I'm* interested in is all that's important to you right now. And what I'm interested in right now is who's behind that door."

Ross's heart was pounding. A trickle of sweat had just slid down Teague's face.

"Right now, Teague!" Byrne snapped.

"Shit." Teague swung away from the door and strode over to the bedroom. Byrne and Ross were close behind. Teague opened the bedroom door, and Ross saw a young girl with long blond hair pull a sweatshirt down over her bare breasts. "Getting a free look, guys?" she said.

"She's a hooker," Teague said.

Her name was Cyndi. She emphasized the correct spelling.

She told them she was eighteen but had no driver's license or any other identification to prove it.

"I like to be driven," she said, shrugging her shoulders.

"You're not a day over seventeen," Byrne said.

She shook her head. "Eighteen last May. The sweet sixteen bit's just a look." She tugged at her plaid skirt. "I can do twenty-five, too. All depends what my boyfriends like." Her tone was light, cocky. But she looked scared to Ross.

"Your boyfriends, huh?"

She glanced at Teague, then back to Byrne. "All of them."

"I don't believe it," Byrne said. "What do you think, Stearns?"

"I think she's fifteen." He noticed her head jerk slightly and felt sick at heart. Trading children for children.

"Yeah, I'd say you're right." Byrne took handcuffs from his pocket. "Turn around, Teague."

"She's a hooker!" Teague said.

"She's a kid."

"Ah, come on, guys," Cyndi said.

"What do you want?" Teague asked. "Tell me what you want."

Byrne handed them the sketches. "Give me some names here. You take a look, too, Cyndi."

Teague looked at the man's picture and snorted. "How the hell do I know? There's not enough here."

"Yeah, well, the cop who identified him didn't have much time. This guy shot him."

"Ah, Jesus, I didn't have anything to do with that. You can

tell enough from the sketch to know the guy isn't me. You can tell that much."

"So who is he?"

"Like I said, no idea."

"And her?"

Teague looked more closely but shrugged. "No."

"Her name might be Nat, or Natalie."

"No."

"How about you, Cyndi?"

The girl looked at both sketches for a long time, but Ross had the sense she was just going through the motions. "Nope."

"Where were you on the evening of July eighth, Teague?"

"I dunno. Where were you?"

"It was a Tuesday night."

Teague squinted. "Yeah, OK." He looked over at Cyndi. "I was with Julia, wasn't I?"

"Yeah," Cyndi answered automatically, no thought included.

"She's twenty-two," Teague said. "Go ask her."

"We will."

"Can't," Cyndi interjected. "She's on holiday."

"A working holiday?" Byrne said.

"Is there another kind? Down in the Bahamas."

"Where? Have you got a phone number down there?"

She laughed. "Be serious. We share an apartment, we don't braid each other's hair."

"Who'd she go with?"

"I have no idea. Just a guy."

Byrne took her phone number and nodded to the doorway. "Take off, Cyndi."

She slid off the chair quickly, grabbed a schoolbag, and headed for the door. "Bye, guys!" she said brightly.

"She's only fifteen," Ross said.

Byrne shrugged. "What can you do?"

CHAPTER 33

Lunchtime, sleepyhead."

The light hurt Janine's eyes, and she turned her face away. Smelled mildew and grease. They were in an abandoned car.

"C'mon, baby, I've gotta go to work, if you can call it that. Look, I got you a chocolate shake, your favorite."

The woman pulled at her arm, and Janine cried out. Moving made her head hurt terribly. It was as if somebody had clunked her with a rock. She asked Nat to leave her alone.

"Oh, baby, you think this is easy on me? I wish I could sleep the day away." Nat's voice had a funny singing sound to it. Janine kept her eyes closed. It still seemed like a dream, one of those where she was trying to run from something, but it was all in slow motion and she just couldn't get away fast enough.

"Sleepyhead!"

Janine felt sharp pain inside her leg.

"Quit it!" Janine slapped the woman's hand away from the inside of her thigh.

"It hurts there, doesn't it?" Nat pinched her thumb and forefinger together. "But Miss Crabby got you up, didn't she? Look, I got to go out for a while, and you can sleep when I do. But I just want to make sure you get something to eat." She raised another bag from McDonald's. "Chocolate shake, burger, fries, apple pie. The works."

The sunlight coming into the car hurt Janine's eyes. She felt sick to her stomach. The woman's face scared her. She was wearing bright red lipstick and dark eye shadow. The makeup made her look pretty and mean at the same time. Nat leaned between the bucket seats to show Janine her clothes. They were different from before. She was wearing a tight red top, a black miniskirt, high heels, net stockings.

"Ta-da." Nat gestured down at her body. "That should stop the boys at lunchtime, wouldn't you say?"

"What're you doing?" Janine looked out the window for the first time. She could barely remember what had happened after they ran last night. But her knees were scraped and her sweatshirt smelled bad. Then she had a quick flash memory of hiding behind a big Dumpster, and the woman crouching beside her as a car muttered outside the alleyway, a big old car with holes in the windshield. And Nat whispering, "I'll do him if he comes down here. I will."

But he hadn't.

"Is that policeman dead?" Janine remembered his eyes opening.

"No, he's OK. I saw a paper this morning. I saved his ass, too, I guess."

Relieved, Janine looked around at the car they were in. It wasn't too old-looking, but it was dirty inside, the window beside the steering wheel edged with broken glass. She could see the hood in front of them was all smashed up.

Nat saw her looking. "It's a mess. Nobody's coming for it soon, believe me."

In the distance, Janine could see the buildings of Boston, and she could smell the ocean. The woman didn't seem to notice that she was sitting on broken glass and little bits of it were stuck to her miniskirt. She even had a small scratch on her leg that trickled blood.

"How'd I get here?"

"Huh? I practically had to carry you. Sleepyhead. I've been busy this morning. I got these clothes, and I'm going to take care of business. A hundred bucks for this outfit, and I can make ten times that by the time it's ready for the dry cleaning." The woman lit a cigarette, drew on it hungrily, and nodded to Janine. "Don't worry. I won't be gone that long."

Janine didn't know what she was talking about. "I want to go home."

"Oh, Jesus," the woman groaned, rolling her eyes. "All I've done for you, I gotta hear this?" She laughed to herself. "My Aunt Barb told me it wouldn't be easy. She said raising kids was tough. Same old, same old, constantly. But you're a good kid." She reached out to stroke Janine's hair, but Janine drew her head away.

"Call my mom. She'll give you money."

"I don't want money. I'll *make* it for us, I'll get on my *back* for it, but I don't want to hear again about calling your mom for money. I said I'd take care of you, and I did more than anybody else could." Nat began nodding as she spoke, her voice rising as she went on, "A goddamn *cop,* Mr. I-Want-to-See-Some-ID, was on the ground when I pulled this thing out and took care of business for you." She patted her purse. "You think your mom could've done that?" Nat reached over and chucked Janine hard under the chin. "That was my *husband* I was shooting at. Don't blame me for missing. I didn't really want to kill the guy. He's had a hard time. And I've made some mistakes, too. I traded him in for you, and I've kept him away, so don't you go telling me who to call and what to do, not when I've done what I have for you."

"You were calling me Leanne. That's not my name."

The woman looked away. Her hand was shaking as she raised her cigarette and inhaled deeply. She blew smoke at Janine, making her cough. "So what? I've been smoking some shit, and I've got what you call a good imagination. Leanne was a great kid—you could do worse, growing up like her, believe me."

"Please—"

"Stop *whining!*"

Janine hesitated. The woman had snapped that last bit so angrily, as if Janine had been nagging at her for hours. But she knew she hadn't. She also knew the woman was making more sense now than she had at other times, and Janine figured she just had to keep trying.

"Please, I know the phone number. I'll call Mom. I won't say anything about you. I promise."

The woman shook her head and her voice sounded very tired, as if she wanted Janine to see how unhappy she'd made her. "No. He's out there. He can show up anytime, anyplace. I'm keeping you safe." She sighed. "It's not easy being . . . it's not easy."

Janine thought maybe she should just run. They were in a huge parking lot and the water was right in front of them. She hadn't been there exactly before, but it reminded her of the times her parents had taken her to the Children's Museum, and when she looked back at the city, she figured maybe she was very close to the museum. Her heart leapt then, because the woman at the counter there was very nice—and she knew Janine's mother. She

always said, "Hi, Beth," when they walked in. She might not remember Janine, but maybe she would.

She would listen.

"I don't see Lee," Janine said.

The woman looked at her sharply. "So you did hear his name,
huh?"

"I won't tell."

"Right." The woman checked her watch. "Look, I gotta go."

"Can I go to the museum?"

"What?"

"The one for children with the big milk bottle. It's near here,
isn't it?"

"No, honey. I've got to work. I don't like doing this, but if
I'm going to, now's the time. Some guys like a little something
around now." The woman touched her breast as she said this,
and then laughed aloud at Janine. "I can see you're a *good* girl,
but I knew that anyhow. Listen, just drink up the shake. I've got
to get going." The woman handed her the drink.

"I don't want the shake."

The woman's smile disappeared. "I said drink it."

"No. I don't feel good after. I want to go home, now."

"Drink it!"

"No."

The woman slapped her.

Janine fell back against the seat and tried to kick the woman
while fumbling for the back door lock. The woman got hold of
her by the waist.

"Help!" Janine cried.

"I don't like having to do this," the woman said, and it
sounded like when the woman had yelled for Janine to stop
whining. It didn't sound real. It sounded like something the
woman thought she was supposed to say. "I'm so disappointed
in you."

"I want my mom!" Janine screamed. "You're not my mom!"

The woman pulled Janine into the front seat and then out of the car. There was no one nearby. Janine screamed for help again. The woman held onto her wrist as she bent back into the car and the trunk lid popped open.

"You made me do this," Nat said tightly. Janine tried to pull away, but Natalie was bigger and stronger, and she yanked Janine off her feet and dragged her to the back. Janine fell to the ground, scraping her nails to the asphalt for purchase. But Natalie was too strong. She simply picked Janine up and shoved her into the trunk. And slammed the lid shut. "Don't leave me!" Janine cried, terrified in the sudden darkness. She found metal on every side. The car was small, and she couldn't lie down straight. "Please don't leave me!"

"You've been a bad girl," she heard the woman say. "So you just stay there and think about disappointing me again."

CHAPTER 34

Byrne said, "It was pretty convenient that the hooker Teague supposedly stayed with was out of town and unable to corroborate his story, I'll say that. And he did remember the date pretty fast." They were on Storrow Drive heading toward Watertown. "Still, that doesn't mean he has anything to do with your niece, just that he doesn't want to get involved any further with the police."

Byrne glanced over at Ross. "It's hard to tell when the dumb ones are lying sometimes. When they come up with a simple story and refuse to budge on it. Now, smart guys try to explain it all away, tie themselves in knots. Such as a guy telling me he didn't have a gun, then hearing from someone else an hour later he did."

"Uh-huh."

"You want to tell me about that?"

"I threw it in the water."

"When?"

"Before coming to the police station. Threw it into the Charles."

"Would you've killed Teague?"

"I didn't."

"Yeah. Well, tomorrow's another day, right? Have you got *anything* that says your prison record got your niece into this situation?"

Ross shook his head. "Nothing definite. It just seems like a hell of a coincidence."

"Yeah, maybe." Byrne rubbed at his chin. "But I see coincidence all the time. Looking at an investigation for what you expect to see will screw you every time. Detective work is like science: You look for what's there. Anyhow, I don't know about Teague."

A cruiser was waiting for them on the Watertown line, and two uniformed officers escorted Ross and Byrne to the first grocery store. "Look, I lied to the woman in here," Ross said. "She has no idea that my brother was in here. She wasn't even sure if there was anyone else here the night her brother was killed."

"Stay in the car then. If it really is the same guy doing these robberies, I'd just as soon keep that possibility down to as few people as I can."

After about twenty minutes, Byrne came back and swung behind the wheel. "Let's go to Cambridge now, confirm what this Muriel Gray told you."

"Did the owner here have anything to add?"

Byrne shook his head as he started the engine. "Just that she misses her brother very much."

At the Store 24 where the clerk had been killed, Ross received a little more respect with Byrne and a Cambridge detective

named Doyle leading the questioning than he had before. But
no more answers.

Muriel Gray wasn't in, and they wasted an hour tracking her
down at her position in the admissions office of Harvard University. "Mr. Jacob," she said, surprised to see him at the door
of her office.

Doyle rolled his eyes at that but didn't take the time to dis-
abuse her of Ross's identity. He and Byrne asked her to again
explain what she'd seen the night the clerk was killed and to pen-
cil out the mask of the gunman. "Why didn't you give us this
before?" Doyle asked. He was a prematurely bald man in his
early thirties, with a scowl that Ross suspected was permanent.

"You didn't ask, and I didn't remember until Mr. Jacob here
asked me."

Doyle apparently didn't have an answer for her, but he managed to convey his disgust without it.

Downstairs a few minutes later, he said to Byrne, "I think it's
time to turn Mr. 'Jacob' here upside down and shake the truth
out of him."

"You know something, Teddy?" Byrne said. "I think you've
got a point."

"You want to take him back to the station?"

"Nah. The feds are in on this, so I'll work it out with them."
Byrne stood with Ross outside the car while Doyle took off.
Byrne said, "He's a putz, too. But then again, so are you. And
now's the time for the rest of the change in your pocket. Tell me
about Crockett."

"What about him?"

"The guy's a professional robber. And we're talking a lot of
money here."

"I know him. He wouldn't do that to us, to me."

"Let me be the judge of that. Let me be the judge of everything you've been doing."

Ross stepped away from the car, feeling a wave of conflicting emotions. Byrne lifted himself onto the hood and waited.

Naturally, Janine came first.

But Ross had promised Crockett silence. The two of them had worked as partners for the past five years, and betraying that trust came hard.

"Her time's wasting," the cop said.

Ross sighed. "Let's go to South Boston."

CHAPTER 35

Ross's mouth tasted sour as Byrne knocked on the door. "Police, Mr. Crockett."

Crockett appeared. He was barefoot, wearing jeans and a white T-shirt. He scratched the stubble on his chin and said to Ross, "Thanks, buddy."

"Can we come in?" Byrne said.

"Yeah, why not?" He gestured toward the kitchen table and sat down himself. He apparently caught Byrne's careful assessment of the room. "It's hard to hide a kid in a studio apartment. But check out the closet. Maybe she's in there."

"I'll do that," Byrne said simply. And he did.

Crockett snorted softly and looked at Ross.

Byrne came back, and joined them at the kitchen table. "You know how it works. Don't pass up the obvious. Eight times out of ten, that's where the answers are."

Crockett lifted his shoulders slightly. "Am I under arrest?"

"Not now. Should you be?"

"Are you wearing a wire?" Crockett looked at Ross as he said this, although he was talking to Byrne.

"No."

"How about I check?"

"Go ahead." Byrne lifted his arms, and Crockett patted him down.

Both looked a little embarrassed, but Crockett seemed satisfied when he was done. "So what do you want from me?"

"Take it from the top," Byrne said. "Tell me your involvement."

Crockett's version matched what Ross had told Byrne on the way over pretty well. He, too, didn't mention giving Ross the time and place to hit the armored car, or admit to dropping the gun off the bridge. Instead, he told Byrne about making the introductions to Datano and staying at the house to act as a bodyguard.

"And you chased down where Teague was living, correct?"

"I made some calls, yeah."

"To who?"

Crockett hesitated, then gave Byrne the names of two fences in Boston. Doing this seemed to make him tired, and angry. He looked at the floor.

"Has he been giving them much business?"

"They didn't say. I didn't ask. I just got the address."

Byrne turned his attention to Ross. "And what did Datano do for you?"

"Try to buy the land at a quarter of the cost," Ross said. "And suggest I take out a contract on the guy."

"Did you?" Byrne's voice was mild.

"No. I didn't think I could trust Datano's people."

"Damn right. If she saw anything, they'd just kill her, believe me . . . so what *did* Datano do for you?"

"Made some introductions."

"To who?"

Ross hesitated for only a second, hoping his trust in Byrne was justified. "A guy by the name of T.S."

"You didn't tell *him* about Janine, did you?"

Ross shook his head.

"Good." Byrne let out a deep breath. "T.S. treats his little psychos like a bunch of cousins. They don't exactly work for him, but he considers them related."

"So you know him."

"Unfortunately. I won't be able to get close to him again. I busted a few of his buddies about two years ago, and no disguise on earth would let me within fifty feet of him now. How'd you get anywhere with him?"

Crockett's eyes narrowed slightly, but Ross didn't need the warning. "I did have that introduction from Datano."

"Yeah. . . ." Byrne looked doubtful, but he shifted gears. "So what happened? He set up anything for you?"

Ross could feel the sweat trickle down his back. But he went ahead and told Byrne about the kid. About how he'd short-circuited the liquor store robbery. Crockett rubbed the bridge of his nose.

"Uh-huh." Byrne finished his notes and said, "Is that it? Are there any murders or rapes you forgot to mention?"

"That's it."

Byrne massaged the back of his neck. "Jesus. Too bad I didn't wear a wire. Turner would've loved this."

"Who's Turner?" Crockett asked.

"FBI," Byrne answered.

"Yuh, he would've loved that, then. Played it before he went to bed every night."

"It's far from foolproof, but you've found your way to a pretty good contact, I'll say that," Byrne said. "There aren't *that* many tall white men robbing stores at any given time in Boston . . . so what did you bright boys have in mind after that? That red hair and ID bit was a once-in-a-lifetime deal."

"I told him that." The corners of Crockett's mouth lifted just slightly. "That's exactly what I told him."

Byrne looked over at Ross. "What next?"

"Next we were going to start recruiting."

"For what?"

Ross gestured to Crockett. "For a truck."

"An armored car," Crockett said. "Recruiting for a guy who knows how to use a shotgun."

CHAPTER 36

Janine started crying when Nat finally let her out of the trunk. She cried because she felt like it; she cried because she had to trick Nat.

Janine didn't put it into words for herself, exactly. But that time in the trunk made her know she was alone in a way she hadn't been before.

She couldn't wait for her Uncle Ross.

She couldn't wait for her mother.

They weren't coming. Maybe they wanted to, but they *hadn't* come for her. So it came down to the same thing.

Janine wished she were strong enough to beat Nat up. She thought about Joey Todd at school, the biggest kid she knew. He was her age, but fatter. When he hit you in the stomach, you couldn't breathe. She thought about him and knew that even if she were as big and strong and mean as he was, Nat would still be able to pick her up and throw her in the trunk.

That adults could do anything they wanted with kids.

It wasn't fair.

"Come on, crybaby," Nat was saying now. "Just get in the backseat and eat your lunch." Nat looked at her watch. "Call it your dinner, now. I was gone longer than I thought. You'll sleep afterward. You can go right through the night. Tomorrow will be better. You'll see."

Nat's lipstick was all smeared and she had that crazy bright voice back. "Got me a little tune-up." Nat touched her nose. "Hey, you save some money, you make money, right? Guy pays me one way or he pays me another. But I got two others that gave me the cash, honey. We get enough, I'll take one of these cars and we'll try a different city. I don't like driving that much, would rather do a bus. Leave the driving to them, like they say. But that's no good, what with that cop getting shot in front of the bus station. I guess they'll be looking for us at the train station, too. And I can't see flying, can you?"

Nat reached back and fussed with Janine's hair.

Janine, more than anything, wanted to bite her, do what she had done to Lee, and make Nat scream.

But Janine wept. Let Nat fuss all the more, act like she was her mother, shushing her and telling her that everything would be all right.

"Here, hon, drink your shake."

"Where are you going now?"

"Nowhere, baby. I'm going to take a little nap myself, right here. You just drink your shake."

Janine took the drink. It was no longer cold to the touch, and when she took a small sip, she couldn't help but make a face. It was warm.

"Don't give me that look. You're the one who wouldn't drink it when I told you to."

Janine sucked at the straw, let her cheeks move in. But she

stuck the tip of her tongue in the straw, letting just a trickle of the liquid into her mouth. Bad as it tasted, she was awfully thirsty. It had been hot in that trunk.

"You drinking that, honey?"

Janine took her tongue away and let the stuff flood in. "Aaah!" she said, opening her mouth as if she were joking.

The woman clapped her hands over her face, laughing. As if Janine were a two-year-old. "Gross! You're doing a 'show-me.' Isn't that what you call it? We did when I was a kid."

"Uh-huh." Janine swallowed and then began to fake it with the straw again. She kept her hands high on the cup, so Nat couldn't see that the level wasn't going down. After a moment, Janine said, "Do your mom and dad live around here?"

"No."

"Where then?"

"They're dead. I lived with my Aunt Barb in New Jersey. Have you heard of that?"

Janine looked at her like she was stupid. "Of *course* I've heard of it."

"Have you been there?"

"No. But I've heard of it. Is that where you and Lee lived?"

The woman shook her head. "New York."

"You were married to him?"

"Still am, honey." Nat lit a cigarette.

"Why'd you marry him if he was so mean?"

She shrugged. "He wasn't—to me, that is. It's different now." She looked at herself in the mirror, then turned back to Janine. "I still don't look so bad, considering. But you should've seen me a few years ago. And he never was handsome, but he had this way about him. Ex-marine, you know. Very tough and smart when it comes doing things. And I liked that."

"He doesn't seem smart to me."

Nat raised her eyebrows. "Oh, is that right, Miss Smarty? Got you, didn't he?" Her voice was silly, but Janine could tell she was angry.

That made Janine angry back: "He killed Daddy."

Nat dropped the voice and sighed. "I know, honey. But it's more complicated than you think , and we've both got a problem with the nose candy. Lee takes what he wants. That's just the way he is."

"Who is Leanne?"

Nat shook her head abruptly.

"Is she your daughter?"

"Drink your shake." Nat's voice was quiet, almost impossible to hear.

"Is she dead?"

"Of course not."

"Then why isn't she with you? Why are you doing this to me?"

Nat reached over and grasped Janine's wrist. She dug her fingernails in slightly.

"Stop it!"

Nat made it hurt more. "Drink your fucking shake."

Tears blurred Janine's eyes, and she slurped more of the shake down. Nat let go.

Almost half the shake was gone. Janine let the tears that had started continue, even though she could've stopped if she wanted. "Can I lie down?"

Nat turned away. "Go ahead. Just finish that up as you do. I'm going to want to see an empty cup."

Janine lay down, and she faked it with the straw for a while. And looked at Nat.

When Nat finally closed her eyes and shifted to be more comfortable, Janine lifted the plastic lid of the cup—and reached down and poured the rest of the shake under the floor mat.

* * *

She fought the sleep.

It wanted to take her. It was like a warm blanket was being drawn slowly up her body. It seemed to start in her legs, and then her belly. She just started feeling heavy. The seat cushions felt soft, and she didn't even feel scared when Nat took the empty cup from her hand.

Janine had to fight wanting to be taken care of.

She had to fight giving it all up for just a few more hours. Through her eyelashes, she watched Nat's head, seeing her move around in the front seat, trying to get comfortable. Janine pinched her own thigh, like Nat had, letting the bright pain from Miss Crabby bring her back awake.

Nat's breathing became louder up front.

Janine sat up, holding her own breath. Nat didn't turn her head. She didn't say, "Lay down," in that mean voice she got sometimes.

Janine looked at the door beside her. The lock was down. She reached over with two hands and quietly lifted it. It slid up smoothly, but the door wouldn't open. She leaned against the door harder, but it didn't move at all.

She shifted quietly to the other door. Same thing.

She almost cried. It was one of those cars where kids weren't allowed to open their own doors.

Her mother's car was like that, and Janine got a sudden image of her mother saying, "We're off," and hitting a button beside her up in the front seat, and all of the doors would make this clunking sound and the doors would be locked.

If this car was like that, Janine knew she'd never get out; Nat would hear the sound. And then she'd find the milk shake on the floor, and her face would get all mad, and she'd say, "After all I've done for you," and she'd put Janine back in the trunk.

Janine began to breathe fast, and she thought she was going to cry.

But she made herself stop. Made herself slow down.

She looked up into the front seat, to see if there were a bunch of buttons on the door beside the steering wheel.

She didn't see any. And the car had a crank for the window. That meant the windows weren't 'lectric. *E*-lectric, she corrected herself. Her dad was always fixing that word for her.

The thought of him brushed at her eyes again, but she pushed it all away, and looked at the door up front again.

That lock was already pulled up.

She drew her feet up and braced herself against the driver's seat. She put her right foot onto the armrest and then had to turn her back to Nat. Janine brought the other foot onto the armrest and balanced there for a second, her back against the ceiling, her bottom close to brushing up against Nat's head. She pressed herself against the driver's seat, and slid down slowly, terrified that when she turned around, Nat would be staring at her, furiously angry.

Once she was on her knees, she almost bolted, almost went straight out that door. But she was sure Nat was looking at her.

Janine forced herself to turn. Nat was still asleep, her mouth open.

Nat's purse was right at her feet. There was a dull glint from inside, and just as Janine opened the door, she realized what she had seen was the gun. And she remembered that Nat had said Lee was out there someplace, and before Janine let herself think much about it, she reached over and took the thing out of Nat's bag. It was heavier than she expected, but she could fit it inside the pouch of her sweatshirt.

She hugged the solid weight to her belly as she slipped out of the car and ran away, free for the first time in eight days.

CHAPTER 37

"Look, Blackie, I gave the kid hell myself for that liquor store thing. I had no idea he'd had a run-in with them the week before." T.S. handed Ross a beer. They were sitting out on the little balcony. "He could've gotten his ass fried."

"Worse, he could've gotten my ass fried." Ross let his lips curl slightly as he sipped at the beer, knowing T.S. was watching. Below, he could see the roof of Byrne's car. "The kid wasn't good enough for the job I had in mind."

"None of these people are too solid. They'd be in another line of work if they were. Shit, you're none too solid, yourself." T.S. downed the rest of his beer and cracked another one. The foam from the first dribbled through his beard. "Of course, that's one of the things I like about you."

"I'm moving forward on that bigger job."

"What's it going to be?"

Ross ignored that. "Tell me what you've got for me."

"All use shotguns. And they're purebreds."

"Purebreds?"

"Like you and me. White. You know I don't handle any spicks or niggers. Datano told you that, right?"

Ross shrugged.

"As for age, they're probably about your age, little younger than me."

"Experienced?"

"Hell, yeah."

"Reasonably good shape?"

"Yeah, any of them can run the frigging marathon for you. But tell me something, even if you're not gonna tell me what the job is—how much money are we talking here?"

"Significant."

"That means different things to different people. How much?"

Ross paused, making it look like he was considering whether or not he could trust T.S., then said, "The guy's cut will be damn near a hundred thousand."

"Holy shit. That's including your partner?"

"Yeah."

"What's he doing on this?"

"Don't worry about him." Here Ross lifted his eyes to T.S. and said coolly, "I see your cut if you come up with the guy we're happy with as twenty grand."

T.S. immediately began to sing his protests, but Ross could tell the big man was floored by the base offer. Ross haggled with him for a few more minutes, then made a show of giving in at twenty-five.

T.S. looked satisfied and anxious to please.

Ross said, "Tell me more about these guys."

"Mean motherfuckers, who'll kill you just as easy as they'll kill whoever you point them at." T.S. looked at him carefully. "Fact is, I might be interested myself. One of the reasons I do this pass-along shit is to keep an eye out for the big stuff. You know I got the weapons, and I've definitely got the balls."

Ross tipped his beer back to give himself time to think. When it was gone, he smiled slowly and lifted his chin toward T.S.'s big gut. "Sorry, buddy. That's why I asked what kind of shape they're in—I need someone riding behind me on a bike."

T.S. flushed red.

"Look, I'm going to trust you on this," Ross said, afraid they were going to lose the whole connection, between T.S.'s greed and wounded dignity. "We're taking on an armored car. But keep that to yourself.

"I want in." T.S.'s face set stubbornly.

Ross widened his smile into a grin. "You're too big, man. You'd bounce me through the armored car window."

T.S. stared at him. "You're taking some chances with me."

"Yeah, drink another beer, and tell me how you're ready to ride sidesaddle."

T.S. held Ross's gaze for a few more beats, before shaking his head and laughing. He reached down into the cooler. "I'll do that. And someday, me and you'll go on a job and you can see just how fast I can move. Either that, or someday maybe I'll just blow you away. How about that?"

"It's a deal. How soon can I see these guys you were telling me about? I want to see all of them, make up my mind."

T.S. cracked the beer, downed it, and tossed the empty down onto one of the cars below. He belched quietly and said, "How about now?"

Afterward, Crockett and Ross referred to the man they met as Surfer. He had a top-floor apartment in Southie overlooking the bay. The place was shabby cool: rock posters on the wall, big stereo system. The smell of suntan lotion permeated the apartment. There was even beach sand on the floor, which couldn't have been that easy to bring up five flights.

"Hey, guys," he'd said when they arrived on his doorstep. "Let's do some beers."

He was tall and blond, and his skin was tanned to a reddish brown hue. He put his feet up on the lobster trap coffee table and said, "So who do we shoot?"

The whole time, Ross was ticking through the details. Surfer was as tall as the gunman, but maybe a little heavier. There was the chilling ease with which he told of his experience, telling stories about robberies without actually mentioning locations or names.

"This black guy behind the counter was looking at me, and I start giving it to him in his own language, saying, 'Hey, you dissing me? You don't like my goddamn sneakers or something?' He didn't say shit, and I said, 'Hey, I'm talking to you, *boy.*' He keeps staring, this injured noble look, like something out of *Roots.* Ba-boom, I let him have it. No more noble savage."

Ross watched the man playact through different voices, all of the voices sounding just like what they were: a California dude mugging through tones and inflections he knew nothing about. Trying hard for some reason known only to himself to entertain Crockett and Ross.

Ross felt certain this wasn't the kidnapper, and he interrupted Crockett before he got into the specifics of the supposed robbery. "We'll be in touch," Ross said.

Crockett showed his false teeth to the man. "Count on it, dude."

Byrne followed them away from Surfer's place and pulled alongside when they parked facing the beach. Another detective was along with him, a young black officer named Jamison.

"You get all that?" Crockett asked

Jamison held up the earphones. "Oh, I heard it all right. That guy just got to the top of my list."

Ross had a small mike taped to his breastbone under a Kevlar bulletproof vest. Crockett had the same.

"You two feel all right in there?" Byrne asked. "I hate not being able to control this better."

"It went fine," Ross answered. "Which means it was a waste. I'm all but a hundred percent sure that it wasn't him."

"Yeah, I guess. I still hate having civilians taking this kind of risk."

Crockett grinned. "What do you think prison was like? Think about that next time you arrest some poor schmuck."

The next one was neat. Short clipped hair, neatly pressed jeans, a navy blue cotton shirt. White tennis shoes. A nice studio apartment in the Back Bay lined with books. He offered them soft drinks and soda water before they sat down at the kitchen table.

Though he volunteered little about himself, he gave them most of the information they requested, and worked toward pulling the details of the job from them.

Ross felt that he and Crockett were in substantially more danger just talking with him than they had been with the Surfer. The man's good manners were brittle and his eyes quick. He was looking for lies, for inconsistencies.

Ross noticed that once the man had sat at the table, his hands never rose above his lap again. Ross was fairly certain there was a gun pointed at his abdomen throughout the entire conversation.

He and Crockett did their best, gave him just enough about the job to appear that they were taking him seriously, but not enough to give away the show. And then they got out of there as soon as possible.

Because there was no way he was the kidnapper. He didn't stand more than five foot six.

CHAPTER 38

Janine couldn't trust her legs to run. Whatever had been in that drink made her legs feel separate from the rest of her, and she couldn't move herself away from Natalie as fast as she wanted.

She looked back.

The car was out of sight. That made her happy and it scared her. She was alone. The sun was going down now, and the summer day was turning cool. She pulled up her sweatshirt hood.

Now that she was out of the parking lot, she looked down the road and was startled to see a big ship—bigger than anything she could imagine any one thing could be—right up close. It was as if the ship had driven right up on land. She realized it was sitting in a big hole in the ground. There were men crawling all over it. There was a muddy lot between them and her, surrounded by a fence with wire on top. She couldn't see how to get around it, where the gate was.

And the idea of going up to them was scary,

It was all too big and noisy. She couldn't think of who she should talk to and if they would care. Just then, a big man with a beard walked past her. "Hard-hat area, honey. Take a hike," he said, not really looking at her.

She backed away quickly. She guessed she should talk to another policeman, but that thought was scary, too, because of what happened last time.

Then she thought of her mother's friend at the museum. The Children's Museum. Mrs. Cranston. The woman who was in the booth in the middle. Not the one where the ropes were, not where you bought your ticket. But the one in the middle where you asked questions, or were supposed to go if you were lost.

The idea warmed her. Mrs. Cranston was a woman who helped lost children.

Janine turned away from the ship. She looked up a long street that headed toward the big buildings of Boston. She remembered Boston had seemed close from the Children's Museum.

In fact, a bridge ran right past the museum and if she took that, she would be away from the waterfront area, away from Nat.

But Janine didn't like the idea of being alone underneath those big buildings.

Instead, she had a sudden thought that seemed too wonderful to believe. Maybe Mrs. Cranston would take her home in her own car, if Janine asked her nicely. "Please take me home?" Janine would ask. And she'd say thank you when she got there.

She yawned mightily before starting up the street, the weight of the gun a cold reminder she wasn't home yet.

She came to a street she had to cross. Cars were passing back and forth quickly, and there was no light. She stopped, confused. Her mother or father always held her hand at the lights.

She looked around at a man passing behind her and started to ask him—in fact, she did ask him—to hold her hand, but he didn't seem to hear her. He just kept going, his head down. She knew her voice had been awfully quiet, she'd felt so shy.

She looked to her left, didn't see any cars. Looked to her right, and didn't see anything there.

And stepped out onto the street.

She was right in the middle when the cab came around the corner.

The tires screamed, and the whole car rocked to a stop right in front of her. The headlights were right in her face, and she'd put her arm up over her head and was trying to say she was sorry when the driver put his head out the window and yelled, "You want to get killed?"

"Please," she said, starting to walk around to him.

"You want to get killed?"

"No."

He asked her again, and she realized didn't really want her to answer. She started to tell him she was lost, but the man in the backseat said, "Come on, will you?"

"The sidewalk, kid," the driver said. "Play on the sidewalk." And his window rolled up, and the car drove away.

She ran across the street from there. She looked back and tried to figure what she'd done wrong. She knew she'd looked right and left, just like her mother always told her. How could she know who was coming around the corner?

Part of her knew she should be able to figure this out, but she just felt so tired. She remembered how she'd felt before, that time with the policeman, and the thought of being that tired was scary.

She didn't know what time the Children's Museum closed, but she knew that she wanted to get there before it did. She kept on down the street.

It was all so noisy and . . . grown-up. There were honking horns, people walking by who talked to each other but ignored her. She kept the gun in the pouch when there were people be-side her. She didn't think about why. It just seemed like the thing to do.

There were smells. She could smell fish. And cooking smells. There were restaurants, and people coming in and out. She won-dered if she should stop in one of those.

But she kept on, wanting to see Mrs. Cranston.

Janine found herself sitting on a bench. She hadn't meant to sit down. She'd just been going along and suddenly she had become so tired she just had to stop.

She knew she'd probably drunk too much of that shake. And the gun was so heavy. Carrying it maybe was a mistake. But the idea of Lee or Nat showing up behind her made her clasp it more tightly.

She got off the bench and stumbled to her knees.

She'd hurt herself there before, and now her leg was bleed-ing again. Janine decided suddenly that she couldn't make it to the museum. She decided in a very clear manner for her foggy head that she needed to get some help from some adult soon. Any adult.

She looked around. There were people still walking by. She saw a little boy.

This brightened her.

A boy, maybe a little older than her, walking with a man and woman. He was wearing a jacket and tie, and they were on their way into a restaurant.

When the door to the place opened up, Janine was hit by a warm smell of food that made her feel sick to her stomach. She made herself get up anyway.

The door was closing as she got there, and it was heavy to pull open. But she did it.

The man and woman were standing, talking to another man

who was behind a tall table and writing something in a notebook. The boy turned as she came in, and she didn't really like the look of his face. He had the same bossy look that Joey Todd had. But he was close to her age, so she went up to him, anyhow.

"Hi," she said shyly.

He looked at her, frowning. "I don't know you."

"My name's Janine."

His eyes focused on her belly. She had both hands in the pouch. When she looked down, she saw that she had pulled the gun out a little ways. She shoved it back in.

"What've you got?"

"Nothing."

"Then go away. You smell bad."

Janine looked down at herself. Her clothes were filthy, her pants ripped, her sweatshirt stained with the ketchup and chocolate from all those burgers and shakes.

She pulled the gun out of the pouch so he could see it. She said, "I do have something."

He looked at her like she was trying to make him look stupid. "Is that real?" he whispered.

"Uh-huh."

He immediately began moving closer to her, moving her away from his parents. "Let me hold it."

"Can you tell your mom that I'm lost?"

"Let me hold the gun," he repeated.

She pulled it to herself, not wanting to let him have it, because it made her feel safer and because he was mean and stupid. "No. It's mine. Just tell your mother."

"Not unless you let me hold it." He pushed her now, his hands on her shoulders.

"Bobby," the woman said. "It's time for us to go in. Say good-bye to your friend."

"She's not my friend!"

Janine saw the woman look at her more closely and frown. The woman said to the man wearing the suit, "Whose child is this? She's a mess."

The boy whispered fiercely, "Let me see the gun, right now!"

"No!"

He grabbed for it.

And that's when the woman screamed, "She's got a gun!"

Her husband strode over, and he seemed tired and mad, and he said, "Calm down, Lucy. It's a toy—"

And the gun went off.

Janine didn't do it. She was holding it in the middle—the boy had it by the handle, and he must've pulled the trigger. She felt part of the gun move under her hand, and then there was the noise. Incredible noise, and a picture beside them on the wall shattered, and the boy was backing away into his dad, his face stark white. "She did it! She did it. She tried to shoot me!"

And the woman was still screaming as she pulled the boy behind herself and her husband. "She's got a gun, my God. Call the police. She's got a gun!"

Janine fled.

CHAPTER 39

Byrne had Ross call T.S. and tell him they wanted to keep going that night, to send the next one over to Crockett's apartment. Byrne rearranged the position of Crockett's kitchen table so that he could observe the meetings from inside the closet. Jamison was stationed outside the building and kept in touch by radio. He was to follow whoever came next if Ross wasn't sure he was the kidnapper.

As if I could be sure, Ross thought as he stood looking out the window, waiting for the next man. Ross felt edgy and irritable. He simply didn't know enough. His own impressions of the kidnapper were gained over the course of a few violent minutes. He'd wracked his brains to remember what Greg had said about the man, but Greg hadn't been able to see that much either. Ross had studied Babcock's sketch, trying to imbue the blanks with detail. After a while, he began to suspect what impressions he had, thinking he'd overanalyzed it all

"You think one person is enough for a tail?" Crockett asked Byrne.

"Olsen barely approved this stakeout as is. It's too much of a long shot. So he thinks he's being generous. . . ." Byrne stiffened. "Speaking of that putz, he just pulled up front."

Ross checked his watch. "The next one's due right now."

Byrne got on the walkie-talkie. "Jamison. Tell Olsen to back off. We got the next one due any minute."

"You tell him," Ross heard. "Olsen's already in the building."

A minute later, he was there.

Olsen wore a sour expression. "Did anybody throw themselves on their knees and confess yet?"

"What's up?" Byrne snapped.

"I'm in on this. Turner's pushing the chief for results, and if this is the extent of our operation, I might as well check it out."

Byrne looked at his watch and said, "Back in the hall and up the stairs, then. Bear in mind, I don't know if the next guy will be him or not, so we don't want to blow our contact with T.S. by screaming cop at this guy. We're going to simply put a tail on him afterward."

"So what's the drill?"

Byrne outlined the plan. "Ross and Crockett, you two do your bit just like before. Keep your conversation close to the vest. If you give too much away, he's gonna figure you for a cop. Ross, if you think it's the guy, my signal will be when you offer him a Pepsi. I'll let the guy walk, and Jamison tails him home. If the whole thing goes wrong, my signal is when you offer him a beer. Keep clear of the closet door and, Olsen, you back me up."

"Got it," Olsen said, going out into the hallway.

"Is he any good?" Crockett asked.

"No." Byrne went back to the window. "But I like to think I am."

* * *

It was hard with the next man.

The others Ross had been able to quickly dismiss as unlikely. This one was the right height and weight. Thin and strong. A sunburned man with horsy yellow teeth and a hard, calloused hand.

He was qualified, too. "I've done stores to banks, and I've done time for both." His voice was neutral. Ross was unable to detect any accent. The man sat at Crockett's kitchen table and said, "I'll do the job. I'm not scared about shooting anybody."

Ross studied him carefully. A lot about him fit. The man had brought a sawed-off pump shotgun, similar to the one Ross had seen the kidnapper use. Yellow teeth, Greg had mentioned that.

But something about the man didn't match. And Ross wasn't pleased with his own reasoning. It seemed all too subjective. The way the man's chin was weak, the way he stood when he first came in. Ross remembered the kidnapper's stance the night he'd killed Greg, the way he'd stood with one hip sprung forward, cocky. This guy appeared too calm. He didn't seem to notice or care about the sound of a board creaking outside the hallway. Ross made a mental note to tell Olsen that he wasn't being quiet enough. If anything, the gunman fit Ross's idea of a dirt farmer who'd turned to murder for a living.

But none of that was definitive. The hard decision was whether or not Ross should signal Byrne to arrest the man. Ross was afraid that if the police picked the man up, he'd find a way to let T.S. know. And that whole contact would be blown.

"I don't think so," Ross said abruptly.

"What?" The man glared back at him.

"We're all done here."

"Am I on?"

"No. We've got to keep looking."

"The hell you say. This is a big piece of change you're talking about, and I'm the guy to get it for you."

Ross said simply, "No, you're not."

The man's lip curled, and he said, "Yeah, well, fuck you, too." But he got up and left, his shotgun well hidden under his coat.

Ross felt the sweat trickle down his spine as he went over to the window to watch Jamison pick up the trail. Ross could feel Byrne and Crockett looking at him.

"Not him, huh?" Crockett said.

"I don't think so." Ross was exhausted but reasonably sure that he'd made the right decision. "Janine's kidnapper doesn't take no for an answer. This guy did."

CHAPTER 40

Janine awoke to the sounds of honking horns and people walking by.

She panicked and brushed her hands down her legs, expecting the rat to be back.

But she was still alone under the restaurant. The one built like old railroad cars that was boarded up. The one across from the Children's Museum.

She had found it last night. It had taken her a long time, because she'd been so tired and there was construction work going on, making everything so confusing. She had come to a bridge not too long after she had run away from the mean boy and his parents. And then she had turned around and gone back up the street again, and had gotten lost behind a big factory with a lot of broken windows.

It had been dark before she had finally come around a corner to find the museum right there. Janine had slumped up against the door and cried when she had realized the place was closed and that Mrs. Cranston was gone. Mrs. Cranston of the red plaid skirts, short gray hair, and glasses. Mrs. Cranston whose *job* it was to help lost children.

It had been the passing police car that had sent Janine under the restaurant. Luckily, there had been a cardboard box under there or else she would have had to sit right in the dirt.

The policeman being shot, and the screaming mother and boy, and the bullet smashing the picture had all become mixed together in Janine's head. Everyone was angry with her: Lee, Natalie, the boy, his mother and father. She had felt certain the police would be very angry with her. Maybe even her mother would be angry with Janine for not coming home.

Maybe it was her fault Lee had killed her daddy.

She had slipped in and out of nightmarish dreams. The restaurant above her was no longer dark. It was full of people who talked and laughed.

Her mother and dad had been up there, too. Her mother's voice had been bright. She didn't seem to care that Janine wasn't there. And her dad had ruffled the mean boy's hair like he used to do with Janine's.

Looking back now, Janine realized that none of that had been real.

But the rat had been there. It had smelled awful, like garbage and rotting meat. And it had been sniffing her right in the face when she had woken up.

Janine lifted the gun now. It smelled strongly, like when she hit a roll of caps with a brick. She hadn't dreamed about shooting at the rat, then.

Looking out at the bright sunlight, Janine considered her position. The lights were turned on in the museum. The McDonald's restaurant beside it was open. Janine's stomach was growling.

But she didn't want to go in there. She knew the people in the restaurant probably didn't know Nat, but she couldn't go in there, after all those burgers and shakes. It just seemed like bad luck.

Besides, it was time to go in and meet Mrs. Cranston. Janine was awfully tired, but her head didn't feel so mushy. She knew most of the things she had thought about last night were dreams. And—as if the idea just landed right in front of her—she realized that she should have just stayed with the mean boy and his parents and let the police come.

They wouldn't have been mad for long once she explained what had happened, and told them that she was Janine Stearns, and that she was lost.

Janine stared at the door to the museum. She wished she had stayed awake the whole night. Maybe she could've seen Mrs. Cranston come in and she could've met her at the door. The distance from where Janine was staying and the front door wasn't far. She could run there in just a few seconds.

But it seemed a long ways away.

Janine wanted the nightmare to be over. But she had been safe under that railroad car for hours. Not happy, but safe. The cardboard box had somehow become comfortable to her, and moving from it seemed awfully hard. Her mind cast forward suddenly, seeing herself living there day after day, this little animal under the restaurant. During the days it wouldn't be so bad. She could watch people, and see boats on the water.

But at night, there would be the rat.

Janine left the box.

The sun was hot on her skin and she was terribly thirsty. Her legs and body felt creaky and stiff. But it was better than the night before. Her body felt like her own, just tired.

A woman was coming Janine's way, her head down as she

talked to her two kids, a boy and a girl. They were little kids. Janine figured about three years old.

Janine looked right and left and didn't see anyone else watching, and then she saw that she was still holding the gun in her hand, and the image of the mean boy came back to her. "You smell bad."

She put the gun back in the sweatshirt pouch and hugged it to her belly. The gun felt hard and dangerous there. She didn't like it, but she wasn't ready to leave it behind either.

It had saved her from the rat.

The mother got to the door first, and Janine waited. The door closed. Now that she was here, her heart was pounding. What if Mrs. Cranston wasn't there? She pressed her nose against the glass. She could see the mother and her kids straight ahead, between the ropes. Buying their tickets. Janine craned her neck, tried to see the center booth where Mrs. Cranston would be. But the angle was all wrong, she could just see a corner of the booth, not see in it.

She took a deep breath, and pulled the door open. It was hard to do with one hand, the other holding the gun to her belly. But she did it . . . and Mrs. Cranston was there!

"Hey!" Janine stepped in the foyer. Mrs. Cranston was talking to some people, a big man with a bald head and a woman in a long gray coat. Janine didn't want to be rude, but the fogginess was out of her head now, and she knew the people who had taken her were wrong and she wanted to go home. "Hey!" she said, again, and Mrs. Cranston looked her way and frowned slightly. She held up her finger and turned back to the woman. Janine stopped short, confused.

Janine looked down at herself and felt at her face and knew she was so dirty, so messy, that she didn't look like herself. And maybe Mrs. Cranston would only know her if she was with her mother.

So she had to tell Mrs. Cranston who she was.

Janine's eyes were still downcast when she realized the man and woman were facing her now, and in her way. She stepped politely to the side, but they moved with her.

Before she could say anything, the man reached down and put his hand on her mouth. He said loudly, "Baby, where the hell have you been?"

He spun her around and wrapped his arm around her belly, pinning the gun to her stomach. "Let's go home, honey." He picked her up, and shoved her through the door.

"Sir?" Mrs. Cranston called. "Sir? Did you find her?"

"Thanks, we've got her!"

The woman beside him was saying quietly, "Don't hurt her, don't."

Janine got past her shock and started screaming then.

Because the woman was Natalie.

The man, she had no idea.

CHAPTER 41

The guy sitting across from Ross was bald except for a blond ruff along the center of his head. His eyes were brilliant green, so much so that Ross suspected he was wearing tinted contact lenses. That, and the man was wearing green leather from head to toe.

Crockett said, "Tell us about your experience."

"Tell me about yours." The man glanced around the room quickly and then snapped back to Crockett. "Keep it in this century, huh?"

"Aw, you've got a sense of humor." Crockett leaned in close. "But I'm on a deadline, asshole, and what I need to know is what you've robbed with a gun and how did it turn out?"

"Places." He blew smoke back at Crockett. "Call me an asshole again, I'll shove your head up your own."

"What kind of places?"

"Stores. You ever do time?"

"Yeah, I've done time."

"Then how good can you be?"

Ross watched the man while he and Crockett continued to spar. The man's nose was running a bit; he clearly was on something. Probably coke. He wore silver studs on his belt and on his wrist guard. Alligator boots with silver heels and toes.

"Are you ready to go this afternoon?" Ross interrupted.

"Right now." The guy slapped his jacket pocket. Ross had noticed the bulge there earlier.

"I told T.S. I needed someone with a shotgun," Ross said.

"Got that in the car."

"Tell me about the stores," Crockett repeated. "You cap anybody?"

The guy sniggered like a teenage boy. He rubbed at his nose. "Uh-huh. You could say that. Look, T.S. said we'd be going in on an armored car."

Crockett snapped, "T.S. has got a big mouth."

"So you're ready now?" Ross said.

"Abso-fucking-lutely. The sooner the better."

"Wearing that?" Ross nodded to the boots, the jacket.

"The jacket stays in the car. It's too distinctive, you know? But the boots, I wouldn't go in without them. Lucky boots. Laid out a guy with them once, too." He pointed to a faint dent on the right toe. "Guy's front teeth. Bastard."

Ross grinned. "Never go on a robbery without them?"

"No way."

It took them a little while, but they got rid of him.

A half hour later, Ross let the last man into the room.

His eyes were deep-set, his face skull-like. He was as tall as Ross. Although he appeared to be losing weight, his build was still very powerful. Pale skin over muscle and sinew. Even though the day was warm he wore white cotton gloves—the kind

Greg had described. His right hand was in the pocket of a black trench coat, but Ross could see he had gauze taped on his wrist, going under the glove. The sawed-off shotgun glinted as the man held it pointing to the floor.

"T.S. gave me this address." The man's voice was quiet. He stood stock-still, his eyes moving about the apartment, taking it all in.

Ross gestured to the bandage on the man's hand and asked what had happened.

"Nothing serious."

"Nothing that's going to hurt your shooting, right?" Ross asked.

"Let's get to it," the man said, pulling the chair away from the table. He sat down so that his weight was forward.

Ross was frightened. There was a coiled power to the man that was hard to define. Ross told himself that the guy before him with the Mohawk could have killed him just as dead.

"Tell me about the job," the man said. "And tell me it's what I want to hear."

"Which is?"

"That it's for serious money, and that it's going down today."

"You've got an appetite," Crockett asked. "Coke?"

"None of your goddamn business."

Crockett shrugged. Crockett's manner was quieter and more deferential than it had been with the guy before, too. But he gave just enough information on the robbery for it to be plausible— he acted as if they needed to hear the man's commitment before actually giving him all the details.

Ross observed the man quietly. He was the right height and weight. The right build. The cotton gloves. The shotgun was a pump-action, like the one Greg's killer had used.

Ross felt this might be the man.

Crockett told the man they'd split the take evenly.

The guy sniffed and said, "It better be even. Or I'm willing to cut it down to a one-way split. You get what I'm saying?"

"Got it," Crockett said. "Let me tell you how we're gonna pull this off."

Ross's mouth went dry. That cocaine sniff, and the phrase the kidnapper had used before. *You get what I'm saying?*

It was the man. Ross was sure of the voice. His heart pounding furiously, Ross worked to keep his tone casual as he said, "You guys want anything? We've got Pepsi in the fridge."

There was a creaking sound from the hallway.

The gunman's head snapped around.

The floor creaked again right outside the door. It was a stealthy, slow sound. Not the sound of someone walking down the stairs at a normal pace, but someone sneaking up.

Olsen.

"How about a beer?" Ross asked.

But by then, the gunman was already in motion. He shoved the table over onto Ross and Crockett. He whirled and the shotgun was out and he put a blast through the door. There was a scream from outside, and then Byrne kicked open the closet door, revolver in hand. But the table was in the way, and the gunman shot him, too. The blast spun Byrne around.

As the man ratcheted another shell into the chamber, Ross rolled to his feet and charged him. He didn't do what Greg had done, grabbing for the barrel. Rather, he took the man in a bear hug and pinned the gun so the shortened barrel stuck out to the right. He ran the gunman back against the wall, breaking through the plaster. He pulled him out and did it again, this time bouncing the man's head off the doorjamb.

The man grunted, and tried to turn the gun up to Ross's face.

Ross slammed him up against the door again, fighting to keep the shotgun aimed off to the side.

And then Crockett was behind him with a knife, and Ross saw his opponent's eyes flicker.

"Crockett!" Ross screamed, knowing it was too late, that Crockett had approached them on the right.

The shotgun blasted again, and Crockett was gone.

Instinctively, Ross loosened his grip, and the gunman elbowed him in the face. Ross held onto the gun, keeping his hand wrapped tight around the action to keep the other man from pumping in another shell.

Ross had a flash of his brother, of his brother's ribs. He squeezed his hand tighter, determined that the pump-action would have to be dragged through bone before another shell could be jacked into the chamber.

But the man let go of the gun altogether.

And with one kick to set Ross up, and another to provide the power, he kicked Ross through the window.

CHAPTER 42

Ross didn't let go of the gun.

Glass rattled through the grates of the fire escape landing as he rolled onto his hands and knees and looked back into Crockett's apartment. Ross was dizzy. It took him a few seconds to take it all in.

The gunman was gone.

Byrne was kneeling on the floor, his right arm bloody. He was saying into the walkie-talkie, "He's coming, Jamison, he's coming. He's got Olsen's gun."

Crockett.

"Oh, Christ," Ross said.

Crockett was on the floor, not moving. Ross's stomach rolled when he saw what the shotgun blast had done to his friend.

The gunman had shot high.

Ross started down the fire escape. The steps were far apart, and it was awkward climbing down with the shotgun in his hand. Ross banged hard against the side rail on the next level.

The gunfire started just as he reached the ground.

By the time he was past the garbage cans in the alley to the front, the man was pulling out in a green Chevy, tires smoking. Jamison was on the sidewalk, clutching his leg. Blood poured through his fingers. He swore steadily while rocking slightly, "Goddamn, Goddamn."

Byrne staggered out of the front door. He called to Ross, "How bad is he?"

The Chevy rounded the corner three blocks up.

"His leg." Ross ran across the street to the motorcycle and swung aboard. He shoved the shotgun into the right sidebag.

"Ross, hold up!" Byrne knelt beside Jamison and began pulling his own belt off to use as a tourniquet.

The radio squawked, and a woman's dispassionate voice said that an ambulance and backup were on the way.

Ross kick-started the bike.

"Wait, goddamn it!"

Ross took off.

Ross twisted his right hand hard, and let the engine scream. By the time he made the corner, the Chevy was out of sight. Ross made up the distance fast by winding the bike up in first and second gears, and then slowing just enough as the intersections came up. The bike had a good-sized fairing—big enough to block his sweatshirt, he figured, if the gunman looked in the mirror.

At the next intersection, Ross hit the brakes and let the bike roll forward so he could see around the corner. It was a main street. No green Chevy to the left. To the right, three blocks ahead, the gunman was forcing the car through a red light. Horns were blaring from oncoming traffic. Ross took a few seconds to take one of the helmets off the clip alongside the bike and strap it on. It had a full-face visor, tinted.

As he wound his way through traffic, Ross searched his memory for the plan Crockett had outlined to the gunman. He couldn't remember Crockett getting to the part about the motorcycle. The word hadn't even been mentioned. T.S. might've mentioned it to the gunman . . . but there was a reasonable chance he hadn't. And, therefore, Ross was going to assume the man wouldn't be expecting a bike to be following him.

The Chevy took a left a few blocks ahead.

Ross had been keeping his speed just a bit over the limit. Once the car was out of sight again, he put the bike on the center line and let the tachometer needle sweep up to red. Car horns wailed as he passed between an oncoming panel truck and a Buick, leaving mere inches on either side.

By the time he was approaching the left turn, he was up to just over a hundred. He downshifted, braked hard, then tucked the bike into a tight turn. The bike wasn't made for that type of performance, and sparks flew as the sidepipe met the pavement.

Ahead, the Chevy was rounding another corner.

Ross kept the car in sight for the next two turns. As it crossed over the bridge into Boston, he noted that the Chevy was going more slowly now. The gunman even stopped for the red light without trying to crowd past the cars ahead of him.

Ross let a few more pass him, so he wouldn't be sitting right on the Chevy's bumper.

And he considered what to do.

The man apparently didn't think he was being followed. Ross could sidle up alongside him and shoot him.

Ross wanted to do it.

His blood was up—he didn't want to slow down and think. He didn't want the fear to have time to creep back. He just wanted to get back at this man. Exact some revenge for Greg and Crockett. He told himself that the gunman wouldn't have been looking into the armored car deal if he had Janine to trade in for $500,000. He told himself that the gunman either didn't have her, or he knew he'd already killed her.

Ross twisted around and reached into the sidebag with both hands and pumped another shell into the shotgun.

As it made its ratcheting sound, he thought, *What other explanation is there?*

And that last question was one he couldn't answer.

Reluctantly, he settled down to following the gunman.

The Chevy rolled onto the expressway, going north. Ross followed a half dozen car lengths behind and stayed in the middle lane while the man pulled quickly into the left. Together, they wound through the heart of Boston, passing the towers of the financial district on the left and the North End on the right. Ross played the tourist on the bike, taking time out to turn his head toward the aquarium; he even raised his hand off the left handgrip in a small salute as another biker rode by.

Whether or not the driver of the Chevy noticed the charade, Ross had no idea. But the car's speed remained steady until the gunman signaled for the exit to Storrow Drive. Ross followed him down the steep, winding turn, and then out along the river. It was a gray morning, and yet there were small boats sailing on the Charles. Ross felt a distinct sense of unreality, driving past people whose primary goal at that moment was most likely a good tack—while his was how to get his niece back from a man who'd just shot three policeman and killed his friend.

A good tack was all Ross had been concerned about plenty of times in his life, and he wondered briefly if he would ever have the chance again.

He pushed those thoughts aside when the gunman took the Arlington Street exit. Up until then, Ross had been following through major thoroughfares. But on the city streets the gunman would be more likely to notice the motorcycle still behind him.

The gunman took the jog to the left and then started down Arlington Street. Ross kept two cars between them. When the Chevy pulled to the right and turned onto Commonwealth Avenue, Ross took a right onto Marlborough Street, which ran parallel. He knew that first block of Marlborough was the only one that ran outbound. After that, it went one-way in the opposite direction. Once he came to the corner of Berkeley, he saw the Chevy flash through the intersection a block up. Ross took a quick turn against traffic and ignored the screeching horn of a cab as he dove down the alley behind the row of buildings on Commonwealth.

The alley was actually a narrow road, full of potholes and occasional patches of slippery cobblestone. It wasn't the kind of road on which Ross would've chosen to wind a motorcycle up to eighty.

But that's what it took to reach each intersection, stop, and make sure the Chevy swept by a block over. And then Ross would twist the throttle and do it again, scrabbling through holes, actually flying a dozen feet out of a deep indentation soon after the intersection of Dartmouth Street. At Gloucester, he took a left as soon as he saw the Chevy go by and pulled up fast to the corner of Commonwealth in time to see the Chevy turn left onto Massachusetts Avenue.

Ross nailed it again, went straight forward on Gloucester. He saw the car crossing the inbound section of Commonwealth. Ross went another block and took a right onto Newbury. He knew he was taking a chance the driver would see him, but he had no choice; he would've been forced to take a left onto Boylston if he'd continued. He stood on his pegs, expecting to see the Chevy flash by then.

But it didn't.

Ross wound the bike out, thinking maybe the gunman had already passed, or had gotten onto the turnpike entrance and Ross had missed it. Or maybe he'd headed up the side street along the turnpike entrance.

Ross stopped at the Massachusetts Avenue light and looked right and left.

Nothing.

His heart was tripping hard. Had the gunman seen him?

Ross leaned forward on the bike, revving the engine in frustration. A patch of green caught his attention and he edged the bike forward, craning his neck.

There it was. So close he'd missed it—the gunman *had* gotten past. The Chevy was facing the wrong way on Massachusetts Avenue, right in front of the subway station.

It was empty.

The gunman had ditched the car and taken off down the subway, Ross thought, cursing himself. He glanced left, looking for a place to leave the bike.

And the man was right there. Standing two feet away.

His hand was inside his coat pocket, and he said, "Just who the hell are you?"

Maybe he'd been waiting in a doorway. Maybe he'd been standing there on the street corner all along and Ross had been too focused looking for the car to notice. Either way, Ross was stuck: In the seconds it would take him to get free from the bike, the guy could empty the gun into him.

The man reached over and lifted Ross's visor. "You a cop?"

"Ross. Ross Stearns."

The corner of the gunman's mouth lifted, and then he grinned. "You're Uncle Ross?"

"That's right."

The guy swung his leg over the back of the bike. "Let's go."

CHAPTER 43

The man grasped the inside of Ross's collar and said, "You're wearing a vest, huh? That means that cop must be still walking." He jammed the gun barrel into Ross's hip. "You've got a big artery right about here. That vest won't help. Now, take a left."

The gunman took the extra helmet off the side of the bike and put it on with one hand, presumably to keep from attracting police attention.

"Is Janine alive?" Ross asked.

"Move it!"

"Not until I know."

The gunman ground the barrel deeper into Ross's hip, but still Ross didn't move. The light turned yellow. The guy said, finally, "She was the last I saw. Now, if you behave, we'll see if your sister-in-law will spring for *you*. I'm not picky, as long as I get my money."

Ross took off. He thought about trying to dislodge the gunman. But from the way he moved with him, Ross figured he had too much riding experience to fool.

The gunman told him to pull off Massachusetts Avenue, and they took the back streets around Northeastern University, until they turned right onto Huntington Avenue, and passed by the Museum of Fine Arts.

Up ahead a few blocks, the gunman snapped his fingers and pointed to the left. Ross took the turn, banking the cycle hard.

"Right there." The gunman pointed to a small factory building, one with boarded-up windows on the bottom floor. It was painted industrial tan, and many of the windows on the upper two floors were shattered. "Home, sweet home." He swung off the bike, opened the garage door, and had Ross park the bike inside.

The gunman pulled the shotgun from the saddlebag and waved Ross over to a broad set of stairs. "You'll have to do the five floors on foot. The elevator's broken." The guy seemed amused. "Good for your health."

The place had obviously been abandoned for some time. Some floors were empty and others were full of machinery tools covered in old grease and dust. The stairs sagged under Ross's feet, and the freight elevator shaft yawned wide and black at each landing, unprotected by safety gates. Ross wondered if the gunman intended to drop his body down there afterward. He was certain the man had no intention of exchanging him alive for the ransom.

But they continued all the way to the top floor, and the gunman gestured for Ross to open a gray door at the top of the stairs. Ross had just the faintest inkling that there was someone on the other side. He half-heard a small rustling noise.

It couldn't begin to prepare him for what he saw in the faint light from the hall skylight.

Janine, bound and gagged, and clearly alive.

*   *   *

Relief stabbed through Ross. But before he could draw breath there was movement to the left. Ross saw the woman, and there was a flash beside her, and the wood jamb behind Ross's head splintered.

The gun fired again.

From behind, the kidnapper shoved Ross in the direction of the flash.

Ross instinctively dropped to the floor. In the half-light, Ross could see a vague shape of a big man. Ross crabbed his way over to Janine and pulled her off the chair, covering her with his body. The woman huddled beside them, her muffled cry eclipsed by the sound of the shotgun blasting from behind.

Teague fell into the light of the open door, his face and upper body blackened with blood. The kidnapper stood over him, saying, in a tone close to bemused, "How about this?"

Ross forcibly shoved aside any thought of Teague, or even Janine. He launched himself off the floor and slapped the shotgun aside. All the fear, guilt, and rage poured out.

Ross simply didn't give the gunman room to move. He crowded him into a corner and tried to break through bone and flesh to the wall behind.

Ross used his knee, pistoning up into the man's groin. He used his elbow across the man's chin.

Having Janine behind him fueled him on, knowing that it all came down to this.

When he felt with fierce exultation that the man had begun to break, he took just long enough to snatch the shotgun away, step back, and crack the man against the jaw with the shortened stock.

The guy fell to his knees.

Ross hit him in the same spot again, sprawling the guy onto

the floor. Ross whirled, the gun leveled against the woman, but her hands were bound in front of her, and she cried through her gag for him to stop.

Ross pumped in another shell and put the shotgun barrel behind the kidnapper's ear.

Janine moaned behind him, and the sound brought Ross up short. Blood dripped off his knuckles, and his breath was whistling in and out.

Janine shook her head violently back and forth, and Ross recognized instantly his position with the gunman wasn't so different than the gunman's had been to Greg.

Ross said, "Hold on, honey. I'm going to tie him up."

But she turned and fled for the doorway, clearly panicked.

"Wait, Janine!" Ross hesitated an instant, and then went after her onto the landing, afraid she wouldn't be able to catch herself with her bound hands if she tripped near that open shaft.

The woman make a noise, a strangled cry.

Ross turned and saw he'd made a terrible mistake—he should've killed the gunman no matter what.

The man had dragged himself into a sitting position, and he had Olsen's gun in his hands. Even as Ross lifted the shotgun, he knew it was too late. The man fired steadily, emptying the gun. Two rounds whistled by harmlessly. One took Ross in the shoulder and set him back on his heels. Another caught him full in the chest, sending him stumbling back. Janine cried out through the gag and tried to reach out for Ross's hand.

She missed by inches.

Ross threw his arms out, but he was right in the center of the elevator entrance. Unchecked, he fell into the darkness of the shaft.

CHAPTER 44

Ross may have screamed aloud. Maybe not. In the second or so of free-falling he threw his arms back, pinwheeling, stretching for something, anything. Every cell of his body cried out with the atavistic fear of falling into the unknown.

Light flashed by, and he was barely aware that he'd passed two floors, and then he felt a blow on the back of his head and realized he was falling along something, and he twisted and grabbed, and then he *did* scream aloud because his hands were being ripped, they were being sliced by free strands of a woven wire cable, and Ross got his leg around it . . . and still he slid.

Until he wasn't.

That's how it felt. He didn't realize at first he had stopped. He was still swaying in the dark, he was still moving, but he wasn't going down.

He wasn't dead.

Ross looked up and saw four parallel cables swinging side by side, in and out of the three windows of faint light that were the landings above.

Blood trickled between his fingers. Ross could taste it, too. He did a brief checklist: shoulder and chest hurting, but no blood there. The vest had done its job.

He shook his head, wondering for a second if he'd hit bottom and was already dead, so unnatural was the sensation of being suspended in the darkness. He rested his head on the cable as a wave of nausea and dizziness overcame him. He ground his teeth and held tight, swinging on his metal lifeline.

The pain in his hands was real.

And so was the strength he was expending hugging the cable. Already his arms were starting to tremble.

He opened his eyes.

Below him about a dozen feet was another open landing.

Ross heard a noise up above, and looked up to see the silhouette of the gunman leaning out at the top-floor landing. The man said, "You hear him hit? I didn't."

His voice echoed down the shaft.

More faintly, the woman's voice drifted down to Ross. He figured she was standing behind the gunman on the landing. "We've got to get out of here, Lee. Somebody could've called the cops with those gunshots."

"I need a frigging flashlight. This guy made a cripple out of Teague, and he's given me trouble at least three times now. I want to see the body."

Ross could hear Janine up there crying. He hung his head, infuriated with his helplessness, and the implication of the man knowing Teague's name.

"Well, maybe the cops will show it to you!" the woman said. "Leave the girl, and let's get the hell out of the state."

"Yeah, right. Jeffers gets fucked again. Why should I be the one to lose out on the deal?"

"You're alive."

"Don't give me this concern shit. You tried to shoot me."

"If I was really trying, you'd be dead," the woman snapped back.

Ross heard the sound of a blow after that. The man's voice was farther away, but Ross could hear the menace clearly. "I'm gonna deal with you later. But right now, I'm gonna make sure Uncle Ross is out of it—and this place passes police inspection. We haven't got time to clean it up right. You hold onto the little chick while I get that mattress."

Ross started letting himself down. He was tempted to try to make it out onto one of the landings. The cable was slack, but not enough to let him swing over to the landing itself. He kept going down, the cable smooth in places and biting sharp with broken strands in others. He couldn't trust the strength of the electrical cables, so he just steeled himself against the pain and kept going. The blood on his hands made them slippery, and his breath was ragged from the exertion.

He was past the ground-floor landing and was on his way to the basement when he heard them up above again. The gunman was barely visible from so far up now. Something big blocked him from view, presumably the mattress.

Ross started sliding down the cable, ignoring the pain. He figured the gunman intended to throw it down to sweep the shaft clean.

Then the sharp smell of acetone filled the air.

Ross slid down the last few feet onto the roof of the stalled elevator, fighting panic.

Ross stumbled over the big pulley on top of the elevator trying to make it to the wall. He got up and lunged against the brick wall, reaching up in the dark for a handhold, looking for something to start his climb up to the ground-floor landing.

Up above, the mattress burst into orange flame.

Ross's fingers closed around a bit of tubing. A wire encased in corrugated metal. He reached as far as he could for a hand-hold and began pulling himself up, hand over hand. He talked to himself under his breath, talked to the gunman up above who was apparently waiting for the fire to catch completely. "Hold it there. Do it right, man."

He was almost up to the landing when the wire broke.

He scrambled against the wall, and for an instant, it seemed as if by sheer willpower alone he could inch upward the final two feet.

But he couldn't. He slid down the smooth face, just as the man above let out a rebel yell.

The mattress was fully engulfed now. Ross landed on the elevator roof and looked up to see the mattress hit the cable and tumble once, then twice, alongside the wall. Ross stepped back, mesmerized. He could see the bluish tinge near the mattress itself, and then bright yellow and orange of the fanning flames. Still the thing came closer, and he knew that even if it didn't hit and cover him, it would turn his little box into a private burning hell.

How long will I be conscious? he thought.

And suddenly Ross went from standing to lying flat on his back.

The breath was knocked out of him and he was in an even deeper darkness. Still he could see the mattress falling, but it was as if he was seeing it through a screen, and then he realized that's exactly what it was, it was the heavy mesh screen of the freight elevator roof.

He'd fallen through the open trapdoor.

And then the mattress hit, rocking his metal cage. Burning acetone dripped and flared onto his shirt, and he rolled to smother the flames, and then rolled again . . . and found that the basement elevator door was open, like those above him.

* * *

By the time he made it past the wall of junk that had been stacked on the basement stairway, Janine, the woman, and the gunman were gone.

When the police and fire engine arrived, Ross was on the sidewalk, sick with smoke inhalation and with the thought that was almost too painful to bear: Ross's own trouble with Teague had been a factor—maybe even the reason that Janine had been abducted in the first place.

Ross could take comfort with only one thing. He knew the man's name. The man had used his own last name and Natalie had said the first. "Lee Jeffers," Ross said, as the first cop approached him. "Lee Jeffers."

CHAPTER 45

There was a minor celebration among the two agents at the house when word came back that Ross had gained the kidnapper's name. Beth had been dismayed that neither of them seemed overly concerned that Janine was still in the kidnapper's hands. It was as if their command over the bureaucracy took precedence over anything as prosaic as returning a little girl to her mother.

The agents made and received a series of phone calls, to their own offices, the U.S. Marines, and finally an important call from a New York City detective. Beth had cornered one of the agents immediately after he got off the phone. He was a young man in his late twenties with a crew cut and a self-important manner that irritated her.

"Yeah, OK," he said, handing Beth a fax off the portable machine. It was a picture of Jeffers, a brutal-looking man with a harsh, planed face. "Ex-marine," the agent said. "Last known job as a welder. He's been arrested a number of times for assault, armed robbery, and murder. Only two convictions, though. Once on an assault charge. Sent to prison for four years. More recently, he served a six-month sentence for abusing Leanne, their daughter."

"A daughter?" Beth had asked. "How old?"

"She turned nine last month. Somewhere in her new home."

"Where was the mother when he was abusing her? This Natalie?"

The agent looked uncomfortable. "You never know."

"What did the detective say?"

"He doesn't know either."

"What did he *say?*"

The agent paused, then said, "His understanding is she didn't do a damn thing to stop Jeffers."

He's aged, Beth thought, when they brought Ross into the room that night.

It had only been a day since she'd last seen him. But his already thin face was more gaunt, with dark hollows at the eyes.

"Sit." She drew out the kitchen chair. Turner, Byrne, and Allie followed him in. They had spent much of the day at the factory going over what remained of the scene. Beth had seen a tape of the burning building on television. The police had kept Ross's name out of the report, but a news crew that had arrived just after the fire truck had turned the camera onto him momentarily.

Beth took Ross's hands. "Tell me about her."

He had already told her over the phone that Janine was alive, that he had actually touched her. But the idea that maybe they were lying to spare her had whispered into Beth's ear that afternoon. Maybe they'd all lied to keep her from being hysterical. Maybe they figured Ross had to tell her face-to-face, and that was what he was here to do now.

Ross looked at his watch. "Six hours ago, she was just fine. Upset, but she looked healthy."

Beth felt the breath shudder out of her. She hadn't realized until then she had been holding it. She took the sandwich that she'd made earlier from the refrigerator and got him a beer. Really, it was just that she needed to move. She thought how screwed up it was—a man tells you your daughter is alive, and you give him a sandwich. A steak for bringing her home?

She broke away from that, thinking as she rejoined them at the table that hysteria was nipping at her mind like a dog.

"Tell me what happened."

He drank the beer but didn't touch the food. And he told her most of what he'd been doing since first hearing about Janine's abduction, about T.S., Datano, Teague, and what had happened at the factory.

"Shit, we should've had T.S. staked out the whole time," Turner said. "Now he's cleared out with all those weapons."

"You can't find out where he's gone?" Beth looked from Byrne to Turner, then back to Ross. "How about that man you first found him through: Datano?"

Ross shook his head. "That's where we just came from. I went into the restaurant, and he told me he couldn't help me. Very polite, but absolutely no help."

"We think T.S. must've gotten to him," Byrne said.

"Your whole stakeout was a fiasco!" Turner snapped.

"I took it as far as I could. Olsen refused me the men I requested, and he wouldn't go to bat with the Cambridge Police for staking out T.S. He said the whole thing was too much of a long shot."

"Well, he got his for being such an idiot."

"As if *you've* got enough men signed onto this—"

"Shut up," Beth said. Her eyes had filled with tears. Angry, bitter tears. "For God's sake, shut up!" She turned to Ross.

"You're telling me this man, Teague, knew you in prison? That this is some sort of vendetta?"

"It's not that simple." Ross's voice was quiet. "Believe me, I've been beating myself up thinking just that. But I've also been thinking about something Jeffers said. . . . He was complaining . . . something to the effect of why should he be the one to lose out on the deal. Like someone else was managing to come out ahead."

"So?" Turner said. "Typical of a guy like that. Teague is laying there with his head blown off, and Jeffers thinks *he's* the one getting the short end of the stick."

"What?" Allie said, confused. "When did he say this?"

"I think it was more than just the two of them," Ross said. "My impression is that they may not have even been working together, exactly."

"My impression is that you're trying to convince yourself and us you didn't drag your family into the shit," Turner said. "If there's any conspiracy going on here, which I don't believe for a second, maybe it's Datano. You dragged that crook into this. Or maybe it was your pal Crockett. He was a thief. He definitely knew Teague—maybe he knew Jeffers."

Beth saw Ross's face flush. "That's bullshit about Crockett and you know it."

"I know no such thing."

On one level, Beth could sympathize with Ross.

On another, she hated him.

"All of this started with you," she said softly. "They followed you to us."

"It's not that simple," Ross said.

"Mrs. Stearns, Ross got us awfully damn close," Byrne said. "We know a lot more than we did before. We've got Jeffers's name."

"And he's got my daughter!" Beth hated herself as she said

it, hated the way her words made Ross's face close down. But her husband was dead. Her little girl was still held by that monster.

There was no containing the thought that just as Greg had feared, all the experts were haggling over the details and still her girl was out there—and Beth hadn't done a thing herself. She had let other people run the show, and still her little girl wasn't home. And after this rage was over, she was going to have to start waiting again, and let their dialogue and speculation around her kitchen table begin.

"Goddamn it, Beth, listen to me," Ross said. "There's more to it than a simple extortion. Jeffers and Teague knew each other, but Jeffers was just as surprised as I was to find Janine behind that door. I know it."

"Stop making excuses!" Beth snapped. A part of her was grateful when she saw Allie grab Ross and pull him away and out the door. Because Beth needed to blame someone, and he was the best candidate. She needed to scream.

But it was just as well Ross didn't have to hear it anymore.

CHAPTER 46

Ross barely listened to Allie's telephone call back to the house. He watched the shadows growing long on a hay field as they passed in her little car. Byrne had handed the portable phone to Allie as she'd pulled Ross out the door, and she was apparently talking to him now.

"We'll be at my apartment. God knows I understand what Beth's feeling, but he's taken enough just now. I want your promise you'll call the instant you hear anything, right?"

She glanced at Ross after disconnecting. "He's given us his word. . . . He's a good guy. You're lucky you've got him on your side this time."

Ross nodded his thanks. He didn't want to speak. The words Beth had thrown at him made him feel mean. He knew well enough she was just lashing out because she was frightened. But he was tired and angry and had done everything he damn well could.

There'll be no place for me if Janine dies, he thought abruptly. *No place on earth where I can hide from myself.*

Allie took his hand. "Put your head back."

"I can't sleep."

"So don't. Just put your head back and close your eyes."

He was going to argue. Tell her to mind her own damn business.

But he still didn't feel like talking. And he liked the feel of her hand in his.

Minutes later, he was asleep.

At her apartment in Back Bay, he followed her up the stairs in a daze. He winced when she snapped on the light. He'd been there maybe a half-dozen times before. They'd had a busy few weeks during their brief affair. Now, unhappy and half-awake as he was, he was hungry for the warmth he remembered there.

The place was simple and elegant: with white-painted walls and original watercolors of coastal Maine scenes. "Wait here." She came back minutes later with his bathrobe. It had barely been used, a gift from Janine, Ross remembered with a painful tug.

"You left this," Allie said. "Hit the shower."

Ross took the robe and went into the bathroom. The steam filled the room quickly, and she knocked on the door and took his clothes to wash. By the time he had dried off, she had a sandwich at the table. "Go ahead and eat. I won't tell you terrible things about yourself as you do."

"Maybe she had the right." The shower had sapped the resentment out of Ross, and all he felt was exhausted and rather useless.

"Nonsense," Allie said crisply. "You've done everything you could. You've gone after Janine as if she were your own daughter. You've sold your inheritance, you put yourself at great physical risk. . . ." Her voice caught, and she looked away for a moment, and then continued as if nothing had happened. "It's obvious to me, and to everyone involved—including Beth—that you'd lay down your life for this little girl."

"Do you think this is all some vendetta?"

Her eyes faltered from his. "It doesn't matter."

"Meaning you do."

"I don't *know*. Neither do you. I admit it's awfully strange that Teague and Jeffers knew each other."

"Is that what you'd say if you were prosecuting?"

"I wouldn't be prosecuting you," she said gently. "You're a victim in this, Ross. It's not your fault."

Ross shook his head, disgusted with himself. "Victim? I'm alive and free. What's Janine going through right now?"

"At this moment, you've done all you can. They'll call if something happens tonight. So, right now, your job is getting rested for tomorrow. And praying that tomorrow includes welcoming Janine home." She put her hand out to him. "Give yourself a break, Ross. Now let's both go to sleep."

He didn't know where he was when he awoke.

It was late, just after three o'clock by her digital clock. He must've called out, because she was awake and pulling him back: "Sssh, baby, sssh."

He lay back down, his heart pounding.

He had been falling in that shaft again, only this time it was his father watching from the top. And there were no cables to catch, nothing to do but fall, and just before he hit, he cried once for help. And he saw it was no longer his father who was watching, but Crockett.

"What?" Her voice was blurred with sleep. "What's the matter?"

"Crockett." He sat up and rubbed his face, trying to clear his head.

"What?"

Suddenly everything Beth and Turner had thrown at him had landed as unassailable facts. All of it was Ross's fault. All of it. "Maybe I misjudged Crockett," he said. "Jesus, I thought I knew him. But he could've done it. Five hundred thousand would've been a big score. All that time in prison, I kept a low profile as best I could, but he knew that the Sands was worth some money."

"And you trusted him."

"I did. I had to trust someone."

"Sure you did." She sat up beside him. "And you may have been right. I mean, wouldn't it have been simpler if he wanted to rip us off to have just done it once we had the cash? Back at the house, before the police were involved?"

"That would've been a lot more straightforward. But it would've meant killing all of us. By using Jeffers and Teague he could've pulled the whole thing off as a blind. Even Janine would've been all right, if she didn't see their faces."

"But it didn't happen that way. And he wouldn't have let Jeffers walk in on the stakeout the two of you set up with the police, would he?"

Ross sagged back against the headboard. "Of course not." His heart calmed down.

She kissed him. "Your brain is just going overtime."

"Good thing I have a trained legal mind waiting at three in the morning."

She smiled as her lips touched his. "Is that all I'm good for?"

The heat swept through him as it had the first time they'd been together. Five years of binding down, of awakening to a loneliness that had pervaded his very flesh, had been burned away by the feel of her throat under his hand, the firmness of her breasts, the soft curve of her belly. The nervousness he'd brought to her bed had vanished.

And it was that way now, made only more intense by his knowledge of her body, and the separation of the past months. He pulled her nightgown to her waist, his breath made short by the sight of her. She stopped him, holding her hands over his. He closed his mind to whether or not it was right, with Janine still gone.

He waited.

Allie didn't speak. She hesitated for just a second, then pulled his head back down to hers.

CHAPTER 47

The next morning, Ross awoke to the sounds of traffic. He sat up quietly so as not to wake her. Purposefully he blocked out thought of anything but taking a moment to look at her dark lashes against her fair skin, the delicate rise and fall as she breathed, the way she tucked the blanket under her chin like a small child.

She awoke to find him watching, and if he was right, he saw a touch of wariness in her eyes.

He tugged at her hair gently and ran his hand down her long, smooth back. "Relax. This isn't where I start making demands."

She smiled at him sleepily, "You might want to consider it after she's back. You could make a good case."

"Thanks, Counselor."

She got up as he took the phone from the nightstand and dialed the house.

Beth answered.

"Nothing from them." She paused. "Look, I'm sorry about what I said last night."

"All right."

"I can't afford to turn you away, and I don't want to. All I want is to get her back."

Afterward, she put Byrne on the phone. He told Ross they had confirmed with Mrs. Cranston at the Children's Museum that she had seen Janine but hadn't recognized her. "We got a witness on T.S., too, not that that'll do us much good. Cambridge Police turned up a guy who said he'd seen T.S. loading a light green van at about the time you were working your way out of that factory. My guess is Jeffers called him."

Byrne also said that Geiler's office had phoned about closing on the property. After hanging up, Ross told Allie, "I've got some work for you today."

She cocked her head curiously.

He told her about Geiler's call. "There's the balance of the sale coming to me. So I guess that means I need a will."

She blanched but said only, "It makes sense."

He watched her personality change as she dressed into a nicely cut but somewhat austere gray business suit. Her face turned cooler as she put on a subdued shade of lipstick and the image of competency replaced her easy warmth. By the time she was on the phone with Geiler's office, she was fully masked by her role. "In any future dealings, I'd prefer you call my office rather than my client's home," she said.

They went to Geiler's office right after breakfast. He came out briefly and shook Ross's hand. Geiler's manner was sympathetic but distant. "I'm sorry my people contacted you so urgently. Any word about your niece so far?"

Ross shook his head.

"Don't worry about any problem from me regarding . . . the situation with your brother's body." He grimaced. "Totally use less, this whole thing. So unnecessary." He looked at his watch. "Well. Let's close this out."

He thinks I'm going to be killed, Ross thought abruptly. Geiler was concerned about the sale getting screwed up if both brothers were dead.

"I'd like to take her to the beach one time when she's back," Ross said suddenly.

"What's that?"

"Janine. I want to take her on the beach at the Sands one day before Labor Day."

Geiler hesitated and then had the good grace to cover his pity with a smile. "Absolutely. All the time you want, of course."

Ross saw that they actually wrote it in. A weekend at the Sands before the summer died for Janine, Beth, and him.

CHAPTER 48

They were back to waiting. They were at the house, Byrne, Allie, Beth, and Ross. Turner's ranks had swelled to eight agents.

Ross felt sour and irritable, and listening to Turner frustrated him. Not that the man's logic was so far-off. If anything, Ross felt he was missing something the man had said, and though he didn't like Turner, he listened all the harder for whatever it was. Some comment Turner had made during the hours of conversation, the endless hashing over the smallest details . . .

"Just about zip on the Black Bloods," Turner was saying. "The gang Teague used to ride with. They've been gone for months. And we haven't had any luck with his buddies at Concord."

One of the agents was a woman who introduced herself as Lisa Taves. She looked a bit like Beth, only a little younger and a lot harder. At that point, Lisa sounded like Beth, too. She and an agent named Peters had been working on Ross's and Beth's voices for hours.

A big aluminum coffeepot stood beside the computer that was to be used during the phone trace. A state map was tacked up on an easel, and Turner was using a flip chart and a Magic Marker to outline their preparations.

He seemed to appreciate the audience.

"Three cars ready to follow whenever the call comes in. My guess is Jeffers will insist that you drop the money someplace, Beth. And he'll promise you he'll release your daughter."

"Just like with Greg," she said dully.

"That's right. And I expect we can trust him just as far as then. So when he calls, Lisa here is going to have to make the case that it must be a face-to-face swap. Frankly, we're hoping he asks just for you, that he assumes Ross is dead. Then Lisa will head out. One of my cars will be actually just ahead of her like this . . . two staggered behind that can switch off. Radio contact the whole way, of course. We'll wire Lisa as well, so we can monitor anything she says, and we've put a transmitter in the case." He showed them how the little electronic device had been inserted just under the plastic near one of the hinges.

He looked at the woman agent approvingly. "Lisa's highly trained. . . . She could probably take this guy out on her own, but she'll have all the backup she needs."

"You're planning on shooting him, then?" Beth said. "Gunfire with Janine right there?"

The woman met Beth's eyes. "We'll do it right, Beth."

Turner continued, "The big question is whether or not Jeffers realizes Ross is still alive, and if he therefore assumes we now know his name."

Turner looked at Ross disdainfully. "Peters is ready to go with Lisa, if that's the case."

"Only one TV station got a shot of Stearns," a young agent

said. "Two newspaper articles referred to an 'unidentified white male survivor.' "

"I think there is a fair chance he doesn't realize I know his name," Ross said quietly. As if he hadn't said the same thing a dozen times already. "When he referred to himself, it was automatic, like a habit: 'Jeffers gets fucked again.' There's a good chance he'll never remember saying it, not like he might remember someone else saying it."

Byrne looked across the table consideringly. "Last night you started to talk about someone else coming out ahead."

Allie glanced quickly at Beth. "Why don't we drop that, OK?"

"No, I'd rather not," Byrne said. He stood and reached for Turner's Magic Marker. "Do you mind?"

"Knock yourself out." Turner sat down.

Byrne said, "I've got no argument with your plans. But let's at least consider the idea that if Teague was involved, there might be someone else involved as well. We can talk motive and opportunity, but lots of times I've found the simplest process is just to take a step back and see who has actually gained something."

Byrne turned to the time line that listed all the major events that had occurred from the moment Janine was kidnapped. He frowned. "We're looking for who's winning, who's losing." He began circling the names of people as they came up: Greg, Janine, Beth, Jeffers, Natalie, Ross, Allie, Crockett, Datano, Geiler, Teague, T.S. He circled the unnamed gunmen by nicknames: Red, Surfer, Mr. Clean, Green.

He put slash marks through Beth's, Janine's, Greg's, and Allie's names. To Ross, he said, "For the moment, we can probably set aside the people you approached yourself after the kidnapping, like Datano, Geiler, and T.S., and the gunmen he introduced you to." He put slash marks through their names. Byrne left Ross's name circled. "Frankly, I think we could cut you out here, too. But if we look at who's got something to win—or something to lose—Turner here could still make the argument that you had something to lose in letting the land be sold because of Greg's failing business."

"Damn straight," Turner said.

"But, again, I don't buy it," Byrne said. "So let's take a look at Crockett."

"Allie and I were talking this through last night," Ross said. "Setting aside the fact that I trusted him, he did know I owned some land worth a fair amount of money. But if he had been working with Jeffers, why would he have let him walk into that sting with us at his apartment?"

"Maybe he wasn't in contact. Maybe something had broken down between them. After all, Teague did try to kill Jeffers just an hour or so later."

"You guys keep playing this old song," Turner said abruptly. "Maybe *he* did it; maybe *he* did it. We *know* who took the girl. We know who has her now. It was Jeffers, and all this speculation is totally useless."

"Geiler said that." Ross spoke without thinking.

"What?" Turner's brow wrinkled.

"Geiler said the whole thing was 'totally useless.' " Ross turned to Allie. "Do you remember?"

She looked confused. "Ross—I don't know. . . . I guess I heard something like that, but so what?"

"It was as if he was disgusted with how this whole kidnapping turned out." Ross stood up. "Impatient, almost."

"Who isn't?" Turner looked to Allie. "I think your client is losing it."

Ross put his finger on Geiler's name. "He's won something. He got the land he wanted at a fire sale price. He is the only one I can see that's come out of this ahead so far."

Allie said quietly, "Ross, I can't see it. Remember, *we* called *him.*"

"No. That's not exactly right." The random thoughts that had been flickering on the edge of Ross's consciousness all day were beginning to come together. Byrne was looking at him carefully. Beth's eyes were intent on him as well. "Before Janine was kidnapped, Geiler had approached us twice, and we refused him twice. He even had his attorney come to see me in prison trying to get me to sell."

"So what?" Turner said.

Ross wanted room to pace, wanted room to think, but the place was so damn crowded with people. He felt the stares of all of them. The agents were taking their cues from Turner, their faces blank with skepticism. Ross said, slowly, "You called it yourself."

"What?"

"Back at the Sands. You accused me of arranging Janine's kidnapping as a dodge. You said what if Greg had been singing this old song about keeping the place intact for his daughter? And what if I wanted to force him to sell by having Janine kidnapped so he'd have to pay a ransom he couldn't possibly meet—not without selling the land? And I told you that didn't make sense, because Greg and I already intended to sell half the land in several parcels."

Ross turned to Allie, his pulse quickening. "And then you and I went through the same thing, only with Crockett. Thinking maybe he pulled it off as a blind, to get the cash. But we agreed that didn't make sense. So take the same idea and turn it around for Geiler. . . . What if he sent Jeffers in to kidnap Janine—not to get cash, but to get the *land?* Hell, if Jeffers was working for him, Geiler might even be getting the cash back. He gets the land and he gets his money back. Maybe he even figured Janine would come home safe. Maybe Jeffers had different plans."

"This is all guesswork," Turner said.

"It's not guesswork that Geiler got the place for three to five hundred thousand less than he otherwise would have had to pay," Ross snapped.

"Small potatoes for a guy like him," Turner said. "Besides, we all knew this: he took advantage of the situation. That doesn't mean he's a kidnapper."

Byrne interjected. "People are killed for a fraction of that all the time. How well do we know Geiler's finances?"

Turner turned to one of his agents, a young man with a crew cut. "Tell us, Hanlon."

The agent said, "From what we can see, his real estate company is reasonably strong, financially. Doing better than most, as a matter of fact."

Turner smiled.

"What about the other holdings?" Ross asked.

"What about them?"

"How are they doing?"

"And *what* are they?" Byrne asked.

The agent looked doubtful. "Shipping . . . and a few others we haven't really paid that much attention to. . . . I mean, it seemed like such a long shot. We knew the kidnapping was a robbery gone bad."

"Right," Byrne said. "Just like all of you knew Teague wasn't involved. Only it just so happened he *was.*"

Turner didn't look too happy with his agent, but nonetheless, he said, "OK. Some sloppiness in our investigation there, I'll admit. But it's still quite a leap from Geiler making a comment about your niece's abduction being 'useless' to nailing him for the job."

"Ross has done all right so far," Byrne said. "Three to five hundred thousand is a fair piece of change for anyone. As far as I can see, Geiler's the only one who has gotten what he wanted since Janine's abduction. He's the only winner so far. And who knows what other reasons Geiler would have for wanting the place?"

"Huh? Nothing but a theory on motive," Turner said. "One that I don't buy, personally. We don't have a speck of evidence."

"So go shake it out of him." Beth's voice was hoarse.

Byrne raised his hand. "We've got to be careful on this. We should stake him out, make sure we can put our hands on him. But we should at least let the night pass, give Jeffers an opportunity to call us. If Geiler is involved, taking him in too soon—"

"—could kill her," Beth finished. She leaned across the table and put her hand on Turner's. "I know you're skeptical. But I'm asking you to do this anyhow. Put the people on it. Give Janine every chance."

Turner withdrew his hand, looking uncomfortable. "Yeah, sure. Wouldn't be the first time we spun our wheels."

Byrne and two agents left to stake out Geiler's condo in the North End.

They called within an hour to say he wasn't there. His lights were out, and the doorman said he had left in a cab about an hour before.

"The doorman's impression was that Geiler was going out for dinner," Byrne said over the phone. "He couldn't remember the type of cab, so it's going to take us time to track the driver down."

Ross noticed Allie was swaying on her feet, and he suggested she find a place to lie down. She refused, saying she would just as soon head home. Her color was wan, and she asked him to walk her out to her car. "I don't know what to think anymore. . . ." She looked at him quietly. "You've got to be careful with this, Ross."

"Meaning?"

She took a deep breath, and Ross felt his chest tighten.

"Ross, on the face of it, it's more likely that Teague and Jeffers got together and tried to make some money and take some revenge. And that's not your fault—but pulling an innocent man like Bob Geiler into it is."

"I might be wrong. But like Byrne said, he's the only one who's coming out ahead on this whole thing so far. And I don't think Jeffers is working alone. It's worth a conversation."

"Ross, accept what *is.*" She got into her car and rolled down her window. "It's like you're trying to shift the blame to make it more palatable. Janine's kidnapping *wasn't* your fault."

"I didn't say it was."

Her face closed. "As your lawyer, I'm telling you, Geiler's not going to take this sitting down."

"Neither am I."

She drove off. He stood out under the moonlight for a few minutes. Thinking that when all was said and done, Allie's desire for respectability was impenetrable. She would always suspect his motives and judgment. She would always see him as an ex-con.

Beth met him at the door. "Allie's gone?"

Ross nodded and reached for Beth's hand. Outside, she walked closely to him; when their shoulders touched he could feel the rigid set of her body.

"What do you think of their plan?" she asked.

He paused, trying to choose his words better. But it came out the same way as he'd thought it. "I think they'll catch Jeffers, or kill him. But I'm afraid for Janine."

She looked at him sharply.

He said, "Look, I don't have the credentials these guys do.

But I've seen more of Jeffers than the others, and I saw him shoot through a door just because he heard a sound outside it." Ross gestured to the driveway packed with big blue sedans, the blazing lights of the full house. "How're they going to hide this whole mechanism once it gets out on the road? Especially with two other people acting like us? Jeffers may not be a genius, but he's not stupid either. He'll go off the deep end if he thinks he's being thwarted."

Beth covered her face briefly. Ross stepped away from her, letting her think. After a moment, she rejoined him and said, almost casually, "Did you know that I had a hard time the first year?"

"What?"

"With Janine. I didn't feel what I should have. Didn't bond. Did Greg ever tell you?"

"No, he never did. Why are you thinking of that now? Janine loves you and knows you love her."

"Does she?" There were tears in Beth's eyes as she looked up. "What can she be thinking now? What can she be thinking about me after all these days?"

"I expect that she wants to be home with you. And if it's any more complicated than that, you'll have years to set everything straight once we get her back."

"You think I should take the money to him myself?"

"No. I think that he would hurt you, too."

"Kill me, you mean." Beth wiped the tears away with the back of her hand. "Enough of that." She stood straighter and seemed to have more focus than a moment before. "Well, he'll have to try to do just that. It's the only way I can see to get between him and her. And that's the job I signed up for the day she was born."

Hours more passed before the phone rang, and Beth and Ross had been arguing with Turner the entire time. The two of them picked up the extension and listened in as Lisa picked up the receiver and said hello.

Ross watched Beth closely, saw her face pale as Jeffers spoke.

"You've got five seconds," he said. "What's Janine's best friend's name in school?"

Lisa looked quickly over to Turner, her eyebrows raised.

Beth said, "Amy."

Turner waved her away and whispered urgently, "Tell it to Lisa! He needs to hear her voice, not yours."

"You get to play again," Jeffers said.

A phone booth in Boston, Kenmore Square," the agent in front of the computer said, and tapped immediately into a Boston Police line. They all waited, the silence physically painful for Ross to bear. He watched Beth and knew it was worse for her. Her head jerked slightly as if she'd been slapped when the agent turned to them, shaking his head. "Gone."

Five minutes later the kidnapper was back on the line. "Now put Uncle Ross on. I saw him on the news, so don't waste my time saying he's not right beside you."

"Right here," Ross said.

Turner slammed his fist on the table.

"What's my name?" the man said abruptly.

"I don't know."

"Bullshit!"

"How could I? You killed Teague. You and the woman sure didn't tell me. How else would I know?"

Ross let the silence fill the line. He could hear the man breathing, almost hear him thinking. Ross kept himself from filling the line with words, from trying too hard to convince the man. Jeffers *wanted* to believe that he was still anonymous, and Ross was counting on that.

Finally, Jeffers said, "There'll be a quiz at every phone booth for the both of you."

"We'll be there," Beth said her eyes locked on Ross's.

"First one you get wrong, Janey dies. First sign of a cop, Janey dies. Go to the farm stand just before the junction of Route 2 and 128, fifteen minutes." He hung up.

CHAPTER 49

"That was the FBI that just passed." Beth turned to look out the rear window. "And two others are following us."

"Don't even look," Ross said. "Jeffers might be watching."

Ross's heart was pounding. It was just after midnight, and the road was clear, making the FBI cars too obvious, to him anyhow. Because Turner had refused to consider Ross and Beth making the actual drop, he hadn't put transmitters on them—and then after Jeffers's call, with only a few minutes to prepare before the first phone booth, they'd only had time to strap on vests and take a walkie-talkie. Turner had reluctantly given Ross a revolver. "Watch yourselves. We're not going to be able to set up the phone traces in time, so he could be anywhere."

Ross kicked the truck up to just over eighty. They passed three farm stands, but the last one before the highway had a phone out front. It was ringing as they pulled into the driveway. Beth jumped out of the truck before it was fully stopped and ran to the phone.

"He wants to talk to you," she said when Ross joined her.

"Uncle Ross," Jeffers said, "tell me your last gift to Janine."

"A hat. A black beret."

"Congratulations. Continue on Route 2, right on Route 16. At the first rotary there's a phone in front of the bank. Be there in ten."

At the next one, Jeffers asked Beth the name of Janine's teddy bear.

"Bartles," Beth said instantly. "Listen, we've got the money; don't hurt her."

"Any excuse," he said. "Any excuse at all, I will. Go to the corner of Mass Ave. and Commonwealth in Boston. Fifteen minutes."

I've joined on," Byrne said over the walkie-talkie.

"Any luck with Geiler?" Ross asked.

"Some. Found the cabdriver who took him out to dinner in Chinatown. Two of Turner's guys are following up there . . . but keep focused on what we're doing now. Over."

Ross glanced over at Beth, knowing the battle between hope and despair in him was a mere skirmish compared to what she must be going through. He put the walkie-talkie on the dashboard, rather than snap back at Byrne just how focused they were.

Jeffers told Beth to name Janine's favorite vacation.

"Disney World." Beth had taken her there with Amy and her mother last year, and Janine talked about the trip constantly.

"Wrong." Jeffers said it with a nasal, talk-show-host tone.

"It is!" Beth said desperately. "For God's sake, I'm her mother—you've got to believe me!"

"Yeah, yeah. She told me about Disney World, but she's picked the trip to the Grand Canyon as her favorite now . . . said it was the best because it was just you, her, and her *daddy.*"

Beth was shaking. "You bastard."

"Careful now. Unless you want to do your vacations *all* alone in the future, get back on Storrow, go south on 93, head to the airport."

Traffic was light, so much so that as Ross and Beth started down the one-way through the Callahan Tunnel, the following FBI cars had to stay quite a distance back, leaving only another car and a truck between them.

The lead FBI car with Peters and another man was only a dozen lengths ahead.

"Do you think it's going to happen at the airport?" Beth raked her hair away from her face, her hands trembling. "He couldn't intend for us to fly someplace, could he?"

"God knows."

The car behind them swung alongside to pass. Ross put the revolver in his lap.

"What?" Beth said.

The car swept by, and Ross began to relax when he saw it wasn't Jeffers. The tunnel was fairly well lit, and Ross saw the young man's face in profile. It took Ross a second to realize who it was—for a moment he'd thought the young man was one of the FBI agents.

But it was the kid. The red-haired kid. The kid who was crazy enough to do anything.

The walkie-talkie crackled, Byrne calling on to the other cars, "That's a fuel oil truck behind Ross! They're not allowed in the tunnel."

Ross grabbed for the walkie-talkie and yelled, "Peters, watch out for the car coming at you!"

Beth screamed as they clearly saw a man rise up from the backseat of the car with a big handgun—a machine pistol. Glass from the FBI car flew as the gun began to chatter, and Ross saw the flash of returning gunfire as the FBI car bounced off the tunnel wall in a shower of sparks.

The kid hit the brakes and swung his car in front of Ross's pickup truck to block the road. Ross hit the brakes. Behind them, the fuel oil truck swung in, cutting them off from Byrne and the FBI agents. Ross shoved Beth to the floor and threw himself on top of her just as the back window of his own truck shattered. He risked a fast look up and saw who was standing in the open doorway of the truck now, a big machine gun leveled at them.

T.S.

Ross ducked down again as bullets punched through the cab. He instinctively pulled the case of money in front of himself and Beth. Once the second burst was over, he said, "Stay behind this," and slipped out his door into the tunnel.

He was so intent on keeping the truck between him and T.S. he almost didn't hear the kid until it was too late.

The kid's shotgun belched flame, and Ross ducked behind the open door. He cried out as a slashing pain cut across his left calf and he fell to the asphalt. He hadn't even realized that the revolver Byrne had given him was in his hand until that moment, and he rolled onto his belly and braced himself as the kid kept coming. Ross fired three times in fast succession. Two of the shots missed, but the third caught the kid under the chin.

Ross staggered to his feet and saw T.S. had left the truck and was running up to them with the machine gun.

Ross pulled himself into the idling truck and dropped the gearshift into reverse. He stood on the gas and aimed for the big man, both with the truck and with his gun out the shattered back window. He emptied his gun and one round apparently grazed T.S. The big man stopped his charge, looking surprised with the blossom of red on his arm, and then he cut loose with the machine gun. Bullets pocked the tailgate until T.S. elevated the barrel, sending the slugs whistling past Ross's face.

T.S. glanced once to the left as Ross sent the truck hurtling toward him, and Ross jabbed the wheel in that direction just as the truck was upon the man.

Ross had read T.S. correctly.

As he jumped left, the truck was there to meet him.

The sickening thud of metal against flesh and bone made Ross cry out as if he'd dealt the blow with his own fist. T.S. was thrown a dozen feet before hitting the tunnel wall. Ross braked to kill the last of the truck's momentum. He could see from the angle of T.S.'s neck that the man was dead.

"Ross!" Beth screamed.

Jeffers was a dozen yards in front of them and closing in fast, a machine pistol in his hand. Ross dropped the truck into gear, knowing his own gun was empty.

Ross headed straight for Jeffers. But unlike T.S., Jeffers showed no indecision. He stood stock-still in the middle of the tunnel, and poured the magazine into the cab. Ross had no choice but to duck down with Beth, knowing that he was driving blind and that Jeffers could step aside like a matador taunting a wounded bull.

When the impact came, it was a glancing blow along the wall. Ross jammed his foot onto the brake, and the truck slid to a halt, sheet metal screeching alongside the tiles.

Ross reached blindly through the cab for something, a tire iron, maybe. Anything to use as a weapon. Knowing their options were gone. Expecting to have the door wrenched open behind him, for the burst of flame into his back.

But when the gunfire sounded again it was farther away. A mere dozen feet, but miles in terms of Ross and Beth still being alive. Ross looked over the sill and saw Jeffers was firing back toward the fuel truck. Byrne and several of the agents had crawled underneath it. One of them had been hit; the others were laying down enough fire to drive Jeffers back behind his own car.

From his angle, Ross could see Jeffers clearly as he slid in another magazine. "Get down! Get down!" Ross yelled.

Jeffers stood and braced the machine pistol against the roof of his car.

Flame seemed to burst from his hands. "Come on!" he yelled. "I'm right here!" Bullets slammed into the fuel truck, streaking the belly of it with oil.

When the gun at last fell silent, Jeffers swung inside his car and took off, the tires spinning. The back end clipped the stalled FBI car and then Jeffers straightened out and headed for the tunnel exit.

Ross got the truck away from the wall and took off after him. In the rearview mirror, he could see Byrne and the agents crowding into Peters's car.

Ross kept his foot to the floor, but still Jeffers pulled away. Glass slid off the dashboard, and it was a nightmarish reminder to Ross of Greg beside him dying.

"Go faster!" Beth said.

"This is the best it'll do."

As Jeffers left the tunnel, Ross saw him reach out the window with something. Ross's first reaction was that it was a gun, and he pulled farther to the right. But he could still see the device in Jeffers's hand, and for a moment Ross thought it was a walkie-talkie.

But then there was a crumping sound, and a flash of yellow from behind. A blast of heat swept through the broken back window as a ball of flame roared up the tunnel.

Jeffers had detonated the fuel truck.

CHAPTER 50

The flames only scorched the back of the truck. The agents following weren't so lucky. Ross saw their car emerge from the tunnel, the tires melted to the rims. Ross slowed before rounding the first corner, staring back over his shoulder until he was certain he'd seen someone moving inside the agents' car.

Ross hit the gas. By the time he and Beth reached the next straightaway, Jeffers's car was just a distant set of tail lights.

Ross brought their own speed up to where the vehicle began to shake before he eased off. Wind beat through the broken window, and he felt the sting of flying glass. Ross switched the plow lights on and cut the head and the roof lights. "Maybe that'll make us look a little different in Jeffers's mirror."

"What're you going to do?" Beth asked.

"Damned if I know." Ross felt through the broken glass on the dashboard and floor until his hand closed around a shattered piece of plastic and metal that had once been their walkie-talkie.

"Damn it. The gun's empty and we've got no way to communicate."

"Get rid of him, then." Beth closed her fingers around Ross's arm tightly. "Run him off the road."

Ross was tempted. But Jeffers was driving a big Ford that could walk away from Ross's truck. And Jeffers still had that gun. It'd be too easy for them to end up by the side of the road, with the truck damaged and Jeffers riding off.

"No."

"What?" He could read the incredulity in her voice even over the rushing wind and engine noise.

"We'd risk losing him altogether. Better to see if he takes us to Janine."

After he turned onto Route 128 North, Jeffers settled down to a steady sixty-two.

"He's not running anymore," Beth said. "He must not recognize us."

"Maybe." Ross considered it. "Or maybe he does, and he figures he'll still have a chance at the money here."

"Either way, it'll give the FBI a chance to catch up."

"*Those* agents certainly won't, not soon," Ross said. In the rearview mirror, the road was empty. He hoped Byrne had made it through all right. "We do have the transmitter in the case. The question is whether there's anyone back there in any shape to follow it."

"Maybe Jeffers just doesn't want to attract highway patrols to pull him over for speeding."

"I think that's likely," Ross said, thinking back to Greg's instructions to take it slow himself, back when the whole thing started, when Ross had driven the opposite direction from the Sands, knotted up with worry about his niece.

Thinking about that ride set him up.

When Jeffers turned off two exits ahead, Ross said softly, "Will you look at that."

The exit was the one leading to the road where Greg had been shot. The road Beth and Ross had taken a million times before.

The road to the Sands.

It hit Beth at the same time. "My God. It's Geiler's now."

Ross pulled off at the very next exit.

"What're you doing?" Beth cried.

"I'm going to try to beat him there."

"We can't be positive that's where he's going!"

"It makes sense," Ross said as he began to push the truck through the tight corners. He'd raced these very roads as a kid, and as long as Jeffers continued to stay close to the speed limit, Ross thought he could outstrip him. He said, "Jeffers needs to take off. Maybe he's stopping by for some money. Maybe he intends to kill Geiler. I know he's not willing to leave witnesses talking—I know that much about him."

When they got to the intersection where the two roads converged, Ross hesitated briefly, expecting to see the headlights of the Ford. But the road to his left remained dark.

Beth said, "Let's keep going. Let's go get her."

The driveway was only a mile away. Neither spoke while hurrying down the twisting dirt road, pebbles knocking up into the wheel wells. Ross's mouth was dry and his heart was pounding hard. The last time he'd felt that way driving down that particular stretch of road had been when he was a teenager coming home late and hoping that his father had already passed out.

Ross doused the lights and traveled the road on memory and the faint illumination of the moon.

Beth peered out into the darkness until they could see the outline of the house against the moonlit cove. Ross pulled the truck over and killed the engine. Faint light glowed through the drawn shades of the main room downstairs. "Nobody pulls the shades with those views," she said.

"Wait behind the wheel." Under the seat Ross found the tire iron that had eluded him before. His head told him to go back for the police, but if Jeffers was indeed headed to the house, there simply wasn't time. "If I'm not back in five minutes, get out of here and call the police."

Beth nodded, her face grim in the moonlight. Ross jogged quietly alongside the road until he was closer. He edged around the house, but all the shades were down on the three sides accessible to him, and he knew the angle would've been impossible from the shore side. Ross eased his way around to the front door and listened carefully. There was something . . . the sound of movement, of a chair scraping, perhaps. Then he heard a woman's voice, too low for him to understand what was being said.

He opened the door and stepped into the living area. Stepped into a place where he'd spent years of his life, where he'd battled with his father and created a friendship with his brother that had lasted.

He didn't know how to react.

Literally, did not know.

For Janine was there, bound to a chair like before, alive and apparently unhurt. Crying out to him past her gag. The woman, Natalie, was there. So was Geiler, bound like the others—but not gagged.

It was Allie who shocked him.

Allie who was tied down, placed beside Geiler. Allie who also wasn't gagged, and who looked not with relief to Ross, but with despair to Geiler.

"Looks guilty as hell, doesn't she?" Jeffers stepped out of the kitchen with the machine gun in his hands.

* * *

He kept Ross covered and snatched away the tire iron. "Thought I saw you following back there. Made some pretty good time, didn't I?"

"We can still get out of this," Geiler said quietly.

"Shut up," Jeffers said. He walked over to Janine and took a switchblade from his pocket. "Easy, Uncle Ross." He sliced the line binding her hands. For a second the irrational idea that Jeffers was letting her go washed over Ross.

But the way Jeffers handled her, the way he hauled her onto her feet, showed he regarded her simply as his hostage.

"Come on, the both of you. Let's go get my money." He waved the gun toward the doorway, the knife in his left hand at Janine's neck.

Once they were outside, Jeffers yelled out into the night, "I know you're out there, lady! If you've got the money, you can come down and get your girl. You don't, then you just sit there while I count to ten, and you'll see me shoot her."

Beth brought the truck down as he reached eight.

She took the case from front seat and strode up to Jeffers and dropped it at his feet. She barely looked at him—her eyes were on Janine—and she said only, "Let go of her."

Janine threw herself into her mother's arms. Beth closed her eyes, and Ross heard her quietly exhale, and he knew that at that moment Beth and Janine were out of the situation, lost within each other.

But the moment didn't last long. Jeffers jabbed at Ross with the gun barrel. "Pick that money up, and take it inside." He told Beth to go into the house and then said to Ross, "And I'm going to give you one chance. You tell me the truth. Do the cops know my name? Do they?"

Ross took a close look at the man. His eyes were even more

deeply shadowed than before. He had several days' stubble on his chin, and his eyes glittered in the faint light. He stank of old sweat and he snuffled slightly, his nose running as if he had a summer cold. "Coke?" Ross asked, lifting the case. "Is that what this has been about?"

"Never mind that shit now." Jeffers shoved Ross into the doorway. He strode across the room, pulled out the switchblade, and cut his wife's ropes and pulled the tape from her mouth. "You've got to make a decision, right now. You with me or no?"

She nodded uncertainly and rubbed her wrists. She stepped vaguely toward Beth and Janine, and then stopped short.

Jeffers raised his voice to include Beth as well as Ross. "You two answer me or people start to die. What's my name? Do the cops know who I am?"

"Get it over with." Allie spoke urgently to Jeffers. "Shoot them, and let us out of here. That case has a transmitter in it and the FBI will be homing in on the signal right now."

"Do it," Geiler said. A trickle of sweat ran down his jaw. "You've gone this far. Just finish it."

"Let Janine go," Beth said. "Please, she's just a little girl! She doesn't know anything."

"She really doesn't know our names," Natalie said. "I've asked her again and again. Please, let her go."

Allie ignored all of them. She said to Jeffers, "Come on. Pull it together one more time, and take these people out of the picture. You can leave a rich man. *We'll* never give you up. We'd face the electric chair!"

Jeffers grinned crookedly at Ross. "How about you, man? You got any last-minute things you've just got to tell me?"

"Just what you wanted to know," Ross said evenly. "Lee. Lee Jeffers."

"No!" Allie cried.

The gunman blanched. Then his grin returned slowly, and he

said to Ross, "Your lawyer there told me all sorts of things after I picked her up at her apartment. She told me about the number of cars the FBI had in place, the way they had agents trained to sound like you and Mommy . . . but this is the first I heard about a transmitter in the case . . . and they promised me no one had a clue on the name. . . . You know what that means?"

"Sure," Ross said.

". . . means the two of them have been feeding me just what they thought I should know, even when I had them tied up and put a gun in their faces."

He shot Geiler.

Jeffers used a short burst that ripped the man's chest open before he turned the gun onto Allie. Her scream was abruptly cut off, and then the gun was swinging Ross's way.

He wouldn't have survived if not for Natalie. He was almost on top of Jeffers, but the gun was in his face, and then the gun chattered, and he was still alive.

Nat had grabbed her husband's arm.

Jeffers elbowed her aside, but it gave Ross the split second he needed, and he grasped the gun with his left hand and kneed Jeffers in the groin. Again and again, he threw short, hard rights into Jeffers's belly and ribs, digging in with all his strength. Getting in close with his head and shoulders. Trying desperately to keep Jeffers from getting his legs back underneath himself or getting both hands on the gun.

Knowing from past experience just how much punishment Jeffers could take.

As they staggered onto the deck, the machine gun erupted briefly. There was a sharp tug along Ross's left thigh, but still he kept throwing those solid right hooks. Told himself to keep breathing, to keep working it. Told himself to ignore that some of Jeffers's blows had landed as well. Blood trickled into Ross's left eye, and still Jeffers showed no sign of collapsing under

Ross's assault. Ross was aware of Beth beside him and he shouted for her to get back, to get away from Jeffers's gun. Ross's breathing was ragged and his arms were shaking, but Jeffers hadn't broken yet.

So when Ross saw a chance to end the fight, he took it.

Jeffers was backing close to the rails, the lightly tacked boards Ross had been putting up when Greg had first called.

Light finishing nails, tapped in only a half-inch or so, for placement.

Ross opened his hand against Jeffers's chest and shoved with all his strength.

The tacked boards gave way.

But Jeffers grabbed at the post with his left hand and regained his balance.

He raised the gun barrel to Ross's face.

"Jeffers!"

It was Beth.

The open case of money was balanced on the rail. She had thrown the kerosene lantern into it and the smell of the oil was strong. She held the lighter over the case, the flame serene in the still night. "I'll burn it. Or you can drop the gun and walk away with the whole case. We don't care about the money."

"Bring it here," Jeffers said, his voice just a croak. He switched the gun to her.

"No."

"Bring it over here. Now!"

"Drop the gun," Ross said.

"Give me the money and I'll leave."

"Once you drop the gun."

"Sure you will." Jeffers took aim again at Ross. "And you all said the money didn't matter."

"Not to us." Beth dropped her hand. The cash burst into flames, and she shoved the case over the rail.

Jeffers cried out as he tried to lunge past Ross, trying to reach for the suitcase handle.

Ross hit him in the face, a solid punch that sent Jeffers reeling. Ross did it again. And then Ross kicked him in the chest.

Even as he fell, Jeffers fired the gun. Several rounds bit into the side of the house just a few feet from Ross's head. But he didn't move away from the edge until he saw Jeffers hit the rocks, fifty feet below.

EPILOGUE

Turner will see that I get fried if we don't make it to the press conference on time," Byrne said. "He wants you right beside him at the podium explaining why it's going to be a tougher commute than usual to the airport."

"You've survived worse." Ross closed his eyes as they waited at a red light. It was good to have Byrne alive and reasonably well beside him. The fire that had overcome Byrne's car in the tunnel had been intense enough to send two of the agents in the backseat to the hospital. But Byrne had ducked down in the seat and kept his foot to the floor while the flames had brushed past.

Byrne had been among the first to arrive at the Sands by following the transmitter. The past few hours had been a blur, as the house had filled with police and FBI asking too many questions too fast. Ross was so tired he felt as if he were wearing lead weights. But his mind was still racing.

The adrenaline, the doctor had said.

They'd just left Beth and Janine at the hospital. The doctor who had examined Janine had given her an essentially clean bill of health but said she wanted to hold onto her for a day or two for observation. Janine had fallen asleep with Beth and Ross watching over her. A single tear slid down Beth's cheek, and she'd wiped it away and said simply, "I wish he were here to see this."

Ross had taken her in his arms and lost himself in her for a time, seeking not to take his brother's place, but to take comfort himself. "Greg's awfully proud of you," she'd said, breaking away finally. "I know he is."

"You, too."

"Better be." She looked steadily at Ross. "I want to thank you. And I'll be selfish and tell you that I hope you don't leave anytime soon. Janine's going to need her uncle, and I'm going to need you, too."

"I'm not sailing away," he'd said, without regret.

Ross opened his eyes and realized that Byrne had been repeating himself. "I'm sorry. I fazed out."

Byrne said, "Tell me about Natalie. Or did you just faze out on her, too?"

"I guess she saw how things were heading and got away."

Byrne looked at him skeptically. "She's an accessory to murder and she kidnapped your niece."

"She also saved Janine more than once, and she saved my life."

"That's something for the judge and jury to take into account."

"Which they'd do right before they sent her to jail. Look, Jeffers pulled her into all of this, and she did the best she could, screwed up as she is." Ross thought about Nat, desperate and fleeing for the Canadian border in the car Jeffers had hidden deep in the brush. The decision to let her go didn't feel good. But after he and Beth had a quiet conversation with Janine, and with Natalie herself, they'd agreed that sending her to prison would be worse.

She'd told them what she knew. "That Geiler told us it'd be a simple job. Snatch the girl, hold onto her a night, and then turn her in. Take the cash. Talk around her like it was a random thing, you know, so when the police interviewed her later it'd sound like something random, like we just snatched her in the middle of a car-jacking. That's what they wanted Lee to do, a car-jacking. Three of those in Boston so far this year." She'd looked at Beth. "They figured you'd have bought that. Lee didn't. He said that if you were stuck out there without a car, and with no proof we'd hurt the girl, you'd have gone to the cops. He told me he'd figured something better. We followed you, and then he told me just to go into that store with him and do what he said. I never expected him to shoot that store owner. But I guess I should've."

Tears had slipped down Natalie's face and she began to explain to Beth directly. "It went wrong from the beginning. I only got into it because I thought maybe I could get your daughter through it . . . do what I couldn't do for my own little girl. I knew Lee was going to do the job, with or without me. We do so much drugs and shit that we needed a score like this. This was a huge score for us. And Lee had worked for Geiler before; the guy owns a shipping company where Lee does some welding. He'd had Lee do some stuff, mess somebody up or burn something, and it'd always turned out all right. This time, Geiler was screaming on the phone after Lee killed the store owner . . . and Geiler was real upset that Lee shot your husband. Said that it would bring the cops in on the whole thing."

"Why was Lee doing the robberies?" Ross had asked.

"Geiler treated Lee like he was a flunky. Told him that he wouldn't advance us any money for coke. That if Lee wanted

money, then return Janine and collect the cash. And then after
Lee shot that *cop* . . . well, you saw what happened. Geiler hired
Teague to hit Lee. Geiler must've figured Jeffers was going to
bring them all down. But before that, Teague caught up with me
near the shipyard.   " She had looked down, ashamed. "I was
hooking. He got hold of me and kept hitting me, and working
on me all night to tell where I thought Janine would go. . . . I
wouldn't have told him about her asking about the Children's
Museum, but I figured by then she would've been picked up by
somebody and at home with all of you . . . but I guess she'd hidden. . . ."

"What about Allie?" Ross asked.

Natalie had shaken her head. "What about her? She had all
of you jumping, what I could see. Geiler, too. I bet he promised
her he could handle Lee."

Here Natalie had lifted her head with a peculiar kind of pride
and said, "And that's where both of them screwed up. They figured they could handle him. I could've told them. I sure
could've."

To Byrne, Ross said, "Did you talk to Turner when I was in with
the doctor?"

"Yeah. He was close to hysterical. This may be a career buster
for him. You know how the FBI dropped the ball on Geiler. They
had done a cursory check on him but didn't make the connection because he's got at least a couple of dummy corporations
between his shipping, construction, and real estate interests.
And the agents that I left behind to look for Geiler in Boston took
hours to find out that he'd been last seen leaving a restaurant in
Chinatown. I'd guess Jeffers or T.S. put a gun on him and kidnapped him. Either way, Turner didn't get around to checking
out the Sands until we saw that's where the signal was going.
Way too late by Bureau twenty-twenty hindsight."

"Did they learn anything more about Geiler?"

"Yeah, they got his lawyer out of bed, and so far they've learned only that Geiler had his hands into a *lot* of businesses, including several sanitation companies."

"Garbage dumping?"

"Garbage and worse. I expect they're going to find he would've made money fourteen ways to Sunday, from the construction of the docks, to legit shipping, to dumping the stuff that'll turn the fish colors that Mother Nature didn't intend. Maybe even some high-volume drug running. We're talking millions of dollars. It's looking likely that the company that owned that factory that Jeffers was squatting in and that employed both him and Teague as welders is going to turn up as one of Geiler's holdings. It'll take months, maybe years, to pull it all together. The thing is, your place was a good choice for him—nice deep harbor, easy access, but still secluded. Positioned well for roads and industry, and zoning. I figure it was the place he wanted and he was used to getting what he wanted. Who was one little family to stand in his way? The fact that you were going to subdivide would've complicated everything and made him jump."

Byrne looked over at Ross. "Which came first? Your refusal to sell the place to Geiler's lawyer or Teague's attack?"

Ross nodded. "The refusal. Yeah, I've been thinking about that. If I was dead, it would've all been left to Greg, and then there would've just been one person to convince to sell. It seems we've been under assault for that place for a while now; we just didn't know it. Including Allie's relationship with me—nothing more than another reason to convince me to sell—money to start a new future."

The sun was rising as they reached Watertown. Ross was so exhausted that it was physically painful to turn his thoughts to her. Ross wondered if any of what she told him about herself was true.

He rubbed his eyes against the brightness of the sunrise.

Byrne said, "All I know about her is what a friend at the district attorney's office told me about an hour ago. And this he wouldn't tell me until I told him Allie was dead. I guess he was afraid of a lawsuit himself. There had been whispers that she'd maybe let a couple of near cases slip through her fingers. Nothing hard enough to justify an investigation, or to even give her a bad reputation outside the office. Let's just say the DA wasn't too broken up when she resigned to start her own practice."

"Organized crime cases? As in Tommy Datano?"

"Not directly. Probably part of Geiler's own smuggling. How much he and Datano overlapped isn't clear. Probably never will be. I'd say it's unlikely Datano was involved in the front end of this thing, because otherwise he wouldn't have helped you at all. No, we'll look into it, but I expect we're going to come down to Allie helping out some part of Geiler's business, then they meet, and get something going . . . and figure a way they can pull off a deal themselves. Hell, maybe she brought you folks to them. You never know."

The light was on inside the store. Ross said, "That's an understatement."

"Yeah, but you know a hell of a lot more than her. You want me to go in with you?"

Ross shook his head and got out of the car. "Thanks."

Byrne let his seat fall back and closed his eyes. "Take your time. Turner can wait."

The bell rang over the door at the Jacob Family Spa, and the woman at the counter said, "Haven't we met?"

"We have." Ross told her his real name, and that he was there to talk about her brother.